GRAVES IN THE SAND

A Cole Williams Novel

by

Brian Boland

Also by Brian Boland

CARIBBEAN'S KEEPER: A NOVEL OF VENDETTA

GRAVES IN THE SAND

A Cole Williams Novel

by

Brian Boland

WARRIORS PUBLISHING GROUP
NORTH HILLS, CALIFORNIA

GRAVES IN THE SAND: A COLE WILLIAMS NOVEL

A Warriors Publishing Group book/published by arrangement with the author

The views expressed herein are those of the author and are not to be construed as official views or reflecting the views of the Commandant or of the U. S. Coast Guard.

PRINTING HISTORY
Warriors Publishing Group edition/August 2018

ISBN 978-1-944353-17-9

Library of Congress Control Number: 2018949366

The name "Warriors Publishing Group" and the logo
are trademarks belonging to Warriors Publishing Group

PRINTED IN THE UNITED STATES OF AMERICA

10 9 8 7 6 5 4 3 2 1

To my parents.

None of this would have happened
without your love and support.

CHAPTER 1 — NORMANDY COAST

IT WAS COOL AND DARK in the room, save for the scattered bits of light that wandered in between the wall and heavy curtain drawn across a solitary open window. The curtain muted an unending chorus of birds outside. There were more birds here than Cole had ever heard in his life. Opening his eyes and blinking a few times, he looked towards the wall as the curtain danced just a bit with the soft morning breeze that snuck through the narrow streets of Carentan. A minor detail lost to others, Cole couldn't help but appreciate the cool and clean air of a morning in coastal France when compared to the stagnant and loud congestion he'd known back in Panama. Careful with his movements, he rolled gently to his left and saw Marie nestled against Isabella's side, sleeping on her back with one of her arms draped over her head. At six months old, Marie had a full head of the same curly dark hair as her mother. Cole reckoned that she had his ears, but just about every other feature of his darling little girl was handed down from Isabella.

The room was a light shade of blue with white accents around the window and door frames. The coat of paint was heavy and masked what had undoubtedly been several other colors over the decades. The walls bore dozens of small imperfections that were well concealed under the latest shade of blue. Barely big enough for the larger bed that Isabella's parents had graciously bought when Cole showed up, and with an antique crib tucked against the corner, Cole rolled onto his back once more and slowly lowered his feet to the wooden floor of the crowded yet modest room. With deliberate steps to avoid the creakiest of the uneven and foot-worn floorboards, Cole pulled on a pair of jeans, the same t-shirt from the day before, and stepped around the empty crib towards the door.

Marie was up each night at some time between midnight and two in the morning. She was easy enough to put down at night in her crib, but she was a child determined to wake up in her mother's arms each morning. And so, each night Isabella would scoop her up, whisper something French into Marie's ear, and lay her down in the middle of their bed. With a few short whimpers, Marie was quickly back asleep for the remainder of the night. Cole stopped at the doorway for a moment to admire them both in the pale morning light, then with delicate precision, pulled upwards on the heavy wooden door to keep it from creaking, and closed it slowly before letting the brass handle latch.

Down two flights of stairs, he found his shoes by the door leading into the bakery. Boulanger Patissier was run by Isabella's family and had been since well before the war. Her mother was the muscle behind the operation while her father ran the administrative side of their small business. Since his arrival, Cole had worked tirelessly to win them over, but it was a daunting task given the particulars of his situation. They had sent Isabella, their youngest daughter, off to Martinique to intern at a hotel and she had returned early back to France, pregnant. To make matters worse, Cole showed up six months later with little money to his name and a newly healed scar on his chest from a drug dealer's bullet. Several weeks passed after his arrival before he could even move around without pain and labored breathing.

Isabella had explained as best she could, but her parents had, from the start, raised obvious and very fair concerns. Her father, a resident of Carentan his entire life, had asked Cole early on about his military background. When Cole tried to explain the Coast Guard, Isabella's father had inquisitively asked in broken English, "Like the Airborne?"

When Cole replied no, her father looked away dismissively and blew a short puff of breath from between his lips before finding something else more interesting to focus on. It was clear that Cole would not easily win this man over.

"Airborne?" was a question Cole was asked nearly each time he or Isabella brought up his past. Isabella tried to avoid going into much detail about the drug-running double-agent chapter of Cole's life, preferring to paint his character in a more positive light, but when it came to the quaint little coastal town of Carentan, if an American wasn't part of the Airborne, he mattered little, if at all.

Her father's response was repeated time and again throughout Carentan—it was, Cole thought, quintessentially French. The town had a long-standing love affair with the 101st Airborne, ever since they had daringly jumped into Northern France in the middle of the night on June 6, 1944 to rid France of the Nazi plague. Indeed, nearly every shop, Boulanger Patissier included, proudly hung American and 101st Airborne flags over their doors and windows to recognize the sacrifice of the allied nations. And while their love for the Airborne was real, the people of Carentan knew little of the Coast Guard and cared even less about Cole's years in the service. Moreover, they were, as a whole, smart enough to know that Cole's story had some mystery surrounding it. An American who'd somehow been in the military yet also spent the better part of a year off the grid and undoubtedly consumed with some activity not entirely above-the-board. Cole could see that some in this town were fascinated by him and others wary of his presence. Only he knew that the truth floated somewhere in the middle.

Isabella was Carentan's most favorite daughter and Cole found himself perpetually held in some form of judgmental purgatory. No one really knew what to think of him. On one hand, he'd been tacitly accepted, but on the other he knew he was viewed with some level of skepticism. None of this bothered him much, but he was committed to winning over Isabella's parents. The rest of the town would come around with time, of that he was certain.

On this morning in mid-June, Carentan was still decorated from the previous week's commemoration of the invasion. Stepping out of the bakery and onto the sidewalk, he took a few deep breaths of the crisp morning air and paused for a moment to take it in. Every shop proudly displayed some artifact from the invasion. From old canteens to well-preserved bayonets and first aid kits, each little shop strived to show that Carentan was indeed grateful. *Perhaps that's why the birds never stop chirping*, Cole thought. Looking around at the rooftops, Cole never could figure out where they all came from or why they chose Carentan, but if there was going to be a constant sound of anything, it could be far worse than songbirds. Panama was still fresh in his mind and if he closed his eyes, he could hear the faint pulsing bass and see the strobe lights from the dance floor of Habana's. On the mornings when he found himself thinking back to the Caribbean, he was quick to shake those haunting thoughts from his mind. If his mind lingered too long, he was inevitably drawn back to that night when he shot David and David shot him. The image of dark red blood, both his and David's, swirling like a flooded river and pooling on the dirty dance floor, gave him the chills. On this morning, he pushed those thoughts aside and focused squarely on his day ahead.

To his left, he saw that the cooler of ice cream bars needed restocking. With that, he went to work. It was just after five in the morning. Back inside, Isabella's mother had already brewed a pot of coffee and Cole filled a mug, dropped in two cubes of sugar and took a short sip before putting the mug down and working his way back to the deep freezer. As he passed the kitchen, he called out, "Bonjour."

Isabella's mother, from somewhere unseen, replied back, "Bonjour, Cole."

He was confident she was beginning to like him. Cole worked tirelessly at the bakery, doing any and all chores he could find to help out. After restocking the cooler out front, he checked on the morning's deliveries. Isabella's mother had laid out a carefully assembled row of bags, each with various assortments of croissants, baguettes, beignets, crispy rolls, and plain loaves of bread. Stepping away from the kitchen for a moment, she started at one end and worked her way down the row calling out names or addresses for Cole to remember. At first it had been a litany of gibberish to Cole, Rue this, Rue that, Rue de la blah

blah blah…, but over the course of several months, he had begun to catch on.

From most men, the French language sounded arrogant to him. But from a woman's lips, it was something delicate and beautiful. Isabella's mother was no exception. When she finished, she looked at Cole to see if he understood. "Oui," he replied with certainty. With that, she smiled at him for just a second, something she had begun to do over the past few weeks. He was confident she was coming around to his presence, and it lifted his spirits to see progress each week.

Finishing his coffee and washing the mug in the sink, Cole wiped his hands and set out with the first of the bags. To say Carentan was scenic in the morning light did it no justice. Downtown had been rebuilt after the war, but its walls still carried many battle scars. There were pockmarked sections of stone that told the story of the fierce house-to-house fighting that took place to take back the town from the Germans. Several of the buildings had undergone refurbishment over the years and had completely hidden the damage, but many more still had original roofs, stone walls, terraces, and columns that showed clearly enough to the careful eye the magnitude of the Second World War.

Rounding a corner onto one of the main streets, Cole heard and saw a construction truck backing up and its crew busy setting up for a day's work. Scowling for a second, Cole shook his head dismissively and continued on his way. It was inevitable that over time the town would eventually conceal its past. As Carentan had expanded after the war, the new construction was mostly of a different type, preferring stucco walls instead of the hand-laid stone that defined old France. The heart of the town was still painted in broad earthy strokes with the same shades of dirty cream stones and grey concrete walls as had defined it during the war. The outskirts were increasingly decorated in pastel colors, but the heart of Carentan remained largely untouched.

∞

BY ELEVEN, he was done with deliveries and back at the bakery. Isabella's mother handed him a small pizza wrapped neatly in paper and taped shut. "With no egg," she said with a smile as she handed it to him. "Merci," Cole replied as he kicked off his shoes and made his way back upstairs. Why anyone would ever put an egg on a pizza, he did not know. Isabella had Marie in her lap playing with a doll. One of Isabella's sisters sat across from her and the two talked casually at the kitchen table, laughing like girls do just as Cole came up the steps. "Bonjour," Cole said as he walked over, kissing both Isabella and Marie on the forehead. Her sister smiled at Cole, then back at Isabella with an expression that only sisters understand.

Unlike her parents, Isabella's two sisters were more accepting of Cole. Older than Isabella by a few years, each were still not old enough to forget the winding path of young love that had joined Isabella and Cole together.

"Huit," Isabella said with a slight smile as she looked up at Cole, indicating that Marie had slept until eight in the morning. There were days when Cole's movement in the morning woke her up and others, like today, where his little girl would sleep well into the morning. This in turn put both Isabella and Marie in the best of moods.

Switching to English, Isabella spoke, "We may go out for the afternoon. Is that all right?"

"Sure," Cole replied. They looked at each other for a moment. She was in many ways the same girl he'd met in Martinique. The labors of childbirth had not extinguished her youthful charm, but she had grown quickly into the role of a mother. Less carefree than before, something about Isabella had changed. For Cole, it was comforting to see how much she embraced motherhood, but he struggled to pinpoint just what it was about her that was different. It was nothing bad, he told himself. As they looked at each other for a moment more, he thought it a new chapter in life and nothing more. Martinique, and their nights with a bottle of wine under a sky full of stars, seemed like years ago.

Isabella turned Marie in her lap to look at Cole and pointed, whispering, "Papa," into Marie's ear. She perked up for a second, looked at Cole and tried to control a giggling smile on her face. Her dark hair was already starting to curl just like her mother's. He couldn't help but smile and laugh to himself. Isabella smiled the same way she had in Martinique when they first met. In that moment, as random as it was, Cole felt weightless. He was, for so many reasons, remarkably happy.

Isabella asked, "What will you do today?"

"I'm going to sweep up a bit, then maybe go for a run. Will you be long?"

"Back for dinner, I'm sure. You could take the car?"

Cole thought for a moment. Isabella's parents had given the OK for Cole to take their car out from time to time when the opportunity arose. Driving gave him access to the monuments, museums, and beaches of Normandy, and it was a way to unwind from the occasionally monotonous work at the bakery.

"Oui. Maybe I will."

"Dinner at five, then?" Isabella asked.

"Oui."

With that, Cole gave Isabella a kiss, cupped the side of Marie's head with his hand, and kissed her gently on her curled hair. Back downstairs, he found the broom and went to work, first in the kitchen. Isabella's mother was done with the baking and kitchen work was all but done for the day. It took him the better part of an hour, but by the time he emptied the pan and took out the trash, it was clean and ready for the next morning when she would be up in the cool pre-dawn air to start baking again.

The shop itself was small and took little time to clean. Cole started with the counters, then on to cleaning the glass dividers, and then lastly to the floor which he swept out and into the street. Finally, he swept off the sidewalk and checked the cooler one more time. By the looks of it, the day was slow. On weekends, the children of Carentan often liquidated the ice cream by noon.

He checked in once more with Isabella's mother who waved him off with a simple, "Merci, Cole." It was a cue to get on with his day. Changing upstairs, he was back down to the sidewalk and paused to look again down the street at the small flags running on clotheslines perpendicular to the road. American, British, and French flags were evenly distributed up and down each line and they flickered back and forth in the steady midday breeze. Cole smiled. Perhaps it wasn't his home, but there was nowhere else in the world he wanted to be.

With the sun on his shoulders, he stepped off and started to trot for a few steps before working into a stride towards the water. He'd only been running for the last two months after his injuries in Panama. It felt familiar, but at the same time he had one lung now that wouldn't keep up with the other. Running now was more about control and restraint so as not to overwork himself. He found that somewhere between an eight and nine-minute mile was a pace he could sustain for a bit. Anything faster triggered a shooting pain in his chest. As he checked his pace and worked his way back and forth between the alleys and roads, Cole looked up to admire the rounded tops of the stone walls and the steeply angled rooftops dotted with patches of green, brown, and yellow moss.

AN HOUR LATER he was showered and into a clean set of clothes. Isabella's father was at the desk on the second floor and Cole called out, "Bonjour," as he passed. Without looking up from his work, he replied simply, "Cole." Stopping and doubling back, Cole caught the keys as her father tossed them at him and said matter-of-factly, "La cuisine est proper."

Cole was pretty sure it meant literally the kitchen is clean, but he wasn't sure if it was a question or a compliment. Isabella's father smiled just a bit, barely enough to even call it one, but it nonetheless seemed a turning point for Cole and the old man. He went back to his work at the desk and said simply, "Au revoir." Cole smiled to himself as he walked down the last flight of steps.

A Nissan Micra was by no means a racecar, but Cole's guilty pleasure was to take the absurdly tiny excuse for a vehicle to the ends of its envelope in the roundabouts, blind turns, and straightaways between Carentan and Utah Beach. Outside of Carentan, the countryside was a series of softly rolling hills and narrow roads lined by hedgerows. It was those same hedgerows that had proven such a challenge for the allied forces, and it was a fact that was not lost on Cole as he worked the diminutive gears up and over the hills. There were sleepy cattle huddled in many of the fields and lush green crops growing in the others. The smaller villages all looked remarkably similar in construction. It was the old style of hand-laid stones, tiled roofs, and low stone walls marking the perimeters. Looking out over the expanse of northern France from the crest of each hill, a picture emerged each time worthy of a painting.

Utah Beach was a quick 20-minute drive, one that Cole had already taken several times. He'd been to Omaha as well and walked the American Cemetery, but he preferred Utah as it was the more quiet of the two. For good reason, Omaha drew tourists each day that visited the cemetery and toured the battlefield. On summer days, it was crowded. Utah, on the other hand, had a bit more of an original feel to it. Other than a museum tucked into the sand, it was relatively undisturbed by modern construction. The dunes were lower and the secluded beach nearly always allowed for a quiet spot to sit and look out on the English Channel. To the east, Pointe Du Hoc jutted out into the channel, concealing Omaha Beach from view.

Cole most often parked a bit down the road, walked a new meandering route each time, and found a spot to sit and catch his mind up with the past days' events. He'd toured the museum as well, but after two visits the displays became less interesting. The trip was more about the beach, anyhow. One picture that was cemented into his memory from inside the museum showed American troops climbing down rope ladders to the waiting landing craft. It was that photo, more than any-thing else, that Cole always found himself thinking about. Sitting on the beach, he'd stare out at the calm blue water and wonder what had gone through the minds of those men as they climbed down to make their mark in history. The sheer will it must have taken to advance towards what many thought would be their death was not lost on Cole.

Most of the white crosses and stars at the Omaha Beach cemetery bore the names, units, home state, and date of each service member's death. He was never certain who had it worst, the ones who died on the sixth of June, or those who trudged through the hedgerows and flooded low plains for months only to be killed later in the summer by Germans who still hadn't found the good sense to accept their fate. With these things on his mind, he preferred the solitude of Utah Beach. That was not to suggest that he ever found answers to his questions and his mind usually turned at some point back to Carentan and his new life. Had there been palm trees tucked back from the water and a rock jutting out from the sea, the beach could have easily been a near-perfect recreation Le Diamant, where he and Isabella had spent one of his favorite after-noons. An hour at Utah Beach was usually all it took and he'd make the drive back, finding a parking spot on the street to return the Micra with no one the wiser about his manner of driving.

BACK BY MID-AFTERNOON, Cole took one last run through the kitchen to clean up. Isabella's mother had cooked something, as a few bowls were dirty and in the sink. He quickly went about cleaning them, returning each to its proper place then swept up some flour off the floor just as she was coming in. Startled for just a second, she said a quick hello and then, "Merci," when she saw that Cole had already cleaned up what she had come back for.

It wasn't much longer before Isabella was back with Marie and Cole quickly scooped up his baby to get her ready for a bath. In a small antique tub upstairs, he'd mastered the art of bathing an infant. With a mat for Marie, he could lay her down and manage to keep the girl happy long enough to scrub her down, shampoo her hair, and dry her off. Cole's routine consisted of a series of out-of-tune noises he could make with his mouth while he washed her. Marie found them hilarious, especially when she'd had a good night of sleep the night before. If she hadn't slept well, it could be a different story, but even under those circumstances, Cole could work quickly to get her dried off and into something warm for the cool summer nights.

Dinner was never elaborate, but it was always good on account of Isabella's mother. Afterwards, Cole usually took Marie into the living room and spent some time with her while Isabella chatted with her parents. His game of choice was to call out body parts and point to them. Marie was just now beginning to point to her nose when Cole did and by the time he'd worked through all the parts of a human face, Isabella was usually there to join him. They'd talk in English, as Cole's French was still not at a decent level for conversation. A rug in the corner with some toys and stuffed animals was a play area where Marie would give crawling a go and work out the last bits of energy before Isabella or Cole put her to bed for the night.

As they sat on a couch, both watching Marie, Isabella put her head down on Cole's shoulder and asked, "How was the beach?"

"Quiet, as usual."

"What do you like so much about it?"

Cole thought for a second before replying, "It's just nice to see the water sometimes."

"You are quiet when you come back from there. I wonder about you, Cole."

He turned to face her. "And what do you wonder about?"

She smiled. "Just what you're thinking. Sometimes you are so serious about things."

Cole poked at her ribs and tickled her just a bit. As she wiggled to stop him, he laughed, saying, "I'm pretty damn serious about you."

"Maybe you could go work on a fishing boat, if you miss the water so much?"

Isabella was serious, but Cole laughed.

"You're telling me you want me to smell like fish every night?"

She shook her head, but continued, "No, but if you miss the water so much....Do you want to be back on the water? Driving boats again?"

Cole smiled and shook his head. "No, not at all. I like this life, our life. And I like those pizzas for lunch over fish, so long as your mom leaves off the egg."

With that, they were both back to their old selves. Cole could feel it and he could see it on Isabella's face that she was happy. But there were these moments, just like this last one, where she seemed to be probing to get deeper into Cole's head. It was as if there was some new element to their relationship that he couldn't quite put his finger on. Was it motherhood? He couldn't see outward signs of it all the time, but he would catch her at random moments as if something was on the verge of troubling her. She'd been entirely carefree on those nights in Martinique and part of Cole longed for that innocence.

It was true that he'd left her at a critical time, but at that point he had no idea she was even pregnant. Nor did he have any intention of being caught with a boatload of cocaine, dragged back to the States, and then turned into a double agent. If that hadn't been enough, he certainly had never planned to end up back in Panama shooting it out with David outside of a whorehouse. *Fuck David*, he thought.

Cole was done with all of that. In the days that followed the shootout, he'd rid himself of the uncontrollable adrenaline that had guided his decisions in the past years. Once he'd found out Isabella was pregnant, Cole more or less felt himself grow out of those reckless ways. Even if he'd wanted more of it, he was smart enough now to know the risks outweighed the reward. When Tony had followed through with his promise to get Cole to France, that was where it all ended and a new life began.

Cole had missed the bulk of Isabella's pregnancy. Maybe that was it? He' been truthful with her and they'd talked at length once he got to France. They had both been candid and Cole was made aware of the strains she'd been through. But once Marie came along, it seemed they were stronger than ever. He thought back to her last question—about boats. Perhaps it wasn't her at all that was different. Perhaps it was simply his past that worried her. Cole hated to admit it, but his dark side worried him at times as well.

Snapping him back to the moment, Isabella lifted her head from Cole's shoulder and looked down at Marie. Cole had not noticed that she'd slowed down considerably from her earlier movements. Isabella smiled and nodded to Cole, looking down at their daughter. She slid down from the couch where they were sitting and scooped up Marie into her arms. Bringing her over to Cole, he kissed her on the forehead and Isabella walked softly across the room and up the steps to put her into the crib, whispering a lullaby softly and in French.

Cole walked to the kitchen, nodded to Isabella's parents and took a Heineken from the refrigerator. Walking back across the second floor, he took a new seat by a window and opened the wooden shutters to look down on the street below. The flags still danced a bit in the evening breeze as the sun made its late June departure. There was light still in the sky at nine o'clock when Cole made his way upstairs to their bedroom. Isabella was tucked in to their bed and he could hear Marie breathing softly in her crib. He stopped next to the crib for a moment or two just to watch her before stepping around to his side of the bed, laying his clothes down on the floor, and climbing in.

Isabella's dark and curly hair was mostly up and over her head, draped over the pillow just as Cole remembered from that unforgettable first night in Martinique. She was facing Cole and as he laid down she opened her eyes with a shy smile across her face. He was lying right next to her, their feet touching when Cole pulled her in close and they kissed in such a way that would have embarrassed her parents. After a few minutes, Isabella lifted her head back just a bit and stared intently into his eyes. With her left arm across his neck and her hand on the back of his head, she reached up and grabbed a handful of his mangled dirty-blond hair. Gripping tightly, she wrestled his head for a second before pulling him in close to her and whispering, "I love you, Cole Williams."

Cole looked at her for a moment and replied, "And I love you."

THE FOLLOWING morning played out much the same as the previous. Cole woke, on his own, shortly after five in the morning, and made his way downstairs to start the day. Cooler than normal, Cole walked quickly to shake the chill from his bones. He made several trips back and forth from the bakery, each time with two full bags. Some were for restaurants, but many were deliveries to the local families around Carentan that had come to rely on Isabella's family for their weekly bread.

After finishing his last delivery, Cole walked a different route back to the bakery. That afternoon, he planned to once again go for a run and perhaps start working on some pushups and pullups if he could find something suitable to hang from. The military doctors that released him had given some clear instructions on when Cole could work out again. He was only supposed to be walking at this point, but he knew his limits far better than some doctor in a starched lab coat.

On the way back, he traced some of the walls with his fingers along edges that seemed to bear holes and deformations from the war and he stopped from time to time to look at them more closely. From local knowledge, he knew of the verifiable damage and some of the intersections that saw the most intense gunfire. With many of the other roads and junctions, there was no way to know for sure what was what, but Cole enjoyed the guessing game and would stop at intersections along the way to draw out lines of fire in his mind.

Back at the bakery, Cole went to work cleaning up in the kitchen. Not long into the task, Isabella's mother called from the store for him. He walked casually from the kitchen and looked for her, but his eyes stopped short of halfway through their scan of the bakery and focused squarely on the shadow of a man standing just inside the doorway.

"Tony?"

Cole stood in the narrow hall leading in from the kitchen for just a second, unsure of what to think.

"Hey Cole, how you been?"

Cole smacked his hands against his legs back and forth to shake off the flour from the kitchen and asked, "What are you doing here?"

Tony never let his gaze leave Cole's eyes.

"We need to talk, Cole."

CHAPTER 2: THE UNRAVELLING

COLE STOOD FOR A moment more, staring across the small room at Tony's silhouette in the morning light, unsure of what to think. He was not supposed to be here. No one from the Task Force was supposed to ever see him again. While Tony had been his most trusted confidant, Cole nevertheless felt the proverbial butterflies in his stomach. A sharp edge pressed at his throat, like the tip of a blade just cutting slightly into his neck. Despite that, he was, in a strange way, partly relieved to see a familiar face. In Tony he saw the boats, the chases, the drugs, the booze, and most of all, the thrill of putting it all on the line time and again.

"How have you been, Cole?"

Cole paused before wiping his hands one last time on his pant legs. He mashed his back teeth together a few times and tried to swallow, but found that his mouth had already begun to run dry.

"I'm all right Tony. It's good to see you."

Tony took a few steps into the bakery and nodded towards toward Isabella's mother, softly saying *Bonjour* with a smile.

Keenly aware of Cole's discomfort, she turned to look at him for a few seconds before looking back down at the floor and walking back out, past Cole and into the kitchen.

"Can we take a walk?"

Cole nodded and walked over toward the door. As he did, Tony patted him on the back twice and followed. It was that gesture on Tony's part that solidified Cole's fears. This was not good.

Once outside the bakery, Cole took a deep breath and asked, "Where to?"

"How about down by the water?"

Cole turned left and Tony followed to his right and just behind.

"What brings you to France?"

Tony paused before replying. "Something has sort of come up, Cole."

"I thought we were squared up after Panama."

"Yeah; yes, we were—or are. We are, Cole."

Cole didn't respond for some time. They walked to the end of the street, into the main square, and down a second narrow curving road towards the marina.

"Am I in trouble?"

"No, it's not that. There are some guys from Homeland Security that want to talk with you."

"Seems to me that Carentan is a bit out of their jurisdiction." Cole stopped and turned to face Tony, who laughed just a bit and shook his head.

"You haven't changed, Cole."

Cole was not in the mood for jokes. "Tony, quit dodging questions. Tell me what's going on."

"Let's walk."

With that, Cole continued on towards the small marina and as the street opened up on the waterfront, there were a few cafes that lined one side of the road and the marina and docks sat on the other. Cole took quick note of three men in dark business suits that sat in the far shaded corner of a cafe. Two made eye contact with Cole as he and Tony passed. *No one wears dark suits in Carentan*, Cole thought. *Especially on a weekday, at a café, in the middle of the day.*

Beyond the road was a small brick walkway with a handful of fountains and benches that lined each side. Once they were standing by the concrete wharf, Cole pressed Tony again.

"Tell me the truth, Tony. What are you doing here?"

Tony hesitated and looked out at the fleet of small fishing boats and pleasure craft that were tied up to the finger piers. He took a long breath, which did nothing but reaffirm Cole's fears that something was wrong.

"There's something going on down in Mexico, and your name came up as someone that might be able to help."

Cole thought about Mexico for a few seconds then pivoted to look back at the cafés. He looked back at the suits, who were still seated around a small table with coffee cups in their hands. Two were just a few years older than Cole, and a third was an older and mildly overweight man. As Cole stared at them, they all made eye contact with him for a second time.

"The suits over at the café?"

"How'd you know that?"

Cole turned back towards the water and scowled. "They don't fit in."

Tony was quiet again and clearly looking for the right words.

"Cole, I wanted to come myself to tell you. This wasn't my idea, but I'm not in a position to stop it."

"I'm not leaving, if that's what you're asking." The tension peaked.

"Cole, you're not going to have a choice on this one."

Sensing someone walking up from his side, Cole turned to see the oldest of the suits casually walking up. As he approached, he smiled a big obnoxious toothy grin and called out loudly, "Is this our man, Tony?"

Tony replied, "It is. This is Cole Williams. Cole, this is Special Agent Johnson with DHS."

With that, Johnson let out a short cackling laugh and extended his hand.

Cole obliged and shook his. As soon as he did, Johnson gripped and pulled hard enough to throw off Cole's balance for a second. Never letting go of his stupid goofy smile, Cole knew at once all he needed to know about Johnson. *Total dick.*

"Happy to have you onboard, Cole."

Cole stared intently at Johnson and replied, "Not sure I follow what's going on here."

"Not to worry, Cole. We'll fill you in on the way."

"I'm not leaving."

Johnson laughed so loudly that Cole was pretty sure most of Carentan could hear it.

He said it again, "I'm not leaving."

Johnson dropped his smile for just a second and replied, "Well, apparently you're the only one who doesn't realize you don't have a choice." With that, Johnson laughed again, and turned to Tony as if to pressure him in to laughing along with whatever Johnson thought was so funny. Tony didn't laugh. He nodded to acknowledge Johnson, then looked back at Cole.

"Cole, we could use your help on this."

"Who is 'we'?"

"Your country, son." Johnson was still loud and increasingly annoying.

"And if I don't go?"

"We either take you with us, or take you to jail." Johnson's arrogant nasally voice was enough to drive Cole towards the jail option rather than anywhere with him. He was clearly enjoying his little power trip.

By now, the other two younger agents were hovering just out of earshot and walking back and forth.

"So, those are your goons who will drag me off?"

In an instant, Johnson's true colors emerged. "Those aren't goons. Those are two federal agents, young man. And yes, they'll take you to jail if that's what you'd prefer. Plenty of charges I can think of off the top of my head."

Cole looked away as Johnson continued, "I know all about you Cole. Your mouth and your bad decisions are your downfall. I can see that more clearly now."

Tony intervened and put a hand on Cole's shoulder. "Cole, let's walk some more."

Turning Cole away from Johnson and taking a step to give them some distance, he turned back towards Johnson. "Can we have an hour?"

Johnson's head wobbled just a bit as he grinned, "That's fine. One hour. We'll have the van ready to go."

Tony nodded, "Thanks. We'll be ready."

As they walked, Johnson called out again, "One hour, Tony."

Cole was shaking. Tony held Cole's shoulder and urged him along, "Cole, walk. Don't say a word. Just walk."

Back at the bakery, Tony stopped Cole just outside. "Cole, get some things packed. I don't have time to say all the things I want to tell you right now, so please just grab some clothes and do whatever you can to say goodbye."

"Fuck this, Tony."

"Dammit Cole. Listen to me. Go pack some clothes. Don't turn this into anything. Not here, OK?"

Cole exhaled through his nostrils and turned to walk inside.

଼

HE FOUND Isabella with Marie in the kitchen. They had just finished lunch. Marie was splashing her hand in a small pool of water on the table and smiling as she looked up at Cole.

In a trembling voice, he asked, "Can we go upstairs?"

"Cole, what is going on?"

Isabella's mother and father both came from upstairs, stood at the bottom of the steps, and didn't say a word. Cole walked towards Marie and picked her up in his right arm, with his left hand around her back. He ran his hand up and down her back and felt his legs getting light under his feet.

"Can we just go upstairs for a bit?"

"Yes, yes, of course. What is going on? Who was that man?"

Cole looked at Isabella's parents as he walked past them then down at the floor as he carried Marie in his arms. There was nothing to say. When he got to their room, the weight of it all struck him and he pressed his back hard against the blue wall before dropping to the floor. Now seated on the hard wood with his legs crossed in front of him, he held Marie tight against his chest and felt her hand playing with his ear. He remembered their games every night and with that simple solitary thought, he fell apart.

He felt the tears first in the outer corners of his eyes, followed soon by the lump in his throat. He fought back as hard as he could, but the tears swelled to the bottoms of his eyelids before spilling over and down his cheek. His right cheek against Marie's, he felt the drops between his skin and hers, only deepening the pit into which his heart had fallen.

His vision now blurred, he felt the first short uncontrollable puffs of forced air through his nostrils that marked the onset of even deeper tears. By the time Isabella came through the door, she could do nothing but stand there with her hand over her mouth and back away from Cole. As she did, she shook her head as if to deny his apparent hopelessness.

"What did they do, Cole?"

He couldn't talk or even acknowledge her question. He just held Marie in his arms and pinched his eyes in a failed attempt to stop, or at least delay, the tears that were now rolling down his cheek. Isabella reached out to take Marie, but Cole wouldn't let go. She then dropped down softly to her knees and leaned in towards Cole. Marie's hand was against his face now and as he opened his eyes, he saw Isabella tuck a long and dark curled strand of hair behind her ear as she tried to comfort him.

Several minutes passed before Cole could compose himself. Each time he tried, Marie shuffled in his arms or moved in such a way that Cole could not escape the reality that he was leaving. Without knowing details, even Isabella had tears forming in her own eyes. Marie was the only one not crying, only because she was too young to understand what Cole knew and Isabella was slowly realizing. He was leaving. Cole thought back to the image of Isabella standing on the pier in Martinique as he throttled ahead on that fateful run. He'd left her crying once and vowed to never do it again. Now, his promise was slipping away.

Twenty minutes or so passed. Half an hour of his time was now gone. Cole ran his fingers through Marie's hair and touched her head with the pads of his fingers. It took something as bad as him leaving to fully realize how much he loved that little girl. For a few moments he forgot entirely about Tony and the others waiting for him and reflected on his own emotions. *Have I taken the better part of the past year for granted? Why, in my last hour with Marie am I only understanding now how much she means to me?* He realized that Isabella still had no idea what was going on.

Composing himself, Cole took a steady breath and looked at her watered eyes. She scanned his back and forth for answers.

"They want me to leave with them."

She shook her head. "When?"

Cole swallowed and closed his eyes for a second, pulling Marie's head against his cheek. "Now."

"Who are they? Is this for drugs?" She said *drugs* softly as her parents were still unaware of those sordid details.

Cole shook his head. "No, they're Americans. I think they want me to do more work for them."

"No. Tell them no."

"I can't. They're taking me either way. Jail, or I work for them."

"But this is France. You are in France. They can't just take you."

At that, Cole found a bit of humor. Not enough for him to laugh, or even smile, but enough to clear his head for a moment.

"At this level, they can do anything they want."

"Tell them no." Isabella did not want to accept it. She was normally quick to understand these kinds of things, but the thought of Cole's departure was overwhelming her.

With less than half an hour to go, Cole passed Marie off to Isabella and pulled his green sea bag from under the bed. There were few possessions that conjured up vivid emotions like the ones Cole now felt. His sea bag was one of them. It bore the harshest of his memories. It had been issued to him when he first reported to the Coast Guard

Academy. For Cole, it was a rough four years of instruction followed by two miserable years on *Delaney* followed by another year where he'd damn near gotten himself killed in the name of a good time. Isabella sat on the floor with Marie and watched him. As he pulled boxers and socks from the drawer, she again said, "No. Tell them you won't leave."

Moving to the closet, he pulled some of his shirts off their hangers and a few pairs of pants.

"Isabella, they're taking me and I can't stop them."

"Then let's leave. We can take the car right now."

Cole shook his head, "And go where? With Marie, where would we go?"

He paused at the closet and looked at her. She was beautiful, her hair a mess and tangled behind her head and an old pair of jeans sitting low on her curved waist. Cole felt the tears again and turned back to the closet to grab what was left of his clothes.

"Wait for me. Just give me a second." He wanted to pack quickly so that he could give the two of them his undivided attention for what precious minutes remained. From the bathroom, he grabbed some basics and returned to their room, pushed them into his sea bag, and cinched the top of it closed. From there, he sat back down next to Isabella and reached his arms out for Marie. Typical of her, she didn't want to leave her mother's arms, and it made Cole smile for just a second.

Isabella now had her head down, against Marie's, rubbing her hand up and down Marie's back.

"What do they want you to do?"

"I don't know."

Cole looked at the clock by the dresser and he had 15 minutes left. *Fifteen minutes and an unknown future ahead,* he thought. He found himself questioning his life again, like he'd done during the back end of his drug running days, but this time it was out of his control and entirely unforeseen. Standing for a second, he stepped up and behind Isabella, sat back down halfway between the door and the wall, and pulled Isabella in close to him so that both of his hands were now also cradling

Marie. He felt the tears once more. *I've taken this for granted,* he thought to himself. *Fifteen damn minutes left.* He tucked his head into the curls of Isabella's hair and took a long breath, fighting back the choking feeling in his gut.

Isabella asked, "For how long?"

"I don't know."

With his head against the side of hers, he looked at the clock again. *Ten minutes.*

Fuck, he thought. It was gut-wrenching. Physical pain was one thing, but the emotional pain that was running unchecked through his veins burned and constricted like nothing else he'd ever felt.

Isabella turned towards him and slowly passed Marie into his arms. As she did, Cole felt Marie's hand again as it ran down his cheek and grabbed onto the collar of his shirt. He loved Isabella dearly, but to feel his own daughter's tiny fingers curled against his neck sent him into another round of tears that quickly pooled and ran down his cheek. She reached up and touched one of them as it ran down to his chin.

"Chin," he said, swallowing and fighting back to regain some decency. As he did, Marie touched her finger to her own chin and Cole was blinded all at once by the onset of more tears, the big kind that seem to rush out unchecked all at once, usually reserved for funerals and other such somber occasions. Isabella was now crying again. With one hand, Cole wiped at his face and mashed his thumb and pointer finger into his closed eyes to stem the tide. He swallowed again and smiled at his little girl.

"Nose," he said. She smiled, reached up and touched at his nose.

"Eye." Again, Marie softly pushed her finger against his left eye.

Cole smiled. He didn't know what Johnson had in store for him, but Cole's specialty in the niche market of boats, drugs, and guns had not proven one with the highest survivability rate. With five minutes left to go, he found in himself a new determination to remember each final minute with every sense afforded to him. With Isabella by his side and her head against his shoulder, he held Marie as close as he could.

"Ear," he said softly. She reached up and touched at his.

"Where is Marie's ear?" She paused for a moment, smiled as she thought out the question and pointed her finger back towards her own.

"You are the smartest little girl in the whole world," he said quietly, again fighting a losing battle to stop the steady drip from his own eyes. "I love you more than the world."

Cole pressed his lips to her forehead, gave her a long kiss, and passed her to Isabella before helping both of them to their feet. Isabella was quiet for no other reason than the incomprehensible magnitude of the situation. Cole walked over to the closet again and from the back corner, he reached for his boots. They had gathered some dust over the past months, but he stared at them for a few seconds with the same look as one would give to an old partner in crime. Each nick and scratch against the leather was its own story of Cole's life, born from some dark alley in the seediest parts of Panama. He set them down on the floor, kicked off his shoes, and slid the leather boots over his feet. They felt familiar on his feet, but foreign in a way as he had not worn them since arriving in France.

Back to Isabella and Marie, he hugged them both and Isabella began to cry. It was typical of her to wait until the last second and her timing was awful as he needed to be moving downstairs at that moment. He held her close and whispered, "I'll be back soon."

"Promise me, Cole."

"I promise. Soon." It was a lie. He hated it, but he had no choice. Cole knew nothing of what lay ahead, but it served its purpose to calm her enough to begin walking downstairs. He pulled his sea bag over his shoulder, looked back at their room for a second, and then turned away before giving his mind another opportunity to bleed itself dry of tears. As his feet touched each step on the way down, Cole composed himself, again pressing his fingers into his eyes to dry them out and he bit down with his jaw to rekindle his long-dormant meanness before encountering Johnson and his thug agents.

Isabella was still sniffling as they made their way down to the second floor. Her parents followed, still not saying a word. Once down in the bakery, Cole saw the silhouettes of the men standing on the sidewalk outside. He hugged Isabella once more and wrapped his right hand around Marie's head and kissed her just beside her delicate and tiny ear. Looking at Isabella's parents, he saw that her mother was also on the verge of tears.

In a thick French accent, she said, "Be safe, Cole."

Cole nodded, then looked at her father, who said nothing, but stood trying his best to seem stoic against a room of crying women. At that moment it occurred to Cole that Isabella's father was certainly not going to enjoy the rest of the day. Cole stepped outside and nodded at Tony, taking a deep breath. The five of them stood on the curb in a loose circle.

Tony asked, "You ready?"

Cole hesitated and stared at him for a moment before replying, "Yeah."

Johnson was next to speak, again in a voice louder than necessary for the occasion, "Well, if we've got all the good-byes out of the way, we should be going. Cole, these are two of my agents, Special Agent Adams and Special Agent Lawrence. They'll be escorting you." He paused before continuing, "I've been told you can be a handful at times." He laughed as he said it, with the same shrill tone from before. Mildly overweight, with a receding hairline and a near-constant smile, Cole was more and more convinced that Johnson was not the type anyone wanted to be around for any period of time.

Cole looked back to Tony, who softly shook his head and looked away as if to dismiss it as a joke. Lawrence spoke up then, in a muted voice, to ask, "We're not gonna have any problems, are we Cole?"

In total contrast to Johnson, and by his tone alone, Cole could tell that Lawrence wasn't as bad as he'd previously suspected. But Johnson's annoying voice and bravado in front of Isabella, who was now standing in the doorway with Marie, was chaffing him. Cole was going to shake his head to indicate no, but before he could, Adams interjected.

Tall, with short blond hair and beady sinister eyes, Adams looked the part of a cocky federal type. With a half grin on his face, he looked over to Isabella, then back at Lawrence and said, "With a piece of tail like that, I wouldn't want to leave either."

Isabella was close enough to hear it and she instinctively took a step back inside. Lawrence said nothing, but Johnson let go another one of his piercing laughs and Cole felt the kind of rage that he hadn't experienced for some time. Cole had a dark side, and he'd worked for the better part of a year to rid himself of it, but Adams was unknowingly stirring the beast. Adams then looked directly at Cole for a reaction, his smile a weird expression that looked more of a practiced pose than a smile. He was picking a fight, which was fine, but he proved himself too much of a prick to do it anywhere but here. And rather than back up his words with force, he was relying on whatever stupid little badge was tucked under his jacket. He laughed as he looked at Cole, rocked back and forth a bit on his legs, and crossed his arms in front of his chest.

In a split-second decision, a reaction, Cole stepped slightly forward with his right foot, balancing the bulk of his weight on the sole of his boot, and drove forward with both his elbows to lean in towards Adams. Before anyone could react, Cole lifted his left foot from the ground, pointed his toe slightly back and angled his foot as it came down hard and fast at a steep angle against Adams' straightened knee. With a pop and an eerie elastic feel, he kicked through and felt Adams' leg buckle backwards.

What followed was too quick for Cole to process, but he heard Adams' scream followed by other yells and shouts. Before he could discern who was yelling at who, Cole found his right arm extended and subdued by Lawrence as he was thrown firmly to the sidewalk. With a knee against the back of his neck, he strained to turn his head and look back towards Isabella. As he did, he saw her just for a second shielding Marie's face from the fight on the curb. Isabella looked at him for a moment and he thought to tell her that he loved her, but her father was already bringing them further inside the bakery. Isabella and Marie were gone. Her father emerged a moment later and yelled at someone, either Tony or Johnson, but Cole couldn't tell who.

He couldn't see Adams, but he could hear the moans and constant cursing, which gave Cole some satisfaction. Lawrence was busy putting handcuffs on Cole when he heard Johnson's agitated and booming voice yell out to get them all in the van. Lawrence was up for a second, opened a door, then returned to pull Cole up by his shoulders and walk him a few steps towards a parked and already running van. He tried to look back once more for Isabella, but Lawrence pushed hard at the back of his head until Cole was thrown into the van. Tony was driving, Adams was in the passenger seat, screaming that he was going to kill Cole, and Johnson was yelling sporadically at all of them to either shut up or move faster.

Cole looked to his left and caught one last glimpse of the *Boulanger Patissier*, wondering whether he would ever see it again. The ice cream cooler, the little pizzas he devoured each day, the old wooden broom that he'd swept up with each day—they all flashed through his mind. Then there was the blue paint on the walls, the white trim with its imperfections and dents. And then there was Isabella and Marie, with their curly black hair and matching smiles. He forced those thoughts from his mind, beginning a new chapter. There would no doubt be little room for pity or empathy. He was going to fight someone else's war, and his mind and spirit were in dire need of hardening. It was one of those rare moments in life, where above the shouting and confusion surrounding him, he thought only of the certainty that his life had changed once more. He had been a fool to think anything different would come of his tragic life.

C'est la Vie, Cole told himself.

C'est la Vie.

CHAPTER 3: LONDON

AS THEY DROVE THE hour or so to Caen, Johnson made quick arrangements over the phone to drop Adams off at a hospital. Not ten minutes into the drive, Johnson had enough of his screaming and told him authoritatively to shut up, which he grudgingly did. From the back seat, Cole still heard Adams wince or grunt in pain when the van took a turn or hit a bump in the road. He smiled to himself, having deduced from the beginning that a shattered knee was just the kind of thing to put a turd like Adams back in his place.

After dropping him off unceremoniously at a hospital, Johnson, Lawrence, Tony, and Cole pulled up at a ferry terminal on the north coast. Before getting out, Johnson turned to Cole from the seat in front of him and pointed one finger, waving it erratically, and told Cole in so many words not to try anything. He was breathing heavily, indicating to Cole that Johnson was struggling to hide his growing unease. Lawrence took off his handcuffs and they made their way through the terminal. Lawrence did the bulk of the work clearing them through Customs as Johnson settled into a seat at the small café inside, his back to the seating area. There was an unending stream of paperwork that Lawrence casually produced before they let Cole through.

Once cleared, he asked, "So what am I, a prisoner?"

"Not quite," said Lawrence calmly, "but you're close to being one with that stunt back there. Just keep your act together for a bit, I think you'll have some more clarity once we get to London."

"Why are we going to London?"

Lawrence looked at Cole for a moment, then away and out to the approaching ferry before replying, "You'll get read in on the project."

"What project?"

"Just sit tight, OK?" Lawrence was not giving up any more information, so Cole went over to a seat in the corner and sat down. Tony soon came over and sat next to him while Lawrence kept a slow stroll around the terminal. Johnson stayed at the café, devouring a plate of assorted pastries and a cup of coffee.

"He's a fat piece of shit," Cole said, nodding towards Johnson.

"For fuck's sake, Cole. Could you just try not to destroy anything or anyone for a few hours?"

"How long is this project gonna run?"

Tony shook his head to dismiss the question. "I really don't know. I think a lot is going to depend on you. You'll have a better idea once we get to London."

London, Cole thought. *Why is everyone so focused on London?*

Cole sat and stewed for the next half hour until the ferry boarded. Once they all found some seats, Johnson did his best to take a nap while Lawrence sat opposite Cole as his babysitter for the trip and Tony sat beside him. It was nearing midday, and the ferry was full of vacationers and a few school groups. Cole watched as kids ran around playing with each other and young families carried their toddlers in their arms. In nearly all of them, he saw Isabella and Marie. The couples' smiles and light conversations only drove Cole deeper into the void. A mother talking to her child, a father holding a daughters' hand, or just a smiling kid playing tag with his friends was all too much for Cole to keep himself together. He tried to sleep, but couldn't.

"Can I take a walk?"

Lawrence looked at Tony for a second as if to ask what would happen if Cole went for a walk. Before either of them could discuss it, Johnson, with his eyes still closed, asked plainly, "Is he going to do anything dumb?"

Tony answered, "No, he'll be fine. Just some fresh air maybe might help a bit."

Johnson, without even the decency to open an eye, asked, "He's not gonna jump overboard or anything?" His lips and forehead were dotted with beads of sweat.

"No, he'll be fine."

Tony then turned to Cole, looked sternly at him, and repeated himself. "He'll be fine."

"Stay with him, Lawrence." Johnson turned his head back to the other side and pretended to nod off.

Walking the upper decks, Cole looked back to the south and saw the disappearing low form of the Normandy coast. To his right was Pointe Du Hoc and beyond that Carentan. *Isabella,* he thought. *Marie.* He remembered the softness of her hair against his fingers. It was painful to think about, but Cole was wholly unable to pull his eyes away from the fading coast. He stood for some time on the fantail, watching the white trail of wake behind the ferry as she rocked fore and aft in a light chop. The wind blew steady but light from the northwest, and it was true what Tony had said. The salt air gave Cole a bit of a break and some time to process. As Normandy disappeared behind him, Cole walked forward and stared out at the English Channel and wondered what he'd find on the other side.

After some time, and with a light sheen of salt mist against his skin, Cole returned to the cabin and sat back down without saying a word. The rest of the trip was uneventful. Once in Portsmouth early in the evening, they hurried off to another waiting van and were on their way headed north. Johnson was back on the phone and seemed to be making an unending stream of promises, all seeming to center around his ability to manage whatever program Cole was now being led into. With time, Johnson's voice faded into the background and Cole focused more intently on the south of England, thinking to himself that it was not that much unlike France. There were rolling hills, open fields, and small villages dotting the landscape. At times Cole could see a playground or schoolyard approaching and he found it easier to look away than to see anything or anyone that might bring his mind back to Marie.

An hour and a half later, with the sun now down, the distant outline of London appeared in front of them. He remembered the first time he'd seen Panama City, with all its lights and pulsing dance music and the excitement of something new. In his current state of mind, Cole looked at London with indifference. After a half an hour of roundabouts and narrow roads, the van stopped in front of a neat row of townhouses on a narrow one-way street.

Tony and Johnson stepped out while Lawrence stayed with the van. Cole then slid out as well, yawned, and followed them as they walked up to the front door of the fifth or sixth townhouse down the road. Johnson knocked. Shortly thereafter, a woman opened the front door, greeted them all, then moved back inside and allowed them in.

"Special Agent Johnson, I presume?"

Stepping forward, Johnson shook her hand and turned back to Tony and Cole.

"Yes, Ma'am. Let me introduce Tony, one of our agents with a background in Central America, and Cole, our resident boat driver and smuggling extraordinaire. Cole will be in-country with the team."

"Pleasure to meet each of you. Please just call me Gail. Thank you for meeting here—far less chances of nosey people intruding. Now let's move into the kitchen and have a little chat."

They all walked through the living room into the kitchen, and took seats at a round wooden table overlooking a small well-kept garden outside.

"Can I get anyone anything to drink?"

All shaking their heads no, Gail pressed the issue. "Cole, you look like you could use a beer."

Reluctantly, he agreed. "That would be great. Thank you." He immediately liked her.

"Anyone else?"

Tony looked just for a second at Johnson then turned to Gail, "Why not? Thanks."

Pulling two Budweisers from her refrigerator, Gail made quick work of popping off the tops before passing them to Tony and Cole, who didn't hide their surprise that she kept bottles of Budweiser in her kitchen.

Gail smiled slightly. "My son, he likes your American beer." She looked down at the floor, lost in thought for a second. Sitting back down, she quickly turned her attention elsewhere. "Let's get down to business, shall we? Tony, would you be so kind as to close that door?"

Tony leaned over and pushed the door to the garden closed and nudged it further until it latched shut.

"All right then, gentlemen. As you may or may not be aware, we have credible intelligence that suggests there is an effort underway to move people and weapons across the southern border of the United States."

With his arrogance taking center stage, Johnson asked, "And who is 'we'?"

"British intelligence." Gail stared back at him with no emotion whatsoever. There was more than a hint of tension between the two, and Johnson was back to his game of trying to puff out his chest and establish himself as the alpha.

He flashed his stupid smile again and laughed out loud. "Can't we be a bit more specific?"

Gail flatly replied, "No, we cannot. We have strong indications of an impending attempt to exploit your southern maritime border and launch attacks within the United States. We have vetted sources both in Africa and the Caribbean who suggest that a transatlantic movement may have already taken place to stage a cell along a route that likely will go as far north as Mexico before making the jump through your Gulf of Mexico."

Johnson asked, "Can you elaborate on your sources?"

Tony looked away, visibly embarrassed. It was clear that Johnson was not going to abandon his power trip.

"No, I cannot, nor will I. We are sharing this intelligence with you as a courtesy. Frankly, Mr. Johnson, your agencies do not have a stellar track record when it comes to protecting our sources. For that reason, and several others, we have agreed to share pertinent information with you, and I'm offering one of our top analysts to embed with your team to give this project the best chance at success. But we will not divulge to you—or to anyone else—the full extent of our ongoing counter-terror operations."

She stared at him. Cole's stomach pulsed for a second as he almost laughed out loud. Johnson sat back in his chair and looked away from Gail. He was defeated. Gail was clearly not one to mess with.

"Well, on behalf of the United States, we thank you for working with us." It was his attempt at redemption, as if to suggest a clown like him spoke for the entire country. Gail slowly exhaled, clearly seeing through Johnson's line of shit.

Tony asked, "Where can we link up with your analyst?"

Gail replied happily, "She'll be down any minute."

Tony and Cole looked at each and both took long sips from their beers. A pause in the conversation followed that bordered on awkward before Gail spoke up again.

"These are dark times for both of our countries. If we work together, I truly believe we have the best chance of stopping this before it goes too far." She paused for a second before looking towards Johnson and continuing. "But if we resort to politics and pettiness, I fear they may have a leg up on us. So for both our sakes, let's please be adults."

Cole took another sip from his beer to hide his smile. Johnson was all but deflated. After a few moments more, Cole heard the steps creaking and turned in his seat to look down the hallway.

Gail called out, "Claire, darling, we're in the kitchen."

From near the front door, a younger voice called back, "One minute."

After another trip up and down the steps, she emerged from the living room. Tall, with long brown hair that rolled off her shoulders in shallow waves, she walked casually into the kitchen and Cole could do little but look away to avoid staring for too long. She was absolutely stunning in a pair of jeans and a loose white t-shirt that hung low over her hips. Nevertheless, Cole was not in the mood for pretty girls.

Gail spoke since none of the men in the room could find anything remotely intelligent to say. "Claire, these are the Americans we've been discussing."

Johnson immediately chimed in, "I'm Michael Johnson, the Special Agent in Charge from Homeland Security. Pleased to meet you."

Funny, Cole thought, that Johnson had started to inflate his ego once again. He hoped that Gail would find another opportunity to poke holes in his bubble of narcissism, but it seemed that for the time at least, Johnson might keep himself in check.

"Claire, this is Tony and Cole. Cole will be travelling with you."

He nodded and offered a slight smile, "Nice to meet you."

It's difficult to get a read on her, Cole thought. She seemed to offer just a passing glance at each of these men now seated around the kitchen table and seemed wholly unimpressed by either their background or the impending trip.

"Nice to meet you too," was all she said back, albeit with a friendly tone.

"I've got one more bag to grab, and I'll be ready."

Gail nodded and smiled at her, watching Claire walk out of the kitchen, down the hallway to the staircase and up. It was the first facial expression he'd seen from Gail that showed any indication of fondness for anything. There was a connection between the two of them, but what that connection was Cole couldn't yet be certain.

Gail spoke. "Claire will send me updates with your progress and we'll pass what we can back to her. She will be your primary point of contact on our end. Agent Johnson, I assume you've compiled the rest of the team?"

"Of course. Cole and Claire will meet up with two more of our guys before Cozumel."

Gail thought for a second. "A total of four seems a bit thin…"

Johnson tried to reassure her. "We've looked extensively at this and feel that a soft profile is critical, but my two guys are top tier operators."

She asked, "QRF?"

"Of course. We'll have one staged along with twenty-four-hour satellite coverage, if needed."

Cole thought back to the Panama and the supposed Quick Reaction Force that hadn't quite been quick enough before he took a bullet. With his fingers, he pressed them against the hardened scar across his chest, as if that would make any difference.

Gail paused again, took a long slow breath and said, "Well, all right then. Tony, would you crack that door open again? It's a bit warm without a breeze."

Tony leaned over, reopened the door, and as he did, Cole felt the late evening air swirl through the small kitchen, a hint of some flower from outside carried in with it. He looked out to the garden where a circular table was surrounded by chairs and a high wooden fence. There were flowers neatly dug into a bed of mulch that ran the length of all three sides. As he sat there and looked out of the large glass window overlooking the garden, he heard the creaking steps again as Claire made her way down one last time.

"Well then," Gail said, "I guess you should be going. It's a long trip in front of you."

Cole asked, "What's in Cozumel?"

Gail smiled, "Has no one told you?"

Cole shook his head.

She laughed, "Sex, drugs, and rock and roll, my dear. Try not to lose your head."

Cole liked her more by the minute. He couldn't quite nail down what it was about Gail, but in less than half an hour, he knew, without a doubt, that she was someone he could get along with.

Johnson interjected, "We will make a quick stop in Mississippi to pick up the rest of the team, and then you'll be on your way, Cole."

Gail chimed in. "Be sure to say hello to Congressman Thomas for me."

Johnson looked taken aback, surprised by Gail's comment.

"Did you think I didn't know? Gene and I have worked together for years."

Johnson stumbled on his words. "Well, no; of course I knew," before he turned to avoid any more of Gail's questions.

Cole thought for a moment. He'd been to Mexico several times on *Delaney*. It was a beautiful country under siege by a horrific drug problem, fueled by North America's unending addiction to cocaine, marijuana, and whatever else the cartels could cook up, ship north, and turn a profit.

They all crowded into the living room where each took a turn to shake Gail's hand and she wished them well. With the front door open and Johnson already outside, Gail called out softly as Claire was the last to leave, "Claire, darling..."

She turned and looked back. "Yes?"

From the doorway, Cole stopped and turned to catch Gail as she called back, "Do be careful down there."

Casually, Claire replied, "Of course. We'll talk soon."

Out on the sidewalk, Cole looked at Claire for a second and was about to ask her about Gail, but she was quick to grab both duffel bags and take them to the back of the van. Beautiful indeed, and she also seemed keenly aware of her surroundings. With her bags loaded, she walked back around, smiled at Cole for a second, and climbed in. Johnson was in the backseat now, Tony beside him, leaving Cole and Claire in the middle. He wanted to talk, but couldn't think of a thing to say. From the front passenger seat, Lawrence looked back and gave a thumbs up.

Johnson snorted, "Let's get going."

Claire was staring intently out the window as the van meandered down some side streets, past a row of small shops, then into a small downtown area before navigating towards the highway.

Cole asked, "So where are we?"

Still looking outside at the streets, she replied, "Chiswick," before pausing for a second. "I grew up here."

The rest of the ride was quiet, except for Johnson and his litany of phone calls that he seemed determined to make in front of all the passengers in the van to demonstrate just how important he was. It was dark, but the streets were alive with families, friends, and bustling foot traffic all out for an evening stroll. Had it not been for Johnson, it might have been a pleasant ride. He was now talking to higher-ups, with most of his sentences either beginning or ending with "Yes, Sir" or "Absolutely" or "We will make that happen." It seemed to Cole that he was blowing smoke and empty promises. He tried to drown out Johnson's incessant ass-kissing, but found it nearly impossible. Just over an hour later, the van pulled up to Gatwick airport and Cole had a mild headache from Johnson's ever-increasing level of bragging.

After clearing a gate, the van continued out onto the general aviation ramp and up to a sleek-looking white jet. *Better than most*, Cole thought as he stepped out to unload his sea bag. Claire had her two bags and as Johnson walked, he looked at Lawrence then back at the van, telling him in his own arrogant way to get his bag for him. Lawrence did it with the same quiet professionalism that he'd demonstrated since Cole first saw him in France. Just as had been the case with his first encounter with Tony, Cole surmised that he shouldn't write off all of DHS just because Johnson didn't know his head from his ass.

Soon after boarding, the plane began a slow taxi before Cole had even sat down. As they climbed out over London in the evening calm, Cole settled into an unbelievably comfortable leather reclining seat, well ahead of even what first class passengers would expect on a major airline. It was a DHS-contracted Gulfstream that roared up above the high clouds and settled in the mid-40s for a cruising altitude to the west. By the time they leveled off, Cole was asleep.

HE AWOKE EARLY in the morning as the plane began a shallow descent. There was a television screen on one bulkhead of the plane with a map indicating their position over northern Florida. Still descending, Cole wondered where they were headed now, but didn't want to bother anyone as he'd long since discovered it didn't matter if he knew either way. He rolled a bit in his seat and looked out the window. Ahead of them it was still dark, but at their altitude he could see the thin orange line on the horizon to the east marking the sun's climb and the start of another day.

He thought back to Isabella and Marie. They were almost certainly asleep in their bed, this being the first night Marie had known without her father. He was beyond the point of tears, the increasing distance between them being enough for Cole to partially detach himself from those raw emotions. It didn't stop him from being short of breath until he regained full control of his thoughts. The sadness was the same, but the pit in his stomach just sat there, unable to draw out any more outward signs of the deep pain he felt. He was fighting with himself and wrestling with the softer side that had attached to him over the past months. He didn't hate his past self, but knew well enough that he would need to rekindle his dark side if he was to survive the task ahead.

To his left, and a row in front of him, Claire was still sleeping in a seat. Her hair was up in a loose bun over her head and at some point she'd acquired a blanket that was tucked across her chest. Cole looked at her for a few moments more then back out the window. She was undeniably gorgeous, which at any other point in Cole's life would have triggered a vast array of feelings. But in this case, with so much of his life up-ended in less than 24 hours, his conscience couldn't stir the same emotions that should have surely boiled to the surface in the presence of such a woman. Just a few years ago, Claire would have sent his heart spiraling off in random directions or at the least triggered some basic conversation to see where it might lead. It occurred to him as he turned to look at her again that he was a broken man. The thought saddened him, but again, it was a thought he kept buried in the deepest pit of his own mind.

Tony was up and walking now, taking a seat next to Cole.

"You gonna be all right, Cole?"

Cole looked back out the window, "Yeah. I'll be fine."

"You're going to meet with a Congressman that has some oversight on this whole thing. I've met him before. He's one of the good ones, OK?"

"What's that supposed to mean?"

Tony laughed, "It means try not to piss him off."

Cole nodded.

The two of them sat for several seconds in the pre-dawn dimly lit cabin without saying a word.

"Cole, I'm sorry about all of this. You're name came up when this whole Mexico situation started to develop. I tried to keep you out of it, but your ass-kicking in Panama made you a popular person for a while. It was too fresh in a lot of peoples' minds to let go of."

Cole thought for a second, then asked, "Would they really put me in jail if I didn't go? You told me that I was free and clear from all of this stuff."

Tony exhaled, "I know I said that; to me you were. But once Johnson had the idea in his head, he brought it all back up and got enough people onboard to bring you back in." He paused for a moment then continued in a muted voice, "Cole, this is just me and you talking, OK?"

Cole nodded that he understood.

Tony continued, "Watch out for him. Johnson is not one to mess with. He's got his sights set on some pretty lofty goals in DHS and he will do whatever he thinks will get him to the top, to include burying you. I can't tell you how sorry I am about all of this. When we get to Mississippi, I'm heading out, but I'll do what I can to keep tabs on you."

Cole looked quickly at Tony, "So you're not coming?"

"No, I've been reassigned off the Central American stuff and they've got me up in Canada now. I came along on this because I wanted to tell you in person."

Cole squinted his eyes for a moment and asked, "Why Canada?"

Tony laughed. "I told you not to cross Johnson, right? Well, I learned that the hard way. He's got me on the sidelines now. So listen to what I'm telling you—if you cross him you might not be so lucky. You're smarter than most, and you're gonna need everything you've got once you're in-country. At the end of the day, if any of this turns out to be real, you could be doing a really good thing."

He patted Cole again on the back and stood up to walk back towards his seat.

"Remember, I didn't tell you any of that about Johnson."

Cole nodded and Tony walked back forward to his seat.

§

THE PLANE TOUCHED DOWN in the calm and thick pre-dawn summer air of southern Mississippi. Cole felt the heat immediately after he set foot on the tarmac. As the plane shut down, there were crickets in the grass just off the ramp and swarms of flies hovering in the glow from the lights that formed a perimeter around the field. Yet another van was waiting along with two more cars and drivers in each. At the van, two men waited and leaned against the hood with their arms crossed. One wore a pair of jeans with flip flops, while the other had on a pair of worn cotton shorts. Both had loose button-down printed shirts and were of average build. Johnson looked at Cole and Claire then nodded towards the two men. Cole and Claire walked towards them as Johnson went quickly to one of the cars and Tony to the other. After dropping their bags in the back, the four of them, Cole, Claire, and the two new guys, met up at the side.

"Welcome to Mississippi, I'm Matt. I think we'll be working together for the next few months."

Cole reached out to shake his hand, "I'm Cole and this is Claire."

Claire extended her hand and shook Matt's hand as well.

Matt then turned to his counterpart. "And this is Harley. He'll be with us as well."

The handshakes repeated and Harley, gripping Cole's hand firmly, asked, "Did you really drop that Adams' guy back in France?"

Cole, pulled forward and slightly off-balance and taken by surprise by Harley's direct question, replied, "Yeah, I did."

Harley gripped Cole's hand even tighter and pulled once more. Cole felt as if another fight might start, but Harley quickly flashed a grin and let go of Cole's hand.

"I hate that guy, total dick. I pulled security for him and his buddies in Indonesia last year. Total suckfest." He smiled, "Nice to meet you, Cole."

It broke any tension between them. Matt smiled a bit and turned back towards Claire. "Claire, not sure what you've heard along the way about this op, but I'm damn happy to have you along. You've got quite the reputation from some of my buddies who worked in the desert with you."

Claire nodded softly and looked at Cole as if to see if he'd caught the reference. He certainly had, and it only verified what he'd already figured out about her. She was as capable as she was pretty. *A force to be reckoned with*, he thought.

Johnson was already in the backseat of one of the cars and being driven off. Cole looked over to the second car, where Tony stood solemnly looking at Cole. He waved goodbye slowly with two fingers from his forehead then towards Cole. Cole acknowledged with a nod, and Tony looked for a moment more. *Dammit Tony, quit freaking me out like that*, Cole thought.

Matt spoke, "Well, we should get going. We've got a congressman waiting on us."

CHAPTER 4: TRUST NO ONE

BAY ST. LOUIS WAS quiet in the first few moments of daylight. Cole thought back to the drives he took to the north across Panama. *The calm before the storm.* Harley was driving the van with Claire sitting next to him in the passenger seat. Matt and Cole sat in the seat behind them, and the rest of the seats beyond that were full of bags and a handful of Pelican cases stacked on top of each other. Claire had one foot tucked up on her seat and her arms crossed around that knee that she held close to her chest. Harley fidgeted with his GPS on the dash and made small talk with Claire as she stared out the window into the southern haze.

"Sorry you got dragged into this."

It caught Cole by surprise, and he turned to Matt and stared at him without a reply. Matt laughed and asked, "Your mind's somewhere else, isn't it?"

Cole nodded.

Matt repeated himself, "I'm sorry you got pulled into this. I know you've been through a bit already."

Cole nodded again, replying, "No sense in thinking about it. I'm here now."

Matt nodded, then turned and looked out the window as there was little else to say. Up front, Harley and Claire had struck up a conversation now and had found some common ground by discussing Middle East shitholes they'd been to. Claire still held her arms crossed around her one knee and leaned her head against her own shoulder. Despite the small talk, she struck Cole as somewhat guarded, as if she was deliberately hiding her true self from the group. Cole knew he was doing the same thing. In all likelihood, Harley and Matt were doing exactly that as well. Not 15 minutes into the drive, Harley took a hard left and another after that, glanced at his GPS, then pulled into a long gravel driveway leading up to a modest well-kept house on stilts surrounded by tall palm trees on a large grassy lot.

Once parked, all four got out and Cole took in his surroundings. Other than an expansive set of steps leading to the second floor, the entire house was elevated well above the flood plain. A nest of fishing gear was tucked against one concrete column. Two boats and a Jeep were parked beyond that, and there was an outdoor camp-style kitchen situated just off the concrete slab that sat under the main house.

From behind two enormous stainless stockpots, an older man appeared in a pair of filthy cotton shorts and a faded Bay Waveland Yacht Club t-shirt. He approached all four of them without saying a word. Just as Cole assumed they were at the wrong house, the disheveled man extended his hand and introduced himself to Claire.

"You must be Claire," he said, ignoring the rest of them.

She smiled, "Yes, Sir. Claire Parker. Pleased to meet you."

"And how is your mother these days?"

Claire smiled. "She's well. Thank you."

The man stood there for a few seconds more, looking intently at Claire until she almost seemed ready to blush.

His smile grew bigger. "I see a lot of Gail in you, Claire."

Harley and Matt looked at each other in quiet surprise, and Matt dismissed it with a shrug of his shoulders.

The man turned then to Harley and Matt, shaking both of their hands, and said, "Matt, Harley, you come highly recommended. I'm Gene Thomas. Great to meet you both."

Both Matt and Harley nodded. Gene Thomas turned to Cole and looked at him for a few seconds.

"And you, you have got to be Cole Williams." He extended his hand to Cole. "Pleased to meet you, Cole. Long way from the Coast Guard, huh?"

Cole nodded. "Yes, Sir. It is."

Gene Thomas excused himself, checked something behind his two propane tanks, and then went about pulling some plastic chairs from behind one of the boats.

"Let's sit," he said, offering them all seats in a semi-circle on the concrete slab under his house. "Let's talk some ground rules." He shuffled in his seat and looked around as if he'd forgotten something. "Anyone want anything to drink?"

Just as quick as he'd sat down, Gene Thomas was up again and rummaging through a large and dirty cooler next to the outdoor kitchen. He tossed some waters and bottles of orange juice to the rest of them and returned to his seat.

"Just a bit too early for beer, but we'll get there, don't you worry."

Harley and Matt both chugged a water bottle each while Claire and Cole had opted for the orange juice.

"Well, OK. Let's talk business." He crossed one leg over the other and settled in his plastic seat. "This mission will be conducted under the auspices of a counter-drug operation, hence the Armed Services Committee and myself being involved. On paper, you are all conducting surveillance and nothing more."

As he spoke, the car that carried Johnson came roaring into the driveway and crunched the gravel as it came to a quick stop. Johnson nearly leapt out of the backseat and walked briskly over to the five of them.

"Sorry I'm late," he called out from across the grass, "My driver apparently doesn't know his way around his own damn state."

Gene Thomas rolled his eyes and mumbled under his breath, "Oh for fuck's sake. Why is he here?"

Cole laughed just a bit and looked to Matt and Harley, who slyly indicated with their facial expressions that they felt the same about Johnson.

Johnson, out of breath, approached and asked, "What did I miss?"

"Nothing much, we were just getting started."

Johnson extended his hand and proclaimed, "It's a beautiful state, Congressman. I really enjoyed the drive in."

"Oh, really? What did you like?"

Johnson stood for a moment with his mouth open, unsure of what to say. He'd clearly rehearsed his line, but not thought much further.

"Oh, just the scenery."

Gene Thomas raised his eyebrows, took a breath, and turned again in his seat.

"Well, grab a seat, Mr. Johnson." Gene Thomas continued, "Where was I? Ah yeah, so...Armed Services Committee has oversight, I'm the ranking guy on these kinds of disastrous things, so here you all are and we are supposed to talk ground rules. One, you are, on paper, conducting counter-narcotics surveillance. Period. Any questions?"

No one said a word.

"Great," Gene Thomas said. "Two, I don't really give two shits about drugs coming out of Cozumel." He paused and thought for a second before continuing, "Well, that's not entirely true, but I care a lot more at the moment about RPGs, shoulder-fired missiles, or angry men from dusty countries that want to come to America and kill women and children. So, your unofficial, yet slightly official reason for being here, or there, is to stop that from happening. Questions?"

Cole couldn't stay quiet. "I don't know anything about terrorists, Sir."

"You will soon enough, Cole." Gene Thomas looked at Claire with a smile and said, "Claire, we owe your folks a debt of gratitude for sharing this with us. I can assure you we've taken every step we can to keep this quiet. It's as compartmentalized as we can get it, and outside of this little shindig, there are only a handful of folks—all of whom I trust—that have any knowledge of this operation."

Claire nodded. "Thank you."

Gene Thomas looked back at the rest of them, turned to face Cole and continued, "What I need from you Cole is to embed yourself with the seediest, dirtiest, creepiest, and most competent smugglers you can find and look for any sign of something more than cocaine or pot coming into the country. Harley and Matt can add a bit of muscle if need be—they're here to help you. Matt has the lead for the American contingent and they'll keep things running smooth between Cozumel and Washington. Claire is, among many things, the ears behind this. With a little luck, we can crack into this network quickly and wipe it out before it even gets started. Questions?"

Cole asked dryly, "You want me to run drugs?"

Gene Thomas looked at him with a straight face and nodded, "Yes. Drugs, migrants; hell, if they want to smuggle bananas, I want you to smuggle fucking bananas. Map out the network. If there is talk of smuggling anyone from the Middle East, eastern Russia, China, Africa, Philippines, I need to know about it and I may need you all to stop it."

Johnson inserted himself into the conversation, "If they cross the border, Homeland Security gets the lead."

Gene Thomas looked up for a second, clearly annoyed, and replied, "Yes, of course. If it gets that far, DHS takes the lead. But hopefully it won't. I want to knock these guys out before they even smell American soil."

Johnson nodded, "Of course, Sir. We all want the same thing."

Matt, Harley, and Claire had all been quiet for most of the conversation. Cole could sense that he was the only one just now learning of the objective.

He asked, "What happens if I die?"

"I'm sorry, what?" Gene Thomas asked.

"If I die, what happens?" Cole was sitting in his seat, an empty bottle of orange juice in his hand, and his face devoid of any emotion. It was a simple question in his mind, but he'd inadvertently stared down at his boots and recalled the first hit against him in Panama. "Who am I working for, and what happens if I die? I've got a daughter in France and I want to know what happens if I die."

Claire turned quickly and looked at Cole. Harley scratched his head and looked away. Matt just looked down at his feet and Claire then looked slowly from person to person for a reaction.

"Well, hopefully it won't come to that, Cole," Gene Thomas said.

Johnson again inserted himself into the conversation, "We will absolutely make sure your family is taken care of, Cole."

Johnson's bullshit was quickly chiseling away at Cole's patience.

"Cole," Gene Thomas said, "Why don't you come with me." He stood up and motioned for Cole to follow him. After climbing the large set of steps that led to the front porch, Gene Thomas opened the front door and motioned for Cole to step inside. As he did, Cole felt Gene Thomas' hand pat his shoulder twice. *Why does everyone feel the need to pat my fucking shoulder?* He remembered Tony's advice to stay calm.

Inside Gene Thomas' study, which was a dark wood panel-lined room with the kinds of antiques and souvenirs one would expect from a Congressman, Gene Thomas sat at his desk and powered up his computer.

"Grab a seat," he said.

Gene Thomas typed for a few minutes, proofed it for some time, then spun in his chair to his printer, pulled the single piece of paper off of it, and proof read it again before handing the letter to Cole. It was, in so many words, a life insurance policy, written on United States Congressional letterhead, and promised $250,000 in life insurance to Cole.

"If that works, sign above your name."

Cole took a pen, set the letter down on Gene Thomas' desk and signed. As he did, Gene Thomas printed a second copy and instructed Cole to sign it as well. Once that was complete, Gene Thomas signed both copies and put one in an envelope before passing it back to Cole.

He asked, "Do you have her address?"

Cole thought for a moment and went to write Isabella's address. Halfway through it, he felt the knot in his stomach again and stopped writing lest he let go of a few more tears. He scratched at his neck, coughed to clear his throat, and forced himself to think of something other than her while he filled out the rest of Isabella's parents' street address. Once complete, he pushed it back at Gene Thomas, who sealed it and went the extra step of signing his name over the back of the envelope. He got up from his chair and went over to a wall safe, where he slid the second letter.

"I'll file this today, Cole. You have my word."

Cole cleared his throat to fight back the last of his emotion and said, "Thanks."

"Now, listen to me, Cole. Matt and Harley are on your side. Don't ever question that. I've known Claire's mother for decades. That family is as good as it gets. You have a team that I worked quite hard to build. You, my friend, are the wild card. This entire operation hinges on your ability to infiltrate, something you've apparently done with tremendous success in the past."

He paused before continuing, "How old is she?"

"Who?" Cole asked.

"Your Daughter."

"Six months."

Gene Thomas paused again. "I know this isn't easy for you, but we are too close to something tragic happening. I gave the go-ahead to snatch you. You can dislike me if you'd like, but I did it because I had no one else with a track record like yours. I need this to work, Cole. I don't want to see any more Americans get killed and that's what these punks are coming here to do."

Cole nodded that he understood.

"One last thing, Cole…"

"What's that, Sir?"

"This is just me and you talking, OK?"

Cole had heard that line before and cut Gene Thomas off. "Is this where you tell me not to trust Johnson?"

Gene Thomas sat back in his leather seat and looked at Cole with nothing short of admiration.

"I knew I liked you the second I read your file, Cole. Yes, I was going to tell you not to trust him. In fact, trust no one outside of your circle once you're in Cozumel. I have a strong suspicion he wants DHS to make headline news and may take some risks to facilitate that. I do not agree with those risks. Nevertheless, he'll have tactical control of the operation."

"How does DHS run something in Mexico?"

Gene Thomas nodded. "That's a good question. Politics are often about power and in this day and age every department and agency wants as much as they can get. In this case, Johnson pulled strings and dropped names until he got what he wanted. I've got most of the oversight, but you'll be answering to him."

He pursed his lips for just a second, looked back towards a painting on the wall and continued, "Sometimes, Cole, the right choice is not black and white. Your choices over the next few months may have far-reaching impacts. Understand?"

"Yes, Sir. I do."

BACK DOWNSTAIRS, the mood had lightened when Cole returned. Gene Thomas introduced them all to his son, Jeff, and suggested they take the boat out to get acquainted and blow off some steam. Jeff, perhaps 20 years old, quickly went to work loading up the Jeep, which mostly consisted of filling a cooler with beer and ice.

Matt and Harley already had beers in hand, and Claire sipped at one as well. Gene Thomas dug his hand deep into the cooler and pulled out a Coors Light, tossing it to Cole. *Cowboy piss*, Cole thought as he imagined a Dos Equis in his mind.

"A plane will fly you in to Cozumel tonight. You've got the day to burn—enjoy yourselves. I'll be here when you get back to see you all off."

Gene Thomas disappeared and Jeff finished grabbing some random supplies from around the house. He was young, athletic, and home on leave from the Merchant Marine Academy. In many ways, he reminded Cole of himself prior to his fall from grace in the Coast Guard. Once loaded, all five of them piled in, and Jeff drove the short trip down to the waterfront and the yacht club. Not ten minutes later, they were all spread out on the deck of a small Boston Whaler, and Jeff was motoring out of the narrow channel.

"Where y'all wanna go?" he asked as they neared the end of the jetty and turned north for the open bay. Matt and Harley were both seated in front of the console on the oversized cooler. Claire was further up ahead, laid out along some cushions. She looked back and showed little interest in any particular destination. Cole, seated next to Jeff, was left to decide.

"Are there alligators up in the swamp?"

Jeff laughed, "Yeah, the whole thing is crawling with them."

"Can we go check them out? I've never seen one."

Jeff grinned, spun the boat hard to the north, and away they went. Harley tossed a beer back towards Cole and another up to Claire as the bow rose up momentarily, the engine surged, and she slowly came up on a plane. With the bow settling back down, Cole smiled without thinking about it. He was, once again, on the water, with that same feeling as when he'd crossed the jetty guarding the Panama Canal and sped out into the open Caribbean. The midday sun ricocheted off thousands of small waves kicked up by the sea breeze that now pushed its way into the bay. The boat lurched with the larger of the waves, but held a course well and the outboard motor screamed in a way so familiar to Cole yet so foreign at the same time, as he had not heard an engine run at speed in many months.

Now on his third beer, and with little food in his stomach, Cole felt the first hint of a dizzy mind and thought back to his days in Key West. The wind tore at his face, and he leaned into it to feel its familiar embrace. Looking to the shore, he watched the docks and elevated houses as they passed and then back in front at the approaching banks of the river that Jeff turned towards.

"Where are we going?" Cole asked.

Jeff pointed ahead to their left, "Jourdan River."

Cole sat and felt his body sway from side to side as the boat powered over the tops of the diminishing crests. Nearing the banks of the river, the water was all but calm and the Whaler screamed past crab pots and derelict pilings left over from long-abandoned docks. Jeff was a waterman in his own right, hugging the turns and working the throttle like he'd no doubt been doing since he was a child. Without asking, Cole could tell the kid knew which banks he could hug and what bends to avoid for the sake of not wrecking against the sandbars concealed just under the muddied surface. Before long, they were still cruising on a plane with the banks not more than 15 yards to either side. When Jeff finally slowed down after another half an hour, he stood up and started checking the shore back and forth.

Harley and Matt were now intrigued by the possibility of getting close to an alligator. They trolled for some time, and Jeff pointed out the disturbed areas of grass marking a recent trail. With the motor now barely idling, Cole took another beer from the cooler and sat down against the railing to soak in his surroundings. His bare feet on the deck, the first hint of a sunburn on his face, and the sweating ice-cold can of beer in his hand all combined to conjure up so many forgotten memories of his days on the water. It was an unplanned moment of introspection—something the sea had always provided and perhaps what Cole had been chasing for so many months.

"Right there," Jeff pointed ahead against the bank. Sure enough, there was an alligator nosed up against the shore, the last few feet of his tail still in the water. Jeff smiled and nudged the boat slowly ahead to get closer. Harley and Matt were pressed against the starboard side and Claire was now sitting up on the bow, all of them staring intently at the alligator. Cole and Jeff were back at the console and Cole moved around as well to the starboard side and aft to get a better look. As they approached, the gator slipped down the grass and into the water just as they approached abeam of where it had been spotted.

With all of them on the starboard side and the boat listing a bit, they were no more then five feet from the patch of grass. "That was cool," Harley said as they each shuffled back for another beer. Jeff had the boat at idle now as they floated with the faint ebbing tide. Harley sat up on the port rail facing forward, his left knee up with his right foot down on the deck. Matt joined him while Cole chugged the rest of his beer, dug into the cooler for another, and Claire, still seated up front, turned aft to face them. Turning, Cole caught her looking back at him before she quickly turned her head away. Cole smiled, remembering his old games with pretty girls. Jeff sat at the console, minding his own business and still scanning the shore a few feet away from them.

Matt lifted his beer, "Well, here's to Cozumel." They each took a long sip.

Jeff asked, "So what are y'all doing in Mexico anyhow?"

Matt replied, "Just doing some sightseeing."

Jeff was smart enough to know it was a lie, and also smart enough to know that his dad kept many secrets from him for a reason. He looked back to the bank again.

"Well, that fella is probably long gone."

"Why do you say that?" asked Harley.

"He's a predator for sure, but they're smart enough to know when to run."

Matt spoke, "I guess that's human nature."

They all looked again to the starboard side and along the grass for any signs of movement. As they did, Claire yelled out, her voice increasing quickly as she did, "Harley, watch out!" As she yelled, she sat up and pointed just as Harley turned to see the gator had surfaced right next to the Whaler, not 12 inches from the port rail and nearly the same distance from where Matt and Harley were seated.

Both of them jumped up from the rail and steadied themselves in the center of the boat, as it rolled with the shift in weight. The gator just sat there on the surface, floating motionless with his right eye facing directly at them in the boat.

"Holy fuck," Harley exclaimed as he shook with an onset of chills up his back. None of them dared walk closer to the port side with what must have been a ten-foot alligator next to the boat.

From the console, Jeff said bluntly, "Well, they don't usually do that."

Harley laughed, "So much for human nature."

No one said a word. They all just stood on the deck of the boat, each of them staring back at the alligator who showed no signs of movement until after half a minute had passed. At that point, the alligator dropped below the surface without even a ripple to mark where he'd submerged back into the muddy river.

"Well, I'm good," Cole said as he reached into the cooler for yet another beer. He was on his fourth or fifth, and was nearing the point when one begins to think they're more invincible than they should. For Cole, it was not invincibility he felt, but rather the increasingly fatalistic sadness that he, at that moment, was like a man on death row. Harley and Matt reached for beers as well, although both of them found it humorous and laughed off the close encounter. Jeff nosed the boat around and pointed her south. He offered Cole the wheel and walked forward to get a beer.

"Just keep it in the center. I'll motion if you need to favor one side or the other."

As Cole situated himself, Claire came back and sat next to him. "Can I sit here?"

Cole smiled. "Of course. Thought you'd never ask." He'd known her for a day, but just her presence next to him was enough to instill the faintest touch of comfort that, for a moment, quelled the dark thoughts in his mind.

He pushed the throttles up halfway and felt the bow surge up and settle just shy of a plane. The wheel felt a bit sluggish in the turns until he pushed the throttles another quarter of the way forward and the bow came back down. Cole checked his wake behind him and smiled at the small rooster tail that kicked up. The wake fanned out behind him and disappeared into the thick reeds of grass lining both banks.

From the corner of his eye, he watched Claire's hair as the wind caught it and sent strands off in different directions. She looked ahead and occasionally to the banks as houses passed by.

Over the wind, he asked, "So, Gail is your mom, huh?"

Claire looked at Cole for a second and, with a half grin, replied, "Yeah."

"So is the spy game some kind of family business?"

Claire turned to look at him squarely in his eyes. Cole realized she was still eyeing him. With the throttle down and the boat screaming ahead, the two of them looked at each longer than they had since meeting back in London. "Something like that, yes."

Cole smiled and looked at her for another moment more before returning his scan to the river in front of them.

"Your mom crushed Johnson in all of two minutes. If that runs in the blood, I sure hope we can be friends."

Claire replied, "Yes. That would be nice."

❧

AS EVENING APPROACHED, they were all once again seated in the yard, and Gene Thomas was feverishly working at a proper crab boil. He had two steaming pots and picked ingredients at random, not taking the time to measure out spices or even taste them before adding them into the pots. Beers in hand again, he ushered them all upstairs where his wife had set up a table and chairs in the dining room. The mood was light, partly from the beer and also from a day on the water. It had all served to at least break the ice.

By the time Gene Thomas dumped both pots on the wooden table, there was a pile of corn, crab legs, sausage, and potatoes that would have fed three times the crowd that was assembled. Matt took on the task of teaching Claire the intricacies of cracking crab legs, and Harley and Jeff recounted the alligator from that afternoon. Gene Thomas seemed somewhat quiet, and it occurred to Cole that he didn't want to take anything away from the four who would depart shortly for Cozumel. Cole surmised that the task at hand weighed heavy on the Congressman's mind. Even his wife had gone over to him and pinched with her fingers at the back of his neck. Cole had read that when Ike gave the order to go for D-Day, he was seen crying shortly thereafter. Watching Gene Thomas, it occurred to Cole that the man was putting himself through many of the same emotions.

As darkness fell and the pile of seafood dwindled, the room grew quiet. The group had moved to couches in the living room, and just as the evening looked to be on its last legs, Gene Thomas spoke up. "Thank you to each of you for coming, regardless of the particulars of your situation."

He looked at Cole and continued, "Jeff will drive you back down to the airport where a plane will be waiting to fly you in. The Commandante at the airport is a friend of mine. He'll let you in tonight with no questions. Once you're there," he paused before continuing, "do your do best."

He looked down at the floor for a moment, then back up and at each of them before wishing them well.

"Give 'em hell."

CHAPTER 5: COZUMEL

EVEN AT TWO IN THE morning, Cozumel was warm. A steady wind blew hard down the length of the runway, carrying with it the heat that still blossomed like an afternoon thunderstorm. From the bleached and cracked ramp where Cole and his companions stood next to the Cessna Caravan that had just brought them across the Gulf, Cole asked, "What now?"

He spoke to no one in particular as he casually dropped his sea bag to the ground.

Matt looked around, but save for a few lights perched high on poles around the airfield, the field was dark and abandoned.

Matt scanned their surroundings for a few seconds more and replied, "We wait for the Commandante, I guess."

Cole and Harley went back to the small plane and unloaded half a dozen Pelican cases, arranging them in a row next to the aircraft. The pilot, who had not spoken more than a few words since picking them up at Stennis earlier in the evening, emerged from the cockpit with two large foot-long magnetic strips. The plane was white with a blue stripe running the length of each side. There was a small registration number on the tail and no other markings. He reached up and affixed one of the new strips over the numbers, and then went to the other side and placed the second strip in the same place. Pressing them firmly with his hand, he then stepped away from the tail. He looked at his work for a few seconds, content that they were straight.

The pilot walked back over to Matt and shook his hand, saying, "Good luck with it all." He smiled at Cole. "I was never here."

The pilot, dressed in jeans and a buttoned shirt, climbed back in and closed the door behind him. Not three minutes later, the single engine of the Caravan was whining and the propeller quickly spun up with

a steady hum. Exhaust blew out and was propelled aft by the prop, forc-
ing Cole, Matt, Claire, and Harley to shield their eyes and step away.
The plane taxied slowly at first, then picked up speed, meandering its
way down the taxiway until it disappeared. The whine of the engine ta-
pered off as the plane moved out of sight at the far end of the runway.
The pilot pushed it up to full power and started a quick takeoff run. As
he climbed up and away from Cozumel, the four of them watched the
Caravan disappear into the night sky until all that was left was the
steady rhythmic blinking of his strobe light and the faintest hint of a red
navigation light.

The airfield was quiet again. Other than the wind that blew incessantly against the craggy low trees that lined the perimeter of the field,
there was no sound. Cole looked to Matt for any sign that he knew what
they were supposed to do. Just as he did before, Matt looked calmly
around the field. Harley was popping open Pelican cases, rummaging
through them for a moment, then moving on to the next one. After the
third case, he called out loudly, "Bingo."

He squatted down low and rummaged further through the open
case before walking over to Matt with four stainless revolvers, two in
each hand.

"Revolvers?" Matt asked.

"You betcha," Harley replied.

"Harley, what the fuck, man?"

Matt now held one in his hand and flipped the cylinder open
quickly before flinging it back closed. Harley grinned and handed one
to Cole as well. They were Ruger SP101s, chambered in .357 Magnum
and each wearing a black rubber grip. Cole, not entirely familiar with its
operation, slowly looked it over and verified just as Matt had that it was
indeed loaded. His mind raced back to the kid getting his head blown
off in Panama. Against the salt air, Cole swore he could still smell the
gunpowder and remembered vividly how the kid had squirmed in his
seat when he realized his time had come. Cole shook the thought away.

"Harley, how, and more importantly why, did you get these?"

"This here is the wild west, buddy. I thought they'd be a bit more appropriate than some plastic fantastic. Plus," he said cheerily, "no need to go track down your brass."

Expressionless, Matt stared at Harley.

Harley continued, "I've got holsters, too. Hang on a second."

As he walked back over to the Pelican cases, he handed one of the revolvers to Claire, but she shook her head and said, "I'm all set, thanks."

Harley held it out for her for a moment more before he shrugged his shoulders, "Suit yourself." He dug through the same Pelican case and produced three black holsters. Checking them individually, he tossed one to Matt and one to Cole. They were leather, with two clips for a belt, and the outside was kydex formed in the outline of the revolvers.

"Did you bring any of the Sigs?" Matt asked.

Without looking up from the case he was now digging through, Harley replied, "A couple."

Matt took a long—and clearly frustrated—breath. Cole was already loosening his belt and affixing the holster to his right hip. Once secure, he holstered the pistol and was surprised at how easily it concealed under his shirt.

"Try not to use that thing, Cole."

Cole looked at Matt with a half-hearted grin, "I'll do my best."

Cozumel was already stirring long-dormant parts of Cole's mind. Having been shot—twice—Cole held a handgun in much higher regard than he did before. With a pistol on his hip and once again in the Caribbean, he quietly let his mind wander and noticed that the thoughts in his head were, at best, of the mixed variety.

Harley walked over to rejoin them and spoke defensively. "Thing? These aren't just things. These are hand-tuned pieces of art. Bobbed hammers, trigger jobs, tritium front sights, and three-inch barrels with matched ammo. Seven pound pull or two pounds in single action. You could whack a dinner plate at fifty yards, no problem."

He handed Matt and Cole two speed strips as well, each holding six more rounds of ammo.

"One hundred fifty-eight grain hollow point sleeping pills. You put one of these anywhere near the ticker, and it's lights out." Harley said with pride.

"Any other surprises, Harley?"

Harley looked at Matt. "Maybe one or two."

Matt stared at him for a moment more and let off a slight smile. He wasn't mad at Harley, Cole was certain. He could see in them a friendship that trumped any of the frustration Matt had. Harley was grinning, and with neither of them saying a word, they were both reading each other as if in a conversation. Cole felt out of place.

"Something is moving this way," Claire said as she looked beyond the terminal towards two sets of headlights running a circuitous route through the parking area. A small car pulled up to the gate followed by a white pickup truck.

Matt and Harley instinctively split to either side of their luggage, putting some distance between them. They faced towards the gate as it opened and watched the car slowly creep towards them, followed by the truck. Cole squinted to make out the details, but was almost blinded by its headlights as it crept closer to them.

"I only see a driver in each," Harley called out softly.

Matt nodded, but never took his eyes off the vehicles, angling his body to afford less of a target should guns become necessary. As they approached the group, both vehicles shut off their lights and circled halfway around the pile of gear. Matt and Harley pivoted to follow them. Cole reached back and felt the grip of his pistol for reassurance, and he watched Harley for the first sign of trouble. Harley was entirely fixed on the vehicles, a calm but serious look on his face. Claire stood casually a few feet from Cole. She was either playing it exceptionally cool or was quickly proving herself to have the kind of steel resolve that comes from hard experience.

"What do you think?" Cole asked.

"About what?" she asked back.

Cole felt like an idiot for even asking. "Nothing, never mind." He laughed to himself.

From the small car, a man hopped out and approached. Matt walked forward to greet him. They exchanged few words, and Matt turned to walk back towards the group. He was relaxed and gave off a sense of calm that Cole immediately noticed, much to his relief.

"It's the Commandante. Let's load up."

They all grabbed their bags and tossed them into the back of the car. Harley and Matt made quick work of loading up the Pelican cases into the bed of the truck, and within minutes, they were off. Cole was seated in the backseat of an absolute piece-of-shit car. Matt sat next to him, with Harley driving and Claire once again sitting shotgun.

"What is this thing?" Cole asked.

Matt just laughed and shook his head. "It is literally a Thing."

Cole didn't get the reference and Matt explained further, "It's a Volkswagen Thing."

It was a convertible, but only in the sense that it had permanently been converted many years ago. The backseat was a bench with no seat belts, and up front, the two seats seemed more appropriate to a high school gymnasium than an automobile. Nevertheless, Harley was putting her through its paces. After a hard blind turn out of the airport, Matt slid across the bench and pressed up against Cole before pushing himself back to his side.

"Harley…" he called out.

Harley replied with a grin, "Sorry, Dad."

Cozumel was quiet as the dawn was still an hour or two away. Cole could smell the salt in the air that rode along hard and fast with the wind coming off the Caribbean Sea. The city sat on the western side of the island, almost directly south and east from Cancun on the mainland. The town was painted in pastel colors and the architecture was somewhere between old Mexico and the new Caribbean. It was most certainly a bustling area during the day when the cruise ships came in, but as Harley followed the truck in front of them and shifted gears with a vengeance, Cole couldn't help but recall the Caribbean he knew with a sense of fondness. He had missed her.

The roads were narrow, with small shops and houses pressed against each other along each side. All but of a few of the homes had high concrete walls and iron gates to separate the occupants from the noise and congestion of the roads. Few, if any, were more than two stories, yet somehow the city felt as if it were smothering itself. The small signs that hung over the shops advertised things like Dos Equis, Coca-Cola, or the basics of standard Mexican fare that served to draw in customers each day. With the breeze against his face, Cole scanned outside as Harley ripped the little Volkswagen Thing through 90-degree turns at intersections, neither the truck nor Harley paying much attention to the stop signs or occasional lights. There were pockets of graffiti on some of the walls, but for the most part, Cozumel seemed to be in good order.

Twenty minutes after they'd left the airport, the truck came to a quick halt at a large iron gate. The driver stepped out into the yellow glare of the headlights, waved at Harley, and motioned him towards the gate. Unlocking it and pushing both gates wide open, the driver returned to his truck and turned to drive in. Harley followed closely behind him. Once inside, the driver left the truck running and proceeded to unload the bed. Harley, Matt, and Cole each grabbed cases and set them down on the manicured lawn next to the small curved driveway. Once unloaded, the driver shook Matt's hand and mouthed, "Ten Cuidado." He handed Matt a set of keys and looked at each of them with stern and almost disapproving looks.

He then motioned Harley to move the Thing to the side, which Harley quickly did, and without another word, the driver backed out, turned his lights back on, and was gone. Harley had parked the Thing just to the side of the gate, tucked against a six-foot concrete wall and out of sight from anyone passing by. Matt walked over to the gate, stepped outside for a second, scanned each side of the street, then closed and locked it.

After unloading the rest of their gear, they each dragged what they could over to an ornate wooden door. Matt turned the keys and opened it up, scanning first before walking inside. Each of them followed and walked into a small ground floor with a living room, open kitchen, and some basic furniture scattered about.

Harley dropped his bag on a large and dark wooden dining room table. Looking around, he spoke, "Well, I've seen a lot worse."

Matt agreed, "Yeah, buddy. This'll do for a while."

They dragged the rest of the Pelican cases inside and set them all against a wall with a large set of windows. Harley, once again, went to rummaging through them, clearly looking for something in particular. With an open floorplan, the house was cool inside. The kitchen was tiled in the Caribbean fashion. The counters, floor, and walls were all varying shades of blue tile, some of them gradient in color, and several areas were painted with tropical themes. The cabinets were an off-white and a single exposed light hung from the ceiling. The living room was similar, but opted for a green theme and the wicker furniture matched the intent of its minimalist design nicely.

Matt was the first up a set of stairs, followed by Claire and Cole. Up on the second floor, there was a narrow hallway and two rooms, one on each end. Inside the first room, there were two single beds, each against a wall and a bathroom at the far end. The room was clean with a tile floor and dark orange walls. A dresser and small table were against the third wall. Matt walked to the window and pushed the shutters open. Cole could see that it looked down on the gate and a small pool that took up most of the walled courtyard. Cole caught a bit of the breeze as it rolled in from the window and against his chest. Looking up, he could see moonlight reflect off the tall palm fronds that were at eye level across the courtyard.

"Harley and I are in here. It's a good spot for anyone coming in."

Behind them, Cole heard Harley enter the room and turned to see him laying two M4 carbines down on the table along with half a dozen 30-round magazines. He looked at Cole and grinned. "I'm gonna sleep well tonight."

Cole was already beginning to like Harley, who seemed to share Cole's penchant for mischief. From his shoulders, Harley dropped his bag by the foot of one of the beds and scanned the room before walking to the window and peering out. While Cole had been consumed by the view of the pool and palm trees, he realized that both Harley and Matt scanned outside with entirely different views. To them, it was a tactical choice, and they saw the window as less of a scenic view and more as a defensive fighting position. With each passing hour, he better appreciated their presence.

Claire was down the hall, and he found her setting her bags down in the second bedroom. Again, there were two beds, one against each wall. She looked at Cole as he walked in and tried to feign a friendly smile, but Cole could already sense her discomfort. He looked around for a few moments more, and watched her as she laid one bag down on a bed and began to pull out the clothes she'd packed.

"I'll sleep on the couch downstairs."

She turned to look at him for a second, but stopped short of it and went back to her bag, saying, "It's fine. I don't mind. Take the other bed."

Cole couldn't quite put his finger on what he felt at that particular point, but it was nothing short of some kind of dull aching emptiness. Claire was wholly consumed by her bag, and Cole stood there feeling as if he didn't exist at all. His mind wandered as he watched her. She was gorgeous, even after 24 hours on the road, and she'd made the outward offer of sharing the room with him, but Cole was aware that she was uncomfortable.

"Nah, I'll take the couch."

She turned and looked at him for a second. Cole, normally able to read a girls' expression, was entirely unable to get even a hint as to what Claire was thinking. She smiled slightly and replied, "OK."

Back down the hallway, Matt stepped out of his room and he looked directly at Cole, asking, "You good?"

Cole, still walking, replied, "Yeah, I'm fine. I'm gonna take the couch."

Matt looked at him for a moment more than he should have, and Cole felt as if the whole team was wondering about him. Back downstairs, he entered the kitchen, found nothing in the refrigerator, and then stepped outside into the courtyard. He walked along the brick patio to the edge of the small pool. Several lights lit up the pool from underneath the water, and it was the kind of thing that should have put a smile on anyone's face.

Alone with his thoughts, Cole took long deliberate breaths and stared up at the stars. There were a handful of clouds, backlit by the moon that sat high over the Mexican sky. It was the same moon that Isabella may have been looking at, halfway around the world. Cole looked at his watch and it was just past four in the morning. He didn't quite know the time difference, but Isabella and Marie were certainly awake by now. *Perhaps she is hurting as bad as I am,* Cole thought.

Matt came up beside him and spoke. "We're gonna get some sleep, Cole."

"Yeah, probably a good idea."

"We'll start checking out the town in the afternoon."

Cole nodded, but said nothing as he stared down at the clear water that slowly swirled below in the pool.

Matt turned to walk back in, saying softly, "See ya inside."

Cole wasn't sure what they had read about him or what they knew about his past. He was beginning to think that he must have been wearing his emotions on his face, as each of them showed some level of concern each time they spoke. Back in the house, Harley had laid out a few more guns, and some comms equipment was spread out on the dining room table, but none of it was set up. Harley chugged water from a glass in the kitchen and walked upstairs without another word. Claire came down right after him and found one more bag of hers by the front door. She turned and began to walk back towards the stairs.

"Goodnight," Cole said.

Turning, she nodded and replied, "Goodnight, Cole."

Placing the revolver on a table next to him, he punched at a pillow and folded it over as he tossed a few times to find a comfortable position on the couch. Pulling a light blanket up to his hips, he rolled onto his side and stared across the dark room. He could hear some of the shuffling upstairs for a few minutes before the house went entirely silent.

It wasn't that he felt an attraction to Claire, although he knew it was something he ought to feel. A girl like her was something special, yet Cole's emotions were numb. He didn't want to sleep upstairs, because he knew she didn't want him to. But more than anything, at that moment, he didn't want to be alone either. It was one of the most basic human emotions, but not something that Cole would ever admit. Hard experience had taught him he was more comfortable by himself, although he thought of that empty bed upstairs, and had a gnawing feeling in his gut that maybe the unending sadness would subside if he just had the company of someone else. They were all new to him, their intentions unknown, as well as their hearts. Cole stared for a few seconds more before he tucked his arms in against his chest and closed his eyes.

MARIE CLIMBED UP on his chest and swayed a bit as she tried to balance on her hands and knees, giggling as she pressed her nose against his. *Papa,* she said, as Cole reached up under both her arms and pulled her tight against him, tickling her neck with his mouth. Isabella rolled over and smiled at the sight of the two of them laughing.

How long has she been crawling? He laid there in amazement as his little girl tried her hardest to balance on her father's chest. *Not long. She just started while you were gone.*

I'm sorry that I left, he said as Isabella pulled herself even closer and tucked her head into his neck. She was playing with Marie's hair and draped one leg over Cole's.

Stop worrying, she said. *It's over now.* Cole ran his fingers up and down Marie's back and she squirmed as he did.

She gets that from you, you know, Isabella said. Cole smiled at the thought. It was true. He was never a fan of being lightly touched and he enjoyed seeing the things that Marie had inherited from him. Isabella kissed at his neck. Marie was pushing again, trying to sit on his chest. Her dark curly hair was longer than when he had left. As she lifted her head and turned to look at Isabella, he admired how it now was down below her neck, in a beautiful tangled mess just like her mother's.

I should get down to the kitchen. Your mom is probably waiting. Isabella looked at him for a second and wrapped her arm around him and Marie both. *She'll have to come get you.* She pulled against him and Marie as Cole rolled his head to sink back down onto their pillow. The birds of Carentan were singing like they always did. Marie lunged to her side and Isabella caught her, pulling Marie across to her chest. She laughed and Cole held on to the little girl's foot, tickling her toes as Marie giggled and kicked.

"Cole."

He was incredibly happy in that moment, his absence now a thing buried in the past and whatever it was that had drawn him away was now only a blurred memory, fast disappearing from the back of his mind.

"Cole."

Isabella's mother can wait, he thought. He closed his eyes and rolled even closer to Isabella, his nose catching the faint floral smell of her hair as he did.

"Cole."

He was happy again, content with his simple life.

"Cole."

"Cole."

He opened his eyes. Claire was seated at the dining room table, turned in her chair to face him. She had a laptop computer in front of her.

"Cole," She said it softly, in a tone that he had not yet heard from her.

He looked at her, unsure of exactly where he was until his mind caught up with his surroundings. In a split second, he was back. *Cozumel*, he thought, still staring blankly at Claire. His breath disappeared from his chest and he struggled to fill his lungs with the morning air.

"Cole," she said again softly, as if to infer some kind of genuine concern.

He blinked, "Yeah?"

Her lips curled in a quasi-smile, and it was clear to Cole that she was not entirely aware of the thoughts consuming his mind. "Are you all right?" she asked.

Cole sat up. "Yeah, I'm fine." He paused before continuing. "Morning."

"Yes, indeed. Good morning."

He pushed the blanket down towards his feet and shook the thoughts from his head, trying hard to hide his concern. *A fucking dream,* he thought as he buried his face in both his hands and ripped at his hair.

Claire asked, "Who is Marie?"

Cole felt an immediate chill and beads of sweat on his forehead. "Why?" he asked.

Claire sensed his apprehension and looked away from him, saying, "No reason. You were just saying *Marie* in your sleep."

"Sorry."

"No, it's fine. It's none of my business."

Cole swallowed and looked at Claire as she typed, then turned once more to face him.

"She's my daughter, back in France. What exactly did I say?"

Claire's eyes were locked on his. "Nothing much, that was it—Marie."

He rubbed both his hands over his face to wipe away the sleep and pressed the palms of his hands into his eyes before moving them through his hair once more.

"So what do we do now?" He asked.

Claire was back to typing at her computer. "I suppose we should get to work."

CHAPTER 6: PICK POCKETS

IT WAS NOON BY THE time they were all casually seated around the kitchen table. Claire had a labyrinth of power cords plugged in and two laptops set up on in front of her. Harley was tinkering with his M4, the lower and upper receiver separated as he field-stripped and cleaned the rifle. He wore a light pair of khaki shorts with an unbuttoned shirt over his shoulders. Matt sat with his feet up on the table and his chair on its back legs, his hands behind his head. He too had on a pair of shorts and a tank-top.

Cole, leaning forward from his seat, rubbed his eyes again and spoke first. "I need a drink."

Harley looked up at Matt as Claire paid little attention to any of them.

Matt, still looking back at Harley, asked, "Wanna check out the town?"

Putting the upper and lower back together, and after the audible clicks of both pins back in place, Harley replied, "Sure, why not?"

"Claire?" Matt asked.

"Yeah?" She had not been listening, consumed by whatever she was doing on her computer.

"We're gonna go for a drive. You coming?"

She was clearly thinking about something. She sighed. "I need to set an antenna up on the roof."

Matt nodded and replied, "Best to do that at night when no one's watching."

Claire acknowledged with a nod. "You're right."

Harley chimed in, "Well, let's go then. I'm gonna go nuts sitting here all day."

They grabbed a few things. Cole pressed the revolver back into his holster and pulled his shirt down over it. Matt and Harley both cinched up their belts and slid their revolvers just behind their right hips. Harley tossed a handful of speed strips with extra ammo onto the table. Matt and Cole each took a few and dropped them into their pockets. Once outside, Harley was busy affixing some kind of sticker to the windshield of the Thing. Cole walked around the front to see that it was an *I love NY* sticker with a heart shape instead of the word *love*. He laughed out loud. As he did, Matt walked around and looked at Harley's work. Cole expected him to be upset, but Matt nodded twice and walked back over to the back of the Thing. Some things were personal, and Matt clearly approved of the not-so-subtle message alluding to the newest front of this prolonged war.

Harley fired up the little car and they all climbed in as Matt wrestled the iron gate open. In the daylight, Cole gave their ride a better look. It was pastel blue with spots of rust around the lower floorboards. There was no carpeting or any kind of interior other than the bare metal floor. Harley revved it a few times and threw it into first gear, idling out of the gate and onto the street. Matt then spun and locked the gate behind them and climbed in. Cole was sitting shotgun with Claire and Matt in the backseat.

"Where to?" Harley asked.

Cole nodded forward, "Downtown is that way."

"You know your way around?"

Cole looked at Harley for a second and replied, "I've been here a few times."

Harley roared ahead, and the Thing jumped and surged as he tried to shift into second gear, but couldn't get it to catch. Back in first and accelerating wildly, Harley again tried to shift into second, but couldn't. Veins bulged in his neck as he tried to force the gear, but it was no use. Just as quickly, he dropped it into third and the little car sounded as if it might stall for just a second before the cylinders fired and the car settled down.

Over the noise and clearly frustrated, Harley asked, "Is this seriously the best we could get?"

Matt, from the backseat, replied over the wind, "Apparently."

Cole motioned for a few more turns, and within minutes they were cruising the main drag of downtown Cozumel. There were two cruise ships tied up as a healthy crowd of tourists strolled aimlessly up and down the boulevard, poking their heads in and out of the shops that sold souvenirs, t-shirts, brightly-colored towels, wooden trinkets, and cheap leather boots. The bars were overloaded with yankees sipping fruity concoctions as bartenders blew obnoxiously into whistles and poured shot after shot of warm tequila. Sitting in the congestion, Cole was agitated within minutes. It was hot and muggy in the midday sun. Harley was scanning both side mirrors and idling along with the traffic. As they neared the far end of the boulevard and the traffic began to spread out, he parked along the main street. "Fuck that traffic. Let's walk," he said.

Stepping out and looking back at the car, Matt said, "Well, we don't have to worry about anyone trying to steal it."

Harley dropped the key into his pocket, "We could only be so lucky."

All four walked back towards the busy part of downtown and took seats at a small outdoor patio that faced an open square littered with more vendors selling the same junk as everywhere else, albeit for slightly more or less, depending on the owner's level of desperation. They were huddled around an old iron table with matching chairs and a Tecate umbrella partially shielding them from the sun.

When the server swung by their table, Cole spoke. "Cervezas, por favor. Dos Equis?"

She returned two minutes later with four dark sweating bottles, setting a napkin down in front of each of them before placing the beers down with a lime. Cole smashed the lime into his and held it inverted for just a second before taking a long first sip. He drained a third of it.

Harley was next to do the same, while Matt and Claire followed with smaller sips of their own.

Cole swallowed, exhaled, and asked, "So what now?"

Matt turned a bit in his seat and leaned in to press his forearms against the table. "I don't think we'll see much during the day other than pick-pockets, but that may not be a bad place to start."

He scanned to his left and right before speaking again. "Let's split up into two groups. Meet back here in two hours. Cole, why don't you come with me?"

"Sure." Cole sucked down the rest of his beer. With nothing in his stomach, he felt the first hints of a buzz. Harley laughed and finished the rest of his as well.

Claire smiled and shook her head before saying to no one in particular, "You Americans…" She took another small sip from her beer and set it down, acting the part of a lady.

"Dos mas…" Harley called out cheerfully as the server passed by again.

Cole laughed and said, "Por favor," as she passed behind him and back into the bar. It seemed that Harley had the same mischievous mind as Cole.

Matt stared at Harley for a second before Harley asked defensively, "What?" Neither of them spoke. It was another of those moments where they seemed to be communicating with each other.

Harley finally spoke again, saying casually and to no one in particular, "I'm just trying to blend in."

Claire, now fully smiling, asked, "With the other drunk Americans?"

Harley grinned, pointed at Claire as if she'd hit the nail on the head, and replied, "Precisely."

Claire and Matt finished their beers just as Cole and Harley inverted their second round and set the empty bottles back on the table. Matt settled the bill and they were up and moving. Claire and Harley disappeared into the thick of the vendors while Matt and Cole made their way back down by the boulevard near the water. They walked slowly and kept pace with the herd of tourists. Cole couldn't help but look out at the rolling green water and whitecaps that boiled up and against the sunburned white rocks pressed against a low wall separating the sea from the sidewalk. He spent more time looking out at the water than he did in front of him, thinking that he'd much prefer to jump in rather than walk in the daytime heat. Several dive boats bobbed at their moorings and danced around as the breeze blew hard from the north. With two beers on his brain, Cole found himself content just to be near the water, even with the early afternoon sun bearing down on his back. His mind was fully preoccupied with his surroundings as the walk gave him something other than home to focus on.

Feeling a tap on his back, Cole turned as Matt nodded back into the crowd, "There's one, right there." He started moving in a different direction, and Cole followed.

"What's right there?" Cole asked as he moved to catch up.

"Our first hit. That kid wearing the basketball jersey."

Sure enough, Cole caught a glimpse as the kid, no more than 15, weaved a path against the flow of traffic with a green purse tucked under his arm. Whatever Matt had seen had occurred in an instant and Cole could do nothing but follow as Matt moved along the perimeter of the crowd, his eyes never leaving the kid.

"He passed it off..." Matt said softly as he switched direction and doubled back. Cole was right behind him, frustrated at his own inability to catch the things that Matt seemed to see so clearly. Within a minute, they were hurrying up a narrow side street where the crowd thinned out. Matt and Cole stayed one block back and now followed yet another kid, maybe 20 at the oldest, as he ducked down another street, this one almost entirely empty. Cole and Matt stopped at an intersection and feigned interest at the merchandise in a window display. The kid ducked through a gate into what was likely a walled house not unlike all the others that were crammed next to each other throughout downtown Cozumel. Matt looked down the street for a second, both sides of which were bordered by two-story buildings and concrete walls. He then motioned with his head for them to move back. As he turned, Cole looked for himself and wondered if Matt had already drawn out in his mind the risks of moving any closer. If that was the case, Cole had a lot of catching up to do. Both Matt and Harley moved with precision, seemingly with their guard raised at all times, but not revealing any outward signs. It was all Cole could do to keep up. On the far side of the street sat another bar where Matt and Cole quickly settled into seats, ordering a round of beer.

To Cole, he instructed, "Take it slow on this one. We're on the clock now."

Cole nodded. Ten minutes later, the kid was walking back down the sidewalk towards downtown.

Cole asked, "Do we follow him."

"Nope. We stay put and see if he comes back."

Cole took a small first sip from his Dos Equis. As he did, Matt asked, "You don't remember me, do you?"

Cole looked at him, confused, and shook his head. "What are you talking about?"

Matt took a longer sip and set the bottle back down, looking at Cole as he swallowed a mouthful of beer. "Panama. I was there with Tony. Harley was there too."

Matt was focused on Cole, looking for any kind of reaction.

Cole asked bluntly, "When I got shot?"

"Yup."

Cole thought for a second, about Tony's promise to have his back and how he'd nearly bled out on the filthy concrete floor of a poorly disguised whore house. For a moment, he thought to tell Matt to fuck off, but at the same time he sensed that Matt was a good guy and Gene Thomas had told him as much. "So what happened with you all?"

Matt nodded as if to suggest he knew the heart of Cole's question and already had a good read on what Cole's mind was thinking. "We were told to stand down."

Cole leaned back and asked, "By Tony?"

"No." Matt shook his head. "Someone over Tony. So we saw you, we saw you give the signal and Tony called for us to move in, but someone came over the radio and ordered us to stand down the op. I was looking right at him when you started shooting seconds later and Tony gave us the go ahead to move in."

Cole asked, "So who was above Tony?"

Matt continued. "I don't know. Someone listening in on the net; Tony never said. But I'm pretty sure that's why he got pulled off the Central America stuff. Tony had the final call since he was the senior guy on the ground, but you should know that it wasn't Tony's fault."

Cole was silent for close to a minute and looked away to let his mind process.

Matt continued. "I know we let you down, Cole. It was a split-second…"

Cole nodded, "I get it, Matt. I was disposable." *Disposable to whom*, he wondered.

Matt stared at Cole hard for a moment before continuing. "That won't happen again, not here."

Cole lifted his head, stared off at the tops of the buildings around them, and looked down to his right. "You think I'm disposable to Johnson?"

"You don't mince words, do you?" Matt asked.

Cole shook his head, "No. Not anymore."

Matt took another sip and stared up the street towards the house. He looked for half a minute before turning back to Cole and said to himself, "I don't like that guy, Johnson."

At that, Cole laughed out loud, and for the first time in days felt a genuine smile across his face, saying, "I don't know of anyone that does."

It was a conversation that needed to happen. Cole felt no grudge against Matt, or Harley for that matter. He thought of Tony and how somehow a top agent had been cast off to Canada for sending a team in to get Cole. Matt had added some much-needed background to put it all in context, and all the clues were there to help Cole better understand the big picture. In many ways, he'd been naïve before. *Not this time*, he told himself. He looked at Matt and felt as if they were off to a good start, now sharing something in common and having a bit of history together.

Matt called out calmly, "He's back."

Cole watched as the same kid walked back up the street with yet another purse. Cole laughed at the audacity of it. Twenty minutes later, the kid was back out on the street and headed downtown again. Matt and Cole waited nearly another hour and saw the kid return once more before Matt called it and they walked back to meet Harley and Claire.

Seated again at the same bar, they sat down to yet another round of beers and shared their afternoon adventures. Harley had managed to buy a bag of pot off the street. Claire had positioned herself to identify not only the low-end dealer, but also his apparent street boss at a boot shop further down the main boulevard where local drug peddlers seemed to deposit a near-continuous stream of profits. Claire had taken detailed notes of a steady flow of Cozumel's petty criminals moving in and out over the course of an hour.

As the sun was setting, they called it a day and swung through a grocery store to stock the house on the way back. Cole offered to cook dinner and had done his best to put together the ingredients for some crude enchiladas. Claire and Matt had filled up baskets as well while Harley man-handled two 24-packs of Dos Equis cans.

Back at the house, Cole did what he could in the kitchen, and the four of them devoured a plate of beef enchiladas and crushed half the beers. He struggled not to think of France as he worked in the kitchen, but managed to find enough small talk with his companions to not let his mind wander. Afterwards, they were out by the pool and drinking still as the moon climbed up and over the midnight Mexican sky. The air was now cooler against Cole's skin and he basked in the tranquility of the moment, his brain blurred by the unknown number of empty cans that were his handiwork. Claire poked at Harley and asked out loud where he'd gotten so good at buying dope. Matt couldn't help but laugh and as Cole stood chest deep in the water, beer in hand, he smiled and took it all in. They were friends now.

FOR THE REST OF THE WEEK, Matt and Harley were up each morning working out as best they could on the small lawn by the pool. Cole joined them most mornings and tried to keep up, but both Harley and Matt proved to be in top shape. They didn't have the outward appearance of being muscle-heads, but it became quickly apparent that, under a veil of normalcy, they were strong and mean when the need arose. They wrestled a bit as well, giving Cole some basic tips in Jiu Jitsu, enough so that each morning Cole was sore and struggled to get out of bed. Regardless of the pain, he enjoyed the challenge.

By noon each day, they'd split up downtown and map out the petty crime as best they could. All but Cole seemed well-versed in techniques to pick up on the slightest clues and by the fifth day, they had a map taped to the wall of their house of downtown Cozumel. On the map, Claire had marked each house or business to which they'd associated some kind of illegal activity. On top of that, Claire kept a detailed spreadsheet of each movement they'd tracked and what had been either stolen or bought, linking both people and the specifics of individuals' movement between places. Harley proved to be the resident expert in buying drugs and had amassed a small pile of little baggies that were stashed in a bowl by the front door. It was mostly pot, but there were a few baggies of coke as well. By Sunday of that week, Matt had suggested a day off. There were no cruise ships coming in that day, which meant the pick-pocket market would be limited, and it seemed like the right time to let their hair down a bit.

Mid-morning, they drove east on a flat and straight dusty road across the island to the far side that faced the Caribbean. Once there, they turned south and drove for some time until the road turned to fine white sand and they'd reached a primitive bar and restaurant tucked back against the low dunes. It was constructed mostly of driftwood, palm fronds, and random bits of lumber, all of which was painted in some places while still bare in others. The roof was scrap aluminum and badly rusted, but served its purpose of blocking the sun. The floor was sand and evenly spaced plastic tables and chairs dotted the covered eating area. There were the familiar Tecate and Dos Equis signs hung on the walls along with a few random bits of Caribbean art. Beyond the quasi-walls, several hammocks were strung between palm trees, and some heavily worn wooden chairs baked out in the sun, near the water's edge. It was, in Cole's mind at least, perfect. As the four of them took seats in the shade, an old woman appeared from inside with a pitcher of water and four cups.

They ordered more beer and the woman offered them the option of grouper tacos or burritos. Just as soon as they'd opted for the tacos, she called back inside and a younger kid, her son perhaps, opened the top of a large cooler, and called out, "Dos mas, Mama."

She nodded and signaled the boy to get to work. From the cooler, he pulled out a massive grouper and carried it back to the kitchen.

As the woman walked back inside as well, Harley spoke. "Kind of puts new meaning to the term *catch of the day*, huh?"

Cole nodded. A wooden boat sat down near the water, too small to take far offshore, but he wondered if that boy hadn't caught the fish that same morning. Harley kicked back in his chair and dug his bare feet deep into the cool sand. "I could get used to this," he said.

Matt asked with a grin, "Claire, thoughts?"

She turned to Matt for a second, part of a smile showing on her face before she looked at Cole then back out at the water, and said, "A day off can't hurt anyone, I suppose."

Less than 15 minutes after they'd sat down, the woman appeared with an enormous steaming plate of fish and corn tortillas along with the standard sides of rice, beans, and sliced avocado. They devoured the food, leaving little but empty plates with a scattering of bottles across the table. It was mid-afternoon and a northerly breeze filled in down the length of the beach. Claire had settled into a hammock shielded by several palm trees and pulled her floppy hat over her head. Matt and Harley had found their way down to the water and were swimming out near a rock formation that sheltered them somewhat from the waves and currents. Cole watched them both from a chair at the water's edge as that damn familiar lonely feeling crept up on him, entirely unannounced. He rose and went down to the water where he dove in and swam after Matt and Harley.

The salt burned his lips and eyes as he dove under and swam hard along the sandy bottom, navigating around some of the larger rocks that dotted the seafloor. Back up on the surface, he powered through the light chop and caught up with them as they neared the edge of the rocks and the open water. Matt was the first one to dive down, followed by Harley and Cole. It was about 30 feet deep, but getting down to the bottom seemed effortless for both Matt and Harley. Cole struggled a bit at first, not having been in the water in almost a year. Nevertheless, he was naturally comfortable once his breathing settled, and he kept up as the three of them swam out and around into the deeper water. Once outside the shelter of the rocks, they popped back up, now close to 75 yards offshore. The wind was steady, and spray lifted off the tops of each crest, blowing cool and hard against their faces. Matt grinned as he shook the water from his face. They were no longer protected, and the waves had increased from a light chop to a true groundswell that lifted them each up then back down as the waves passed. In the troughs, they couldn't seen land at all. Harley laughed at it and kicked onto his back.

As the three of them bobbed, Cole looked back to see the shoreline moving quickly. They were in some kind of current that carried them along with the wind steadily to the south. Harley didn't seem to care at all, but Matt was clearly watching the coast and took note of their movement. He took a few more kicks in place before starting a strong stroke towards the shore. Harley was right behind him, and Cole needed only a second or two to realize it was a race. He was five yards behind when he kicked hard and dug his head into the back of a wave and started swimming. Despite the struggle to keep rhythm with the waves lifting and rolling him, Cole was smiling and laughing silently to himself, the ocean rocking him like a loving mother.

Once back on shore, the three of them ordered another round of beer and sat down in the sand at the water's edge. Cole felt the water drip from his hair and down his back. With the sun on his shoulders and still out of breath from the sprint in, Cole took long, exaggerated breaths between sips of beer. He could smell the sea in the air and could sense immediately that both Matt and Harley were also enjoying the moment.

"Did you tell him?" Harley asked.

Matt nodded and looked over to Cole. "Yeah. He knows."

Harley was now looking at Cole, and he sniffed at the air for a second before a serious look came across his face. To Cole, he asked, "We good?"

Cole nodded that they were, saying simply, "Yeah, we're good."

Harley waited a moment before pressing the issue once more, "We've got your back, Cole. And we gotta know if you've got ours. You got anything you need to say, say it."

Cole smiled. He really didn't care about a few seconds of a delayed response, but it seemed a big deal to both Harley and Matt. Cole looked at both of them. "Which one of you picked me up?"

Harley nodded towards Matt.

Cole continued, "I would've been dead if it wasn't for you guys, and Tony. I made my own decisions back in Panama, and I don't blame anyone else for where I am today. Relax, both of you. Let's just get this shit over with." He smiled and said, "And maybe we'll have a bit of fun along the way."

They all tapped bottles and finished off the rest of their beer. It was late afternoon, bordering on early evening, when they made their way back up to the bar. Claire was up again, seated at the wooden bar, and sipping on some kind of mixed drink with her legs crossed. Matt looked at Cole for a just a moment and winked, indicating to Cole that he was not the only who found her remarkably attractive. There was no one else on either end of the beach, and the bar was all but abandoned. The kid sat on a low stool by the bar, at the ready to serve them beer, but otherwise the whole place was theirs.

"I'm building a fire."

Harley was on the move collecting bits of driftwood and dried out palm fronds from around the beach. He piled it all up halfway down the beach towards the water. Cole and Matt pitched in as well, and after nearly an hour, they had a four-foot pile nearly as wide as it was tall. The kid brought a rusted can of kerosene over from the bar and doused the base of the pile with it, looking at Harley as he did, and saying with a grin, "Fuego!"

As he said it, the boy lifted his hands high over his head and smiled. Harley did the same, laughing as he mimicked the kid. The past week's work had been long hours in the heat, and while it had netted some valuable intel, Cole had felt bogged down by it and sensed the rest of the group felt the same. They'd come together over the first week, but there was still some unspoken distance between them. As Harley tossed matches at the fire and cursed each time they extinguished, Cole couldn't help but laugh at him. Claire came over and sat down upwind of the pile, but close enough that Cole wondered if she'd need to back up if Harley ever got it lit. Matt brought a new round of beers over as well and sat down a few feet from Claire.

Just as he did, one of Harley's matches caught the kerosene and the pile came to life. Flames ripped up from the bottom and quickly overtook the entire pile with cracking sounds as the wet bits of wood hissed, swelled, and split. Harley yelled out into the sky, "Fuego!" He took another beer from Matt and plopped down on his side in the sand. Cole took a long breath of the thick air tainted by smoke.

To the east, the late afternoon sky was now overwhelmed by a light orange tint, with the brightest shades lingering out over the water.

Thick grey smoke shot upwards from the flames and trailed off briskly with the wind. Out over the water, towering cumulus clouds hung low, their bases well below the horizon and their tops bright red from the setting sun. Above them, the clouds were lighter shades of yellow and streaks of orange marked the trailing tips of the high clouds above them. Overhead, the sky was a dark blue, bordering on the black that would soon mark the night's arrival.

Cole walked closer to Claire and sat down next to her. She looked at him for a second with the expectation that he would say something, but he didn't.

"Cole...?"

"Claire..." He smiled.

She smiled at him and asked, "Are you drunk?"

"Are you drunk?" He asked back.

"A little."

Cole looked at the fire, then back at her. The sky was darker by the moment, but her face was painted in deep shades of red and orange from the fire. *Don't say too much*, he told himself.

"I like you, Claire." He said it matter-of-factly.

She laughed and shook her head as if it made no sense.

"What exactly does that mean?"

Cole took a long sip from his beer before replying. "Nothing really, I guess. Just an observation. I mean it, though. I like you."

"Well, thank you, Cole. I like you too, I think." They both laughed.

"How about me, Cole. You gonna talk sweet to me, too?"

Cole and Claire both looked over to Harley, who was grinning as he sat on his side in the sand. His hair was a wild mess and his face wore a crazy expression that was further exacerbated by the flames. Had it not been for the shit-eating grin on his face, he would've looked downright terrifying.

Cole said, "Nope, nothing sweet for you, Harley. Not yet, at least."

They sat around the fire well into the night, at times talking casually and at other times entirely quiet. When the wind backed off, Cole could smell the salt in the smoke from the burning driftwood. Harley told a few stories, and Cole gave them all a rundown of some of his finer moments running boats. None of them spoke of home or the things they missed. It had become clear that each of them was focused squarely on the days and weeks ahead. Hours later, as the fire dwindled to mostly smoke, the pile all but ashes, Cole looked up to the sky and saw the moon, nearly full in the midnight sky. To the east, its light reflected in glimmers off the sea beneath it. Cole was looking east. Somewhere, well beyond the horizon, it was almost morning in France. He felt the weight against his chest once more and forced his eyes closed and squinted for just a moment to push away those thoughts. *Don't go there*, he told himself. *Not now. Not here.*

CHAPTER 7: FORTUNE FAVORS THE BRAVE

COLE WOKE FROM HIS sleep on his back, laid out on the cool sand a few feet from the pile of ashes that now softly smoked upward in the still morning air. The sky was a flat shade of grey and Cole smelled the hint of the last smoldering bits of wood buried under a pile of ashes that was nearly five feet across. His head was swollen, and he knew before even moving an inch that the morning would be slow going. He sat up and scanned his surroundings.

Harley was still asleep, on his stomach with his face cocked to one side. It was as if he'd been knocked unconscious mid-sentence. Cole laughed at the sight of him. Further down the beach, near the water's edge, Matt was sitting and staring out at the Caribbean morning. It was as dark and nearly as foreboding as the grey sky that blended seamlessly against it, concealing the horizon far to the east. Cole watched Matt for some time, motionless with his arms draped over his knees in front of him. Lightning struck somewhere in the distance as the horizon was a haze of white for a moment, its crack too far to hear the thunder that would follow.

Still seated, Cole turned to see Claire in one of the hammocks behind them. She'd clearly had the good sense to find a proper place to sleep. Cole's back was covered in sand and his hair was as well. Standing up and shaking himself off as best he could, he made his way down to Matt and took a seat beside him.

"Good night, huh?" asked Cole.

Matt, still staring off at the distance, replied, "Yeah. I think we needed that."

The two of them sat for some time without saying a word as the colors slowly started to morph with the rising sun. It was less than a perfect sunrise, as there were still heavy clouds out over the water that blanketed a blurred stain of orange where the sun was trying to sneak through.

"What's on your mind?" Cole asked.

Matt turned to look toward Cole, and replied casually, "Thinking about my boys at home." He paused before continuing. "Just wondering what they're up to."

Cole nodded, feeling bad for a second for interrupting him, but Matt didn't seem to mind. "I guess you're on the road a lot, too, huh?"

Matt nodded. "Yeah. More than I'd like."

"So what's your story?"

Matt grinned before laying back with one elbow dug into the sand. "I was in the Coast Guard, like you." He looked at Cole for a reaction.

Cole squinted. "Get the fuck out. How'd you end up doing this?"

Matt exhaled and laughed at the same moment before continuing. "I was twenty-three and assigned to this thing called the Drug Interdiction Assistance Team. We were tearing it up all over South America for a few years until the Coast Guard got nervous and pulled the plug."

"On boats?"

Matt tilted his head to indicate it was a complicated answer.

"Yeah, sort of. We'd start out on these small boats and run up rivers in Bolivia to find the drug camps. The camps were always off the rivers, so we'd end up off the boats and running into these camps to clear them out then blow it all up—faces painted up, automatic rifles—full-on Rambo shit."

Cole was impressed. "I never heard that before."

Matt continued, "Yeah, not many people have, but we were up and running for a few years before the admirals got cold feet about Coasties picking fights in third-world countries. They pulled us out after my third year and stood the whole thing down."

"So then what?"

"I ended up on a buoy-tender."

Cole laughed. "Sorry. I don't mean to laugh at you, it's just…"

Matt nodded and laughed as well. "Yeah, no. I get it. I still had Bolivian mud on my boots, and all of a sudden I had a chief yelling at me to scrape barnacles off a buoy. I was young, angry, still hopped up on adrenaline, and couldn't handle that so I popped smoke and got out."

"So you ended up here?"

"Not exactly. I took a pretty circuitous route. Started out at State, did contract stuff for them for a while, went to the DEA for a bit, a few more contracts after that, some private security stuff, then got picked up for this gig."

"So is *this* CIA?" Cole asked.

Matt was quiet, smiling slightly, and looking at Cole. He clearly wasn't going to answer the question. Instead, his facial expression changed and he looked back out at the water. The sky was now changing from grey to blue and a light breeze stirred up, slowly creeping onshore from the sea.

"The thing is, I'm thirty-nine. I could be retired from the Coast Guard by now if I'd stayed in. I could be getting a check every month, working some no-stress day job, and be home every night with my kids..." Matt paused and squinted at the horizon.

Cole asked, "You think you'd be happy?"

Matt turned his head softly from side to side as he mulled over the question before replying, "Yeah, maybe not. Who knows. This hasn't been an easy route, either. Most of these guys are former SOF types. The SEALs with their damn tridents, the Rangers with their tabs, and Marines with their globe and anchor—then there's me, a fucking Coastie. I left the service with nothing but a nametag. It's a tough group to crack into, and they've got their cliques just like a bunch of teenage girls."

Cole nodded. He understood where Matt was coming from and thought back to his days on *Delaney* and the struggle to fit in. The boredom of cutting circles in the ocean and the monotony of shipboard life were things Cole and Matt both had experienced.

Cole spoke. "Harley seems like a good dude..."

Matt nodded firmly. "Yeah. Harley's a different beast altogether. If you can keep up with him, he doesn't care where you come from. That's why I brought him along on this one. A lot of other guys wouldn't stand working under a former Coastie."

"So what's his deal?"

Matt looked back up the beach at Harley, who will still laid out in the sand. He laughed at the sight of him, now starting to stir just a bit. Turning back towards the water, he explained Harley as best he could.

"He was a SEAL. They wanted him to go be an instructor and Harley wasn't done pulling the trigger just yet, so he punched and got picked up pretty quick on the civilian side. So long as he gets to kick in a few skulls and shoot some guns, Harley's a happy camper."

Matt popped up to his feet, and said, "Let's go. I'm tired of feeling sorry for myself."

Cole followed him up the beach. Claire was at the bar, talking with the older woman who had poured four glasses of water. Matt kicked at Harley as he passed, and Harley worked his way up to his feet. After chugging the water and settling up from the night before, they all started a slow march up the beach to their Thing. Harley fired it up as the rest climbed in. Cole was looking forward to the drive back and some wind across his face to shake the last bits of booze from his brain.

After hitting third gear, Harley came alive with a grin on his face, driving like a madman. Cole held on to the side of his seat as Harley worked the gears and the back end drifted through the turns, sending a cloud of fine sandy white dust up in their wake. Once headed back west, towards downtown, Harley opened the little car up, gravel flinging up and bouncing loudly off the undercarriage. Two minutes later, they passed a police truck tucked in against some palms. Harley calmly watched the rear-view mirror until a smirk appeared on his face. He still had sand all over his neck, and his hair was in full-vertical Viking-mode. Cole turned in his seat to see that both Matt and Claire were also looking back. In the middle of the dust kicked up from the Thing, there was a set of flashing blue lights.

Harley red-lined the Thing. Cole expected Matt to be upset, but he stared intently at Harley to see what his next move would be.

"I'd hold on to something," Matt said to no one in particular. Cole did as he was instructed and then looked forward. After 30 seconds of a straightaway, Harley took a series of turns to shake the cops. He slowed down and waited as the sirens drew closer. Pulling over to the side of the road, Harley scanned his side mirror until the cops crept down a parallel road, stopped, backed up, and turned towards the Thing. Harley then opened her up again and tore down a new series of roads, reversing his route twice.

"You ready?" Harley asked.

Matt replied calmly, "Yup."

Two turns later, Harley was miraculously at the gate of their small villa, and Matt jumped out, effortlessly unlocking and swinging the gate open. Harley pulled in and parked against the wall, concealing the Thing from prying eyes outside. Matt swung the gate closed and sauntered in towards the house. Cole made eye contact with Claire, who looked back at him for any reaction before she smiled at him and shook her head. As the sirens from the cops droned off in the distance, it occurred to Cole that luck had nothing to do with Harley ending up at the villa.

THEY SPENT THE majority of the second week much as the first, mapping out the movement of petty crime in and around Cozumel. With an intricate web connecting the dots, Matt and Claire had whittled their list of targets down to the boot shop and one house that seemed particularly busy. By the third week, they'd gone nocturnal. Starting early in the evening, all four of them would set off from the house, still in groups of two, and scout out the town. Drugs were clearly moving in and out of the shop, but they'd yet to figure out where they came from.

Halfway through that week, Harley and Cole were seated at a small bar tucked up against the rocky beach on the southern side of the town. They were nursing their beers and impatiently waiting for midnight. Harley had his feet up on the chair next to him, and Cole was leaned forward in his seat, his elbows against the table and his chin pressed squarely into the palm of his right hand. They'd sat for hours each night, usually moving between two or three bars, hoping to catch some movement. Cole found it boring. This night was shaping up to be yet another bust.

Without moving, Harley spoke under his breath, "There's Shorty."

Shorty was a nickname they'd given to one of the suspected middlemen. He was sitting on the seawall 20 yards or so from the bar, on an unlit patch of cement. Without pulling his face from his hand, Cole looked to his right and recognized the pudgy frame of Shorty. Cole walked to the bar and ordered another round of Tecate. He'd yet to finish any of the others, but couldn't bring himself to take the last sips as the beers had all gone flat and warm. Back at the table, he handed one to Harley and pressed with his pointer finger to sink the lime into his own.

Twenty minutes passed and Shorty still sat by himself, occasionally talking on the phone, but otherwise just sitting and facing the dark water that separated Cozumel from mainland Mexico. A handful of boats were moored out in an unofficial anchorage of sorts off the bar. They bobbed and turned in the late evening breeze. Harley was watching as a small center-console trolled slowly through the moorings towards the bar. Cole watched as well, and noted that Shorty paid particular attention to the boat. Once within five yards of the shore, Cole heard the driver rock the throttles into reverse to hold her in position. A second guy on the bow tossed four backpacks onto the shore, where yet another kid was busy scooping them up and bringing them up to the bar. Once there, he tucked each of them behind the counter and waited.

"This is promising," Cole said without much emotion, still setting himself up for Shorty's appearance to turn out to be yet another dead end.

The bar was far from busy. Well off the beaten path from downtown, there were a handful of lost tourists busily gulping down colorful rum drinks. A few locals were tucked in the corner of the bar, minding their own business and drinking beers at about the same pace as Harley and Cole.

Several minutes passed and yet another group of kids, none older than 20, materialized from the shadows. Each quickly took a bag from behind the bar and disappeared into different directions. Harley was busy texting Matt with one of the dozen or so disposable phones they'd purchased. When he was done, he looked at Cole with an expression of genuine satisfaction. Shorty was gone, having confirmed that whatever was in those bags was on the island and on its way. Half an hour later, Matt texted Harley back that all four bags had been dropped off at the house.

Harley finished off his beer, let out a loud burp, and said quite happily, "Now we're in business."

They settled their tab and walked back towards downtown. All four of them met up at Senor Frog's, one of the more obnoxiously decorated tourist bars in Cozumel. The floor was still moving at full speed and offered enough noise and distractions for the four of them to find a corner and talk without risking anyone overhearing. Matt brought over four beers, and they sat at a high-top table in the corner.

Sitting down, Matt asked, "So, Shorty's our man, huh?"

Harley nodded. "It's looking that way. He was babysitting whatever came in on that boat."

"Drugs?" Matt asked.

"Apparently so," Harley replied. He was staring off at the bartender who was popping tops off beer bottles as quick as she could to meet the insatiable demand of the multitude of gringos. Matt stared at Harley for a moment more before smiling and looking at Claire, who also was aware of Harley's sudden focus on the bartender, who was younger than any of them, a bit shorter than Harley, and pretty with almost black hair and fair skin. Claire also smiled as Harley seemed to be at last showing his softer side.

Claire asked, half-joking, "Should I go talk to her for you?"

Harley's eyes never left the bartender. "Nah, I can handle it." He turned and looked at Claire with a grin. "But thanks."

Harley was up and moving towards the bar, where he quickly settled onto a stool and waited his turn. Moments later, the girl passed by and he managed to snag her into a brief conversation before returning with four more beers, his mouth flared in an even bigger smile. Taking a giant sip from his fresh beer, Harley spoke plainly without looking at anyone in particular. "Brittany."

Matt shook his head for a moment and took a long sip from his beer as well. "Well, here we go."

"Anything I should know about?" asked Claire.

Harley was mentally consumed by something, most likely rehearsing lines or trying in vain to balance his lustful chi. Cole couldn't help but laugh and take another sip from his beer.

Matt replied to Claire's question, "Nah, it's just gonna be one of those nights."

Over the next hour or so, Harley bought most of the drinks, taking each round as an opportunity to strike up conversations with Brittany. It seemed to be working, and as the night began to slow down, Harley was affixed to a bar stool, and Brittany was idling more and more by Harley's seat. Claire had struck up a conversation with a group across the bar, a mixed crowd of 20-somethings that was touring around Central America. Matt and Cole were left with a table and a growing pile of empty beer bottles.

Well after midnight, the bar was still loud, and all that remained were the serious drinkers. Claire's group was picking up and moving on, saying the kind of slow goodbyes that come from newfound quasi-drunken friendships. As Claire walked along the length of the bar and made her way back to Matt and Cole, a guy about her age backed up his stool and blocked her path. Cole looked at Matt, who was already laser-focused on it. Claire smiled, seemingly polite, and tried to move around him. The guy was a tad on the scruffy side and mildly overweight. He and his friend, seated next to him, had been at the bar all night. Claire tried to walk around the first guy, and he blocked her path with his arm, trying to woo her with what he failed to realize as an utter lack of charm. As he did, the second guy stood up next to Claire and put his arm around her waist, low enough that he was pulling himself against her hip.

Cole looked to his right over towards Harley, who by now had paused the conversation and was also patiently watching and waiting. Claire pushed off from the one holding her hip just as the first guy wrapped a finger through one of her belt loops and pulled at it. Claire was quick to drive the web of her hand into his throat, which threw off his balance, and he fell awkwardly against the bar. She yelled something at him, not quite loud enough for Cole or Matt to hear, and the two drunks seemed to get the message, but not before the second guy smacked at her butt as she finally broke free and continued toward Matt and Cole. She looked back quickly with a fiery stare and the two guys laughed to themselves before returning to their drinks. Brittany made her way over to them, and from the body language, she tried to get them to leave.

As Claire sat back down, Harley was already making his way back over to the table as well. Matt asked, "You all right?"

With complete calm, she replied, "I'm fine." She even managed to smile as she said it. If Claire was troubled, she showed no outward signs. It was her nature, Cole surmised. Matt and Harley were not so calm.

"That dude is gonna lose a few teeth," Matt said.

"It's fine," Claire said. "Leave them alone. They're just drunk."

Harley's jaw clenched for a second as he watched Matt for the go ahead.

"Leave them," Claire said with more force. "A bar fight is not the kind of low profile we should be keeping."

"Won't be much of a fight." Harley was staring back at the two guys, who were totally oblivious to Harley or Matt's growing rage.

Brittany was too far away for them to hear her, but it was clear she'd refused to serve them any more drinks. They mouthed off to her as well before she turned her back on them and walked away. Both the drunks were now left talking among themselves as they finished the last drops of beer from their glasses. Harley walked back over to Brittany and talked quietly with her in a corner.

"Matt," Claire said, "Don't make a scene."

Matt just smiled. The two drunks were getting up from their stools and clumsily made their way over to the bathroom. Harley was ten yards behind them, concealing something in his right hand against his chest. Matt took a long steady breath and turned to Cole. "Watch the door."

Matt was up and quickly moved in behind Harley as the two of them followed the drunk guys into the bathroom.

Claire appealed to Cole, "Cole, don't let them…"

Before she could finish, Cole cut her off and stood up to cover the door as instructed. He turned back to Claire as he walked and shrugged his shoulders, "Like I can stop them?"

At the door, Cole leaned against the frame and listened intently over the pulsing Calypso music that blasted from the speakers. He heard a series of thuds, and at least one of the two drunks repeatedly saying *no* until his words were muffled, then muted. A few more spaced out thuds followed, and Cole couldn't help but laugh. An older gentleman approached the door, and Cole sternly shook his head and spoke, "You don't want to go in there right now."

The man looked at Cole for a second before a final pronounced thud echoed out of the bathroom. The man wisely turned and walked away.

Harley cracked the door open and looked to Cole, asking, "Clear?"

Cole shrugged his shoulders, not entirely understanding how exactly a bar at two in the morning could be clear of anything. "Sure," he replied.

Harley pushed the door open, and Matt kicked the two dudes out of the bathroom with his foot. They stumbled forward into the bar area and no one seemed to notice, at least for the first few seconds. Then, a moment later, one by one, the bar took notice and silence ensued.

They were both naked, save for the Duct Tape over their mouths and binding their hands. One guy's arms were around the waist of the other and bound together with an excessive amount of tape. The other's hands were wrapped securely around the first's hands, so that all four hands were interlocked. It forced them into an uncomfortable pose where the one behind was constantly bumping awkwardly into the one in front. They moaned wildly, but their words were inaudible under the tape. Their eyes were wide and looking frantically about in what amounted to nothing less than total shock.

The bar slowly broke out into laughter. The two of them fell over as they tried to make their way towards the door. Claire stared at the two of them in bewilderment. It didn't take her long to laugh. Despite her initial protest, she couldn't help but find the two drunk men's predicament entirely laughable. As the bar broke out into an increasingly raucous laugh, Matt slipped out and around back to Cole and Claire. Harley was back at the bar returning the roll of Duct Tape to Brittany. They spoke for a few minutes more before Harley returned to the table.

Matt said, "We should go."

Claire was smiling at the two of them. Cole looked once more at the two morons struggling to their feet. Each time they stepped, they were on each other's feet and made no significant progress towards whatever route they were trying to take. A particularly overweight and ruddy-faced woman grabbed hard at one of their ass cheeks as they tried to shuffle, which only sent them into a further state of disorientation. Cole laughed out loud. It was too damn funny to not watch. Matt nodded at Harley and the two of them looked at each other in approval.

℘

WELL PAST MIDNIGHT and back at the villa, Cole, Matt, and Claire sat around the kitchen table, nursing their last drinks for the evening. Over the moans of Harley and Brittany upstairs, they talked casually about the days and weeks ahead, in a failed attempt to ignore the wild sex.

Matt spoke. "We need to talk to Shorty."

Claire thought for a second before replying. "That's risky, out of the blue like that."

"You got any other ideas?"

Harley or Brittany, it was hard to know which was which, cried out loudly and Cole closed his eyes, looked down at his lap, and shook his head with a quiet laugh.

Claire was also laughing. She thought for a moment and said, "The chatter has been quiet for two weeks now. My guess is they're moving this way."

Matt asked, "You've got someone embedded with them, don't you?"

Claire looked at Matt with a poker face.

"Sorry," Matt said. "Not my place to ask that."

Claire was quick to answer, "It's fine. We're just a bit sensitive to letting our secrets out."

It was as much of an answer as anyone could ask for, and helped to explain the tension between Johnson and Gail back in Chiswick. Perhaps Johnson had his suspicions and wasn't as stupid as he looked or sounded.

"So what do you think?" asked Matt.

She took a long breath. "We need to make a move, I agree. I just don't know how to do it."

Either the bed frame knocked hard against the wall, or one of the two of them upstairs fell to the floor. More moans were followed by a series of higher and higher pitched shrieks before the upstairs fell silent. It was almost three in the morning.

"Well, maybe now we can get some sleep," Claire said with a hint of humor.

Cole thought about sleep. He was fast growing to despise it. He dreamed of Isabella almost every night, that they were together again and back in France. They were all active during the day and most days went by without much trouble, but at night, when Cole was alone on the couch, he found himself unable to think of anything else. He took a long breath and looked off at the far wall.

As he did, Harley and Brittany made their way downstairs. As if nothing had happened, she casually said goodnight to the rest of them and Harley walked her out into the courtyard and towards the gate. A minute or two later, he was back inside and sitting at the table with them, a look of satisfaction across his face.

Claire, testing Harley, said bluntly, "She could be a liability."

Harley smiled back at Claire, "Nah, she's fine."

Matt asked, "And how do you know that?"

"I searched her pretty good." They all laughed. Between the beer, the two drunks tied up to each other, and Harley's escapade upstairs, they had plenty to smile about.

Harley abruptly stood up and said, "I'm getting some sleep. We've got work to do tomorrow."

"You mean today," Cole corrected him.

They all separated and the others headed to sleep. Cole sat alone at the table, staring at the couch on the other end of the room. He gritted his teeth and ran his hands across his face, driving the palms of his hands into the sockets of his eyes.

Keep it together, he told himself.

CHAPTER 8: DOLDRUMS

THE NEXT WEEK WAS brutally slow. They had the local network mapped out as best they could and continued to follow the petty crime each night, but it did nothing more than confirm what they already knew. Claire labored over her laptop more and more each day and spent considerable time in the early hours of the mornings up on the roof with a satellite phone. Matt had given Cole the go-ahead to try and give Isabella a call, but she had been out both times he tried. Her father had recognized his voice and asked a series of questions, all in French. Both times only served to raise Cole's frustration with the whole ordeal. Harley and Matt, on the other hand, worked out harder each day, and that alone seemed enough of an outlet for whatever frustration they may have held.

By Saturday morning, they were seated around the kitchen table as midday approached. Harley and Matt had put Cole through a workout, and he was increasingly convinced that his shoulder had been separated when Harley had slammed him onto his back during one of their rolls. Cole sat at the table with ice over it and tried to move his arm in a circular motion to stop the tingling.

Harley laughed as he pulled a handful of beers from the fridge and asked, "Feels good, doesn't it?"

Cole stopped his arm's movement and looked back at Harley with an inquisitive stare. "What feels good?"

"A little bit of pain—let's you know you're alive."

Cole thought on it. Harley had a way of revealing his true identity in little bits of random commentary. He thought back to the bullet that had grazed his shoulder in Panama, the burning sensation, the blood down his back, and the realization that he'd won once all the shooting had stopped.

"Yeah, I suppose it does."

Matt nodded before returning his gaze to the map on the wall.

Harley returned and rolled the beers around the table at Matt and Cole. He held a third and fourth in his hand.

"Claire, beer?"

She looked up from her computer and shook her head. She was becoming increasingly preoccupied with her computer as each day passed.

"Suit yourself."

As was becoming custom, Harley and Cole took long sips while Matt did a far better job of pacing himself with the day's first beer. Harley crushed the first can in less than a minute and popped open the second.

Matt was looking intently at Claire. After a long pause, he asked, "Any chatter?"

Without looking up, she shook her head. She finished typing something and closed her computer, pushing it into the middle of the table. "We should have heard something by now."

They all sat and stared at nothing, knowing that Claire was right.

"Will you know for sure when they're here?" asked Cole.

Claire nodded. "If things are still in place, then yes."

"If what's in place?"

She turned to Matt and stared blankly at him. The silence bordered on uncomfortable.

Harley chimed in, "Come on Claire, who do y'all have with them?"

"It's nothing against any of you. I just have some very specific orders about what I can or can't say."

Matt smiled. "Well, that tells me all I need to know."

Harley had pulled his M4 from its Pelican Case and was field-stripping it for the tenth time since they'd landed in Cozumel. Much to his consternation, he'd yet to fire it. As he man-handled the forend off, he spoke without looking up. "I say when they get here, we roll in, off these dudes, and hop a commercial flight home—first class."

Claire, for the first time, looked genuinely mad.

"You've been 'offing' these people for ten years, dropping your bombs and burying them in caves. Tell me, Harley, how is that war going?"

He was running a cleaning swab through the barrel and spoke without looking up from his work. "It's been a hell of a good time." He laid out two cardboard packages of M855 ammo and proceeded to load up two magazines.

She nodded at the ammo and asked, "So is that your solution?"

Harley paused, looked up, smiled and rolled one round across the table to Claire. It careened in a wide semi-circle until Claire delicately placed her flattened hand on top of it to her right.

"Steel core perfectly sums your kind up, Harley," she said.

Matt and Harley looked at each other in a bit of surprise. Once again, Claire knew more than she ever let on.

"Go on," Matt said.

Claire picked up the green-tipped round and stared at it for a few moments. Had it been anyone else, the move would have been overly dramatic, but with Claire she was thinking intently about something.

"A varmint round would be far superior for a lightly dressed adult male target in this environment. Immediate expansion, better accuracy, and less collateral—assuming you can hit your target."

She looked back at both of them with a smile. There was no tension, and for that Cole was grateful. It was another moment when he couldn't help but stare at her until she looked his way, and he tried unsuccessfully to turn away before she caught him.

Matt scratched at his head and looked down at the table before speaking. "We need to make some progress. Anyone got any ideas?"

Harley, changing subjects, perked up. "Shit; I almost forgot. I got credentials."

Matt was watching with curiosity as Harley rummaged through yet another one of the Pelican Cases.

"Found 'em," he called out as he walked back over to the table and dropped four blue American passports on the table. He tossed one at Matt, looked at a second before tossing it at Claire, and then the third at Cole. He tucked one into his own front pocket. Cole opened his and stared in wonder at a picture of himself with a last name of Dover and a first name of Benjamin. There was a street address he didn't recognize, along with several pages of stamps from various Caribbean countries.

"Harley, you can't be fucking serious."

Defensively, Harley called out, "What?"

Matt placed his passport back on the table and looked directly at Harley, asking in disbelief, "James Bond?"

"I thought it suited you," was all Harley could manage as he tried to keep a poker face.

As the two of them played a staring game of chicken, Claire exhaled loudly and asked, "Who is Bambi Stilts?"

At that, Harley lost and laughed the kind of laugh that takes one entirely by surprise.

"Cole, what'd you end up with?" asked Matt.

"Benjamin Dover. I don't get it."

"Harley. Fuck."

Cole asked, "Who is Ben Dover?"

As he said it, the words clicked. It was elementary school humor, and had taken him by surprise. "Do I have a wife named Eileen?" Harley threw a wadded-up napkin at him.

Claire was still looking over her passport. To no one in particular, she asked, "What is Bambi Stilts? That sounds like a go-go dancer's name." She seemed neither upset nor impressed.

Harley was bent over double, laughing to no one but himself.

"I'm sorry, Claire. I didn't know at the time who you'd end up being, but it seemed like a good idea."

Matt interrupted, "Harley, how the fuck did you get these through admin?"

"I know the girl who does credentials."

Claire quickly chimed in, "You mean you slept with her."

Harley, grinning from ear to hear, pointed at Claire and replied, "Don't judge her."

"I'm judging you, Harley—not her," she replied.

Cole, watching them all, interrupted. "Wait. Harley, what's your name?"

They all paused. Harley smiled.

"Pancho Nutz, with a 'z' in Nutz."

Matt pushed back with his feet, raising the front legs of his chair, and crossed both his hands behind his back. Staring at the ceiling, he mumbled, "Of course, you get the cool name. I'm gonna get fired before we even finish this thing."

Harley, his laughing now under control, replied, "Relax Matt, I got your back."

Matt smiled, "I know you do, bud."

&

BY THE LATE AFTERNOON, as they were readying to head out for another night, Cole asked Matt if he could try once more with the phone. Out in the grass by the pool, he dialed Isabella's number and felt his hands shaking as he did.

She answered. "Cole?"

"Isabella, I've been trying to call, I'm sorry it's taken me so long."

She opened up with a long list of questions. *Where are you, what are you doing, are you all right,* and *who are you with?*

"I can't really say much, but I'm OK."

"Where are you?"

At that he laughed. "I'm not supposed to say."

"I'm worried about you."

"Don't be," he tried to tell her.

She asked a second time, "Who are you with?"

"They're good people. I'm working with good people."

With the same concerned voice, she asked, "Are there girls?"

It was out of nowhere, and the question caught Cole off guard. *Why would she ask something like that?* His pause was long enough for Isabella to take note and her tone changed almost immediately.

"What are you doing, Cole?"

He was at a loss for words, and his silence did nothing but make the situation worse.

"Cole, talk to me."

"I'm fine, I'm just not supposed to say much about what we are doing or where we are."

With a tremble in her voice, she asked, "When are you coming home?"

The word *home* put a lump in Cole's throat as it brought with it an image in Cole's head of Marie. He knew without speaking that any word he spoke would bring with it a choking feeling, but at the same time his silence was doing nothing but confirming Isabella's fears.

"Are you with someone else?"

"No," he flatly replied. He was defensive. "Isabella, listen to me. It's nothing like whatever you're thinking."

Cole was smart enough to know that his past did little to quell her fears, and she knew—at least from her perspective—enough of his history to wonder. But Cole wasn't the same as he'd been in Key West, or Panama, or anywhere else for that matter.

"Is there another girl?"

She'd gone for the kill shot. When or how those thoughts had crept into her mind, Cole didn't know. But they were there, and from halfway around the world, there was almost nothing Cole could do.

"Isabella, whatever you're thinking, it's not that."

"Cole." She was emotional. Had she yelled at him, Cole could have managed, as it would have brought with it a young man's natural instinct to create distance from a scornful woman. But that wasn't Isabella. She'd never been that way, nor was she now. She was hurting, of that much Cole was certain.

"Cole, please come home."

He ran his fingers through his hair and grabbed at it as he looked up at the early evening sky. "Isabella, I can't."

She asked, "Who is she?"

"Isabella, no. I love you. There's no one else. Stop thinking that."

Silence ensued. Cole looked back over towards the gate. Harley and Matt were talking about something as they both casually leaned against the wall of the villa. Claire, standing in front of the Thing, was looking at him, and this time she didn't look away when their eyes made contact. Cole was the first to look away and he stared back down at the ground. *Damn her for being so pretty,* he thought. It wasn't her fault, but she didn't make things any easier.

"Cole, can you come home?"

Stop saying that, he thought, but stopped short of saying it.

"I can't."

Matt was looking at Cole now, which was enough of a reminder that he had to break off the call.

"Isabella, I will come as soon as I can. But I can't right now."

She asked, "Do you still love me?"

It was enough that he felt the onset of tears, but there was no way he'd let himself break down now. He couldn't find the words to stop their conversation from spiraling out of control. "Yes, of course I do. Don't think that, Isabella."

Matt motioned with his head to move along.

"I'll finish this as soon as I can, I promise. We need to get going now."

"Cole, please. I love you."

"I love you too. I'll call soon, but I gotta go."

He hung up and walked towards the Thing, frustration growing in his mind. As he neared the far side, he threw the phone against the wall and it broke into three pieces, the battery flying off with the cover.

"Nice, Cole. Now we're down to three phones." Matt patted him on the shoulder as Cole climbed into the Thing.

"Why does *everyone* pat me on the fucking shoulder?"

Harley climbed in after him and patted him on the shoulder just to rub it in and reaffirm the fact that no one was going to cut him any slack. Harley stopped for a moment then continued patting him on the shoulder until Cole laughed.

"Fuck you, Harley."

"Fuck you, Cole."

Matt climbed in the driver's seat, idled forward, and Claire worked the gate open.

∾

DOWNTOWN, THEY SPLIT into two groups again. For whatever reason, Matt and Harley had gone off on their own, leaving Claire and Cole to keep eyes on the boot shop. From a bar across the street, they watched as the steady stream of Caribbean thugs and vandals moved money and merchandise into the back.

Cole was powering through his third or fourth beer. Without looking at her, he was certain that Claire was watching him, maybe even concerned after the phone call. When she spoke, it confirmed what he was already thinking.

"Are you all right, Cole?"

He put his beer down, relieved in a way that she had even bothered to ask. "I'll be all right."

She tilted her head to one side, in the way a girl does when she has genuine interest in a conversation, and pressed him. "Is she mad at you?"

"I think so."

There wasn't much more to be said, as Claire knew well enough that 1,000 miles of distance did nothing but exacerbate an already tense situation. As he looked back towards the boot shop, yet another kid rolled in with a backpack.

"You're not going to pat me on the back, are you?"

Claire laughed. "No, I wouldn't dare. But if you want to talk, we can."

Cole nodded to say thanks and looked at Claire for a few moments more, their eye contact for the first time not seeming even the least bit uncomfortable. He thought of Isabella again and his promise to return.

"I'll be back," Cole said as he stood up and started a quick walk towards the store.

"Cole," Claire called out to no avail.

He walked across the street, paused for some traffic that passed him, then continued up the sidewalk and onto the air-conditioned floor of the boot shop. It was a polished white tile floor with floor-to-ceiling shelves of boots. Without looking at any of them, Cole worked through the small gathering of patrons to the back of the store. A young girl working the counter tried to stop him, but Cole nudged her aside and pushed open the swinging door that led into the backroom. As he stepped into the dimly lit space, he was immediately pushed against a wall with an outspread hand firmly against the back of his head. It knocked him off balance for a second as his cheekbone was smashed into a bare wooden wall. He felt the unmistakable barrel of a gun against the back quarter of his neck. Pressing his hands against the wall to steady himself, he felt an odd grin spread across his face. Harley was right. *Sometimes it takes a bit of pain to feel alive.* The room smelled of dust and leather. Whoever had smashed Cole into the wall didn't let up the pressure.

Someone, from the far side of the room, asked casually, "Who that fuck are you?"

Cole thought for a second. He was now back in his element where uncertainty and quick thinking reigned supreme. Despite a gun to his head, Cole felt comfortable in his current surroundings. *Pull the trigger if you want*, he thought.

"I'm a boat driver."

"What the fuck are you doing here?"

Cole tried to turn his head, but couldn't move under the pressure. He strained for a second, then relaxed against the wall.

"Looking for work."

The man in the corner, again speaking with no urgency, said, "You want to sell boots?"

Cole felt whoever was smashing him against the wall reach into the small of his back and pull out the revolver. He was now entirely at the mercy of the crew running the boot shop.

"No, I want to drive boats."

"I don't know shit about boats."

Cole knew better. "I think you do."

The handful of people in the room spoke quickly and in Spanish, so fast that Cole couldn't understand the conversation. From the inflection, he gathered that they were talking about him.

The man asked, "Are you DEA?"

"Not even close," Cole replied.

"Then what are you?"

"I drive boats."

The man pressing Cole against the wall let him go, and Cole turned to see an older Hispanic man in jeans and a black t-shirt sitting against the far wall. The man nearest him fondled Cole's revolver, flipping the cylinder open, then closing it and pointing it into the corner of the room.

From the corner, the man spoke again. "I never seen a cop carry a revolver."

Cole replied, "Me neither."

It occurred to him that the next few seconds would make or break the deal he was trying to broker. In the larger context, it was reckless to have walked in so brazenly, but all of them had known that time was running thin to get the ball moving. Moreover, Cole was sick and tired of sitting around. If he could end it quickly, even if that meant a less-than-ideal conclusion, he was ready.

"What you know about driving boats?"

Cole took a long breath and steadied himself. "I know how to get a boat from point A to point B without anyone knowing I was even on the water. I think you might have a need for that kind of service."

They talked more, in fast and argumentative Spanish, and Cole rested his back against the wall, feeling the odds turning a bit in his favor. When they finished speaking, the fat guy who'd pressed Cole into the wall raised Cole's revolver and pointed it at his head. The fat guy even went so far as to cock the hammer. The room was entirely silent, so quiet that Cole could hear the subtle clicks from his gun as the hammer dropped into place. He turned to square off with the fat man now pointing a loaded gun at him.

"You can either pull that trigger, or give me back my gun."

From the corner, the man in charge shuffled a bit in his seat. The fat guy looked with uncertainty back and forth from Cole to the boss.

"Why you think he won't shoot you?"

Cole looked at the guy in the corner, and replied, "You don't want my brains all over your office. If you're going to shoot me, you'd do it outside in some alley or backroad."

The man smiled and laughed. "You right. What's your name?"

"Ben," Cole replied. He had to work not to laugh at his new last name, hoping that the boss man wouldn't ask for his last name too.

"Well, Ben, my name is Juan, and I do use some boats from time to time, but I'm not hiring."

Cole asked, "Can I get my revolver back?"

"Not just yet," he replied.

The rest of the occupants in the room, maybe four or five total, said nothing and didn't move even a single muscle in their lanky bodies. They were mostly older men with leathered faces who looked at Cole for answers as to why some gringo had just walked in to their lair.

Juan asked, "Why you wanna drive boats? In Cozumel?"

Cole was quick to answer, "I like it here, but I'm running low on money."

"You here by yourself?"

Cole replied, "Just me and a girl."

"She spend all your money?"

Cole laughed, and so did most of the men in the room. They'd found some common ground.

"Something like that."

"How much you trying to make?"

"How far are you looking to move cargo?"

The two of them stared casually at each other in a game of wits. The pudgy guy finally lowered the revolver, most likely only because his arm had grown tired of holding it up. No one but Cole seemed to notice. He felt relieved, although he'd been fairly certain that if he was going to be shot, it wouldn't be inside.

"I need a pickup later this week from Playa del Carmen. Easy trip back and forth. I pay you $100."

Cole knew the old man was playing games with him to see how much Cole knew of the drug trade. He smirked, "I can make more money waiting tables."

Juan was quick to reply, "Then why don't you?"

Cole was even more quick with his response, "It's boring work."

They each paused. Cole broke the silence. "There and back, five-hundred dollars for the first run. If you like it, we can renegotiate something more permanent."

Cole knew he was likely underbidding the competition. Juan most certainly knew the same thing.

Juan thought for a moment, then asked, "You know anything about a gringo boat driver making trouble down in Central America?"

Cole shook his head.

"I hear stories about some cowboy motherfucker that was running drugs and shooting up his bosses and shit. He was supposedly bad news. Rumor is he got killed. Where you been before Cozumel?"

Cole couldn't help but smile. His reputation had preceded him.

"I worked out of Florida for a while, then moved down into the islands for a bit, on the east side. Came over here to try something different, but I've never been to Panama."

Juan rubbed slowly at his neck.

"OK, Ben. You swing through Tuesday, after the sun goes down. I'll give you keys to a boat."

Juan nodded for the pudgy one to return Cole's revolver, which he did. Cole tucked it back in his holster. He nodded at Juan, said, "Gracias," then turned to walk out, figuring that if he was going to get dragged out back, now was the time. Halfway through the boot store, he could smell the warm salt air again and it occurred to him that he'd pulled it off.

Back across the street, he walked towards Claire, still seated at the bar and trying hard to mask the concern she had over his whereabouts for the past 15 minutes.

"Are you all right?" she asked.

Cole smiled. "Yeah, I'm good. Let's get moving."

As she stood up, Cole took her hand with his and wove his fingers tightly through hers. She looked at him for a second in disbelief and Cole spoke softly, "I told them me and you are together."

He winked at her, and Claire smiled before turning away and shaking her head slowly. Cole held onto her hand, wondering if she could feel him trembling.

CHAPTER 9: THE ARRIVAL

BY SUNDAY, THEY WERE all at their usual spot, drinking their first beers an hour before noon. Harley had managed to acquire three sets of fins and masks along with two crude spear poles. He had also convinced the boy and his mother to let them use the small boat to head out beyond the reef. As Harley finished up his beer, he was setting the elastic bands in the spear poles, screwing in the tips, and giving each a quick glance before setting them down in the sand. He couldn't hide a grin creeping across his face.

Claire sat in a corner of the bar, her feet up on a chair in front of her as she stared out at the sea. Her face showed an expression of calm, but Cole wondered what thoughts were going through her head. Matt nudged Cole to break his focus, and the three of them pushed the boat down to the water's edge. Feeling the warm water swirl around his feet, Cole pushed once more, and the boat slipped into the water and floated up a small wave as it broke on the shore. Harley and Matt both jumped in, with Cole pushing farther and farther until he was up to his stomach. He jumped over the side and landed his bare feet on the wooden deck. On the small transom sat an outboard motor that was held together by the boy's sheer determination. His mother had confirmed that each day her only child set out on the sea by himself to fish just off the reef. On days when a swell rolled in from the north, she'd lose sight of him for the better part of the morning while he worked to bring in a day's worth of fish for her to cook.

Cole flipped the rusted lever that allowed the motor to drop. He pulled with force at the pull cord, and the engine burped twice before roaring to life. It ran slow and lurched a few times against its mount with Cole certain it would die, but the old engine slowly worked its way up to an idle that never quite found a rhythm, but seemed decent enough for the quick ride out past the reef. Cole drove, his left hand around the plastic pipe that served as a steering arm. The bow was pointed and dug up and into the waves before falling down the backside. The larger of the sets threw Cole off course if he didn't meet the crests at just the right angle. It was hard to handle, given its inability to get anywhere near a plain, but the old boat's character left Cole happy to be on the water. There was a part of him that couldn't help but think back to his first run off the Florida Keys to Cuba and back. As it was, Cuba wasn't too far east, and as he chugged ahead, Cole's mind wandered to years past. He was a different person now—part of his youth surely lost on an empty beach on the north coast of Cuba.

Passing the reef, Cole throttled back to idle again and circled, looking down at the abundance of colors below. Beyond the reef, the water was a brilliant shade of blue and clear down to the bottom, some 20 or 30 feet below them. The boat rode up and down on the swells, but well beyond their breaking point. They were more rhythmic and subtle than on the ride out. Harley and Matt were already suited up and sitting on the wooden rail. Harley grinned as Matt turned to Cole and asked, "You good to wait here for a bit?"

Cole nodded. Harley and Matt were over the side, spear poles in hand, and disappeared under the water. Cole sat on the rail and took a long breath of the salt air, with a hint of the gasoline that wafted up from the small plastic tank at his feet. The boat rose up and rolled slightly down the back of a wave, and as it did, Cole closed his eyes and felt the breeze blowing softly against his face. It was enough that he could forget nearly everything in that moment. He would have let his mind rest, but to do so struck him as shallow. He'd talked with Isabella the morning after he'd brokered the boat driving deal. She had seemed more inclined to talk, but Cole was certain that her unanswered questions still festered. When they spoke, it felt nothing like their relationship had before, now more a series of partial thoughts that meandered delicately around what each of them knew had the potential to turn the conversation toxic. It was the onset of some unknown illness, and Cole felt powerless to stop it.

Harley and Matt popped up 20 yards farther from the boat and looked back to Cole, who waved as they both flipped and kicked hard back down to the bottom. Cole looked east, towards Cuba, and smiled. He was now eager to get in the water himself. Harley and Matt popped up once more, Matt huffing loudly when he reached the surface. He was weighed down by something, and Harley called out to Cole, motioning with one arm. Motoring 40 or so yards over, Cole could see Matt's shoulders straining, and that he was kicking hard to keep himself up.

"What is it?" Cole asked as he pulled up next to the two of them.

Harley was laughing at Matt's struggle. "Yellowfin," Harley said as he swam around Matt and grabbed hard to help pull the fish up to the surface. Cole reached over as well and between the three of them, they pulled the fish up to the side and over the rail. It flopped down on the deck, the spear still sticking out from its side, and blood ran with the water off the side of the fish, pooling in the lowest part of the boat. Matt and Harley hung on to the side to catch their breath as Cole stared at the dying fish, now barely moving as it tried in vain to kick for the water. When it was finally still, Cole stared at its eye, staring upwards into the bright midday sky, where gulls were already circling the small boat.

As he pulled himself up and over, Harley spoke. "You're up, Cole." Already at the rail with a mask and fins on, Cole rolled over the side and took Harley's pole. Matt and Cole then pushed back from the boat while Harley pulled himself effortlessly up and over into the boat. They kicked a few yards farther before Matt rolled and looked down under water.

"There's grouper on the ledge, but they're quick little fuckers if they see you."

Cole smiled. "Let's give it a try."

They both dove under the shallow slope of a passing wave and were underwater. As they descended, Cole knew the trick was to stay calm and kick with a soft rhythm. Strength only burned oxygen, and patience paid far better dividends underwater. As he took long graceful kicks, he cleared his nose three times, estimating that he and Matt were perhaps 25 or 30 feet down. At the ledge, which was dark save for a few spots of bright coral and some sponges, he spotted a medium-sized grouper as it descended away out of range. Matt had been right.

Not long after his first descent, Cole turned and kicked back up to the surface. Matt followed and broke through the wave next to Cole. "Try Again?" he asked.

Cole nodded and took another dive down. They repeated the same process three or four more times, and with each dive, Cole was growing confident in his breathing, so that he could stay down at the bottom longer each time. On their fifth ascent, Matt tapped Cole's foot as they broke the surface and pointed back down. Looking through his mask, Cole saw a school of almost a dozen tuna swimming towards the reef from the depths. They were no more than 15 feet down. Taking a long breath, Cole followed Matt's lead, and they both descended to the side of the school. The school, bundled together, seemed to view Matt and Cole with part curiosity and part fear before they turned nearly 45 degrees to create some distance. Cole had already extended the band and was gripping the pole near its base. He let go and watched it launch forward towards a fish before the pole veered off and slowed until the line of paracord around Cole's wrist caught it. They both swam to the surface.

Matt smiled, "It takes some getting used to."

Cole was busy retrieving the pole as Harley guided the boat closer. They'd been in the water nearly 45 minutes.

"You two done yet?"

Matt laughed at Harley, "You want another try already?"

"Just gimme a pole."

Cole pulled himself to the boat, not wanting to admit that his bad lung was burning. "Here, take mine. I'm out for a bit."

Pulling himself back up, Cole felt the sun on his shoulders and the salt water running down his back. He ran his hands through his hair and wiped his face clear, then sat back near the engine as it purred along at idle. Matt and Harley were already underwater. Alone, on the boat, Cole took a few long breaths to steady his breathing and returned to his earlier self-reflection. He felt good, at least for the time being. They'd been out on the water for almost two hours. Harley and Matt popped up twice and looked back towards Cole. Taking a bearing on them before they disappeared again, he trolled in their direction, back towards the exposed reef.

Once in their general area, Cole went back to scanning the sky and towards the shore. Claire was nowhere in sight, most likely still tucked up in the same quiet corner. He wondered about her again. There was a mystery around her that Cole couldn't help but be interested in. He looked back around at the water, waiting for Harley and Matt to pop up. A few more seconds passed, and they still hadn't emerged. Looking down into the water, there were too many distortions from the waves and wind for him to make anything out, but he saw what seemed to be their shape moving slowly on the bottom. Pressing his mask against his face, he leaned over the edge and buried his head for a second to see that it was the two of them together, still 20 feet down. Cole popped up, pulled the strap over his head and looked again. They were still together, but moving more slowly than they should. *Perhaps they're on a fish*, he thought. Pulling his fins on to help, he popped over the side to check once more, and this time he could see clearly enough that Matt had one arm around Harley and was kicking full-speed for the surface.

Cole took a deep breath, rolled, and dove for them. Seconds later, he reached down for Harley and Matt looked at Cole, pointed up, and sprinted for the surface, leaving Cole with Harley's limp body under one arm. Cole continued kicking for the surface, but made little progress until Matt was back down and latched onto Harley's other side. Cole gasped for air once he finally pushed through the surface and Matt was trying to keep Harley's head above the surface with his free hand. In a calm but forceful tone that Cole had to yet to hear from Matt, he called out, "Get him in the boat, now."

Cole hopped up and over, then reached down to grab at Harley's armpits. He wasn't able to pull him more than halfway out of the water. Seconds later, Matt was in the boat and pulling as well, with Harley's body being dragged over and onto the deck. Matt quickly rolled him to his side and hit his fist with force against Harley's back.

"Damn it, Harley," he mumbled as he rolled him on his back. Leaning down, Matt gave one long and forceful breath into Harley's mouth. His chest swelling, Harley coughed and seized up uncontrollably while Matt tried again to get him to his side. Harley lurched forward and hacked out several mouthfuls of water onto the deck. He coughed a few more times and winced as he grabbed at his chest.

Just as quickly, he regained some level of composure and looked up at Cole, startled for a second. It was a subconscious expression, his body trying to catch up with his mind. The boat was rolling, the engine was idling, and Matt sat back against the side, completely out of breath and smiling. Harley looked at Matt and broke out in a smile as well.

"Where's the fish?" asked Harley.

Matt laughed out loud and shook his head. "For fuck's sake, Harley."

"Well, I'm not leaving the damn thing. I know I hit him."

Cole was unsure of what had just transpired under the water.

Harley looked at him with a sly grin, "What's your problem?"

"Nothing."

"Well, let's go find him then. Matt, where's your pole?"

"I dropped it to pull your dead ass out of the water."

Harley shook his head in disapproval. "That was dumb."

"Let's go, Cole."

Matt pulled at Harley's shoulder. "Seriously, dude, you've got enough water in your lungs for one day. We'll go find him. I think your pole is wedged on a rock."

Matt looked at Cole, who hesitated for a second.

"So you want to go get the fish that nearly killed Harley?"

Matt nodded back at Harley. "If we don't, he will. Plus," he said with some reluctance, "it's a grouper."

Cole pulled on his fins and mask and hopped over the side. Once both of them were back in the water, Harley leaned over, draping his arms over the side and still looking to be on the verge of exhaustion.

"Don't lose him."

"Shut up, Harley," Matt said as they backed away from the boat and flipped over to dive down. Sure enough, on the sandy bottom, ten yards from the reef, a good-sized grouper was swimming in a half circle with a line extending from its side down to Harley's pole. Perfectly wedged under a rock, the fish was trapped and mortally wounded. Not far from it, Matt's pole was on the bottom. He motioned for Cole to grab it, then towards the fish. With the pole in his hand, Cole extended the band and gripped twelve inches short of the tip, hovering six feet from the grouper that still had some fight left in him. He let it go, and it struck just behind the head of the fish. For a moment, it kicked even harder, then slowly rolled to its side and sank with the weight of the pole. *More an execution than a hunt*, Cole thought.

Matt had retrieved Harley's pole, and the two of them swam for the surface, the fish trailing ten feet behind them. Even without a fight, the weight of the fish nearly exhausted Cole on the ascent. Harley motored up, his nose now bleeding. Matt handed his line over, and Harley pulled the fish up the rest of the way to the side of the boat. Once all three were back onboard, they lifted it with several grunts and got it on deck. It dwarfed the tuna that Matt had caught earlier.

Matt joked, "That grouper punch you in the face, or what?"

"Mine is bigger than yours," Harley replied flatly.

"Mine didn't nearly kill me either."

Harley looked at Cole with a prophetic grin. "If you don't push your limits, you'll never know where they are."

∞

EARLY THAT EVENING, they'd built another fire as the woman cooked up a plate of grouper for them all to eat. The boy joined them, but ate in silence. He seemed to have grown fond of his new friends.

Harley, Matt, Cole, and the boy ate like animals, stuffing their face with the largest bites they could take. The fire was lined with a growing spread of empty beer bottles. Claire ate with some manners, delicately picking at her plate and sitting more upright than the others. "What happened to your nose, Harley?" she asked.

"Nothing much. Just got in a little tussle with this guy." He lifted his plate to show her the filet of grouper.

"Nothing serious, I hope."

"Nah, it was nothing."

She stared at him for a moment more, then to Cole before looking back at the water. "You all need to think just a bit more before you go off and get yourselves killed. Each of you."

Harley, with his fish stunt, and Cole with his soiree at the boot shop, both knew there was truth in her words. Matt, on the other hand, looked genuinely offended.

Defensively, he asked, "What did I do?"

"Nothing yet, but you're no better than either of them."

Harley cut in, "This grouper is delicious."

"I mean it, Harley. There are consequences if we don't do this right."

Claire was hiding something and it induced a moment of sobriety, at least for Cole. He wasn't entirely certain that Harley or Matt caught on to it like he did, but there was something more going on with her. As she looked down towards the water, her arms draped around her knees that were tucked in close against her chest, it was if she was closely guarding some secret. Cole wanted to ask, but at a time affording more privacy than they had at the moment.

"Want some more Grouper?"

Claire smiled at Harley. "No thank you, Harley, but it was quite good."

She had a way of controlling the tone of a conversation, taking it to different levels that suited the point she was trying to make. And just as quickly as she would come down on one of them, she'd lighten the mood as if nothing had happened.

With dinner over, Harley and Matt stayed near the fire, contributing to the growing collection of bottles. Claire started a conversation with the boy and practiced the little bit of Spanish she'd picked up thus far. Cole walked down to the water and took a seat, staring out at the last bits of light that briefly painted the Caribbean sky. His long shadow walked a slow and meandering course to the east, and he found himself thinking again of Isabella. The breeze kicked up and lifted his face for a second and as he stared at the horizon, he tried to remember what she looked like sleeping in their bed. The image was partly blurred.

Taking a long breath and concentrating, he tried again, but to no avail. It had only been a few weeks, but he felt like he was losing parts of his most treasured memories. He thought back to Martinique and could recall the clothes she'd worn on their first nights together, the way her hair had rolled with the wind, and even the food they'd eaten together. But her face was vague at best. He tried harder, but there was no change. *Maybe it's the beer*, he thought.

✼

AS THE SKY LIGHTENED the following morning, Cole woke with a familiar hangover. He was in the sand, having rolled several times through the night until most of his body was covered. Sitting up, he dusted off his shirt and tried to clean the sand from his face, but his hands were covered. Harley was already up, poking a stick into the ashes at some of the smoldering wood and seemed lost in his own thoughts.

Cole asked, "You good, Harley?"

Looking up from the smoking pile, Harley smiled. "Never better."

And with that, Harley was his same old self. It had become a norm of sorts among the group to maintain an image of invincibility. Cole appreciated it and did his best to blend in, despite the ghosts that haunted him nearly each night and the understanding that underneath it all, they were mortals like the rest. Harley, perhaps in a moment of contemplation about his brush with death, cast aside whatever thoughts had crept into his mind the second Cole asked. It was, for Cole at least, far easier to keep things like that inside. There were times where each of them would let slip some simple statement or observation that peeled away another layer of the emotional masks they all wore, but for the most part it was an unspoken rule for each to keep their nose to the grindstone.

Cole stood up and walked down to the water's edge. The Caribbean was calm and dark, its true shade of blue just beginning to reveal itself with the morning light. He bent down to wash his hands. Realizing just as quickly that he was entirely covered, he took his shirt off and waded in, swimming out in the morning stillness. The water, almost cold without the tropical sun beating down on it, soothed his swollen head enough that Cole dove down to the bottom and swam along the sand and rocks for some time before doubling back. Standing again at the shore, he looked east once more, towards Isabella and wondered if he'd ever see her again.

HARLEY BEAT THE COPS again on the drive back. Cole laughed out loud as they pulled in to the gate and Matt closed it behind them. All but Claire proceeded inside and flopped themselves down on the chairs that lined the living room. Cole realized he wasn't the only one with a thumping headache. Claire flipped open one of her two laptops and scrolled through something.

Matt spoke. "We'll lay low today and tomorrow. Where are you meeting up Tuesday?"

Cole replied, "The boot shop, after the sun goes down."

Matt took a long breath and thought for a bit. "We'll have Claire drop us off a few blocks away. She can run you to the shop then head back here. I assume you want to watch for chatter?"

Without looking up from her computer, Claire nodded. "Yes; that'd be preferred."

Looking at Harley, Matt continued, "We'll split up. I'll stay near the boot shop and Harley can work down by the water. How long of a trip is it, Cole?"

Cole leaned back in his chair, wishing he could jump in the cold water again to stem the headache. He replied, "An hour, tops. Unless they hold me up over at the mainland."

"Claire can track your cellphone, but you're on your own until you're back on this side."

Cole thought for a second and replied, "I know."

Harley and Matt laid up for the rest of the day. Cole did the same, taking some time around noon to cook up a pile of scrambled eggs and sausage for them all. Afterwards, he slept until late afternoon on the couch. Claire had settled into a hammock by the pool and when he woke, he could see that she was still awake, slowly swinging one of her long tan legs to keep the hammock moving.

※

MONDAY WAS MORE of the same, with Harley and Matt running a full inventory of their equipment. An array of cool-looking shit was scattered on the kitchen table. There were ear pieces, small radios, ammo, magazines, a few more pistols, and one MP-5 submachine gun, to which Harley seemed to have taken a real liking to. He field stripped it, cleaned it like he did with every other gun, then reassembled it and set the sub-machine gun down.

They comms-checked both of their radios and set up a third for Claire at the table. Afterwards, Harley and Matt rolled a bit out on the lawn and Cole joined in, working hard at the basics Matt and Harley had shown him. Cole knew they both went, at best, half-speed with him to let him catch up. After an hour, he was spent and lounged for the rest of the day into the night, falling asleep sometime after midnight.

Tuesday morning went slow. It was the same waiting game from Panama. The boredom was only exacerbated by the desire to go and do something, anything, other than sit and idle away the day. Matt, Harley, and Cole all took a bit of a break in the afternoon and hung out in the pool. Claire came out in the late afternoon and sat down at the edge, dipping her feet into the water. "They're on the island."

Matt looked at her and asked, "Who is on the island?"

Claire kicked a little at the water. "The ones we're looking for. They're here."

She seemed somewhat relieved, or even happy, when she said it.

"How many?"

"I don't know."

"Where are they at?"

"I don't have that yet, but they're here."

Harley chimed in, "So how do you know that?"

"Signals. They've pinged here and there is some traffic elsewhere to confirm it."

Matt and Harley knew better than to ask anything else.

"There's some kind of package as well, at least from the chatter."

Harley ducked his head underwater, re-emerged and shook his face dry, blinking to clear his eyes. "Why don't we just go whack 'em?"

He knew the answer, but asked as a workaround to see if Claire would say any more about who or what she had in addition to the little bit of news she'd offered up.

Claire just smiled. "You're cute sometimes, Harley. There is a time and a place for you. Don't you worry."

"Should we pull Cole off tonight?" Matt asked.

Claire shook her head. "I don't think so. This is our first direct line. I think we need to keep moving forward."

Matt nodded and climbed out of the pool. "All right, then. Let's start getting prepped."

CHAPTER 10: MILK RUN

JUST AFTER EIGHT IN THE evening, Cole strolled into the boot shop. The girl behind the corner seemed to know why he was there, and she nodded towards the back door. Pushing the door open and walking in, Cole smelled the tanned leather and sawdust, remembering his last encounter there. It gave him the chills, as he thought back to the dark room in Panama on his first night and the concussive blast that rattled his brain. Cole quickly re-focused on the task ahead. Juan was seated in the corner, wearing jeans and a black t-shirt, and Cole wondered if he might end up killing Juan, just as he had David. Cole had opted for shorts, his running shoes, and a linen shirt, halfway unbuttoned. The two looked at each other in a game of wits.

Juan smiled. "Hola, Ben. You are ready?"

"Si, ready to go. What do you need me to do?"

Juan didn't hesitate to fill in the details. Cole was to take a boat from just north of the cruise ship pier over to Playa del Carmen, pick up five backpacks from a pre-coordinated spot on the beach, then drive them back to the same bar where Shorty would be perched to oversee the drops. Deliver the bags, drop an anchor, and someone would be waiting to bring him in with a dinghy. It seemed simple enough.

An hour later, Cole was downtown and walked out on a concrete pier that jutted out into the water. A cruise ship was still tied up at the big pier further south, and downtown was still bustling. Just as Juan had promised, a small center console with a single outboard engine bobbed gently on the south side of the dock. With the key from Juan, he fired up the 50 horsepower motor and checked the boat. It seemed to be in all right shape. Nothing fancy—it was an open hull with more nicks and dings than Cole could count, but the deck was dry and Playa del Carmen was no more than 12 miles away. He'd be back in less than an hour.

Casting the lines off the pier, Cole swung the boat around and pointed it west, motoring slowly past the towering cruise ship. Once on the open water, he throttled her up and the bow rose quickly, holding for a few moments as she rocked from side to side, unsure of its ability to reach a full plane. Seconds later, the bow dropped back down and she rode hard over the two feet of chop that rolled in from the north. He could already see the faint light of Playa del Carmen, and Cole felt no hesitation at all as Cozumel slowly disappeared behind him. His thoughts briefly drifted back to his first run to Cuba and the wonder with which he'd stared at the outline of Havana. It was an easy run, and Cole was halfway there before he knew it. He stared up at the stars and moon over his head. As the boat screamed along, the air was cool with the boat's bow surging into the front of swells before driving upwards and over them. He steered a bit north of his needed course to steady the boat and focused on the backlit shoreline ahead.

He had no GPS, but Juan had instructed him to get within 100 yards of the long pier downtown then turn north, looking for two side-by-side red lights that would mark his rendezvous. Once he was within half a mile, Cole turned south to compensate for the trip over and headed directly for the busiest part of the town. Settling the boat down to ten knots or so, he found the pier, then turned north again and trolled up along the coast, parallel to some small swells that wrapped around from the north. Nearing 11 p.m., the town and beaches were still busy with people. It seemed like an odd spot, but then again it was perhaps so brazen that no one would even think it was a drug deal.

Within 15 minutes, Cole spotted two bright red lights shining out towards the water. He idled over into two or three feet of water and saw four men standing at the shoreline. He nudged the boat up on the sandy bottom, and two men carried several packs out to him. They nodded, said a cordial hello in Spanish, and tossed the bags casually over the rail and up forward. The two men then pushed Cole's boat back out and waved goodbye. It was so simple that Cole could do little but laugh.

He sped back across and before midnight, he was idling through the scattered moorings that bobbed off the beach from Shorty's usual hangout. Grabbing one of the mooring balls and tying the boat off to it, a boy drove a small dinghy out, and Cole tossed the bags down. He shut the engine off and left the key, hopping over the side to the waiting boy in his small skiff. Once at the water's edge below the bar, Cole hopped over and carried three of the bags while the boy got the other two. They set them down behind the wooden bar and Cole looked around, noting that none of the patrons even bothered to look up from their nightcaps.

Down the sidewalk, Cole spotted Shorty looking at him. He walked over, and they each nodded at the other before Shorty smiled with genuine appreciation for Cole's work and handed him an envelope. Tucking it in his pocket, Cole looked around once more, then parted ways and started walking north, back towards downtown. The sidewalk was mostly dark, with the street to his right and the water to his left. A low wall separated the sidewalk from the rocky beach and the occasional stand of craggy trees.

After less than five minutes, Cole looked back and noted that someone, a guy maybe his age, was closing on him and staring at the same time. A minute later, Cole looked again and confirmed what he already thought. With the revolver on his right hip, he wasn't overly concerned, but at the same time he knew that shooting a gun would draw more attention than he needed. Cole turned to confront the stranger. The guy, who was Cole's height and build, slowed down about ten feet from Cole and drew a knife, saying something in Spanish that Cole couldn't understand. The knife, however, said all Cole needed to know. He looked beyond the guy at the headlights of several cars coming down along the main road that paralleled the sidewalk. *Come on man, don't do this,* Cole thought. To his left there was a row of parked cars and small trucks, and to his right was a waist-high concrete wall painted white with a blue streak across the top. Cole took a long breath and reached for his gun. His attacker lunged towards Cole with the knife in his right hand.

As the two were nearly converging, Matt emerged at a full sprint from behind a parked pickup truck and shouldered violently into the guy, driving him against the white wall. Off-balance and trying to steady himself with his right hand, Matt made quick work of grabbing the wrist that held the knife and spinning the guy so his back was against and over the wall. Matt bumped him hard one more time to throw him further off-balance and reared back before delivering a solid uppercut into the guy's jaw. He reeled back in pain, but Matt didn't quit, firing off three more punches. The guy tried to fight back, but Matt had the clear advantage, keeping the guy off-balance. He swung at Matt a few times, his right hand still wedged against the wall by Matt's left hand. Matt threw two elbows into his head before reaching down at his waist. While he did, the guy hit as hard as he could against the side of Matt's head, but Matt easily ducked his head into the guy's chest, and used his forehead to press the guy further against the wall. From his waist, Matt pulled a small fixed-blade knife, and in one fluid jab, drove it upwards and pressed hard into the guy's left side.

The fight was over, the attacker now doubled over in pain and thinking only to shield himself from any further injuries, but Matt didn't let up. From less than ten feet away, Cole could only watch as Matt drove the knife again and again into the guy's torso with a vicious level of efficiency. Matt countered each attempt the guy made to protect himself and kept stabbing and slashing. If the guy raised his left arm to shield his face, Matt drove the knife in low to which the guy instinctively lowered his arm and bent further to cover a new wound, only to be met with a driving blow to his neck or chest or even armpit. Several times, Matt threw a fake jab only to clear the guy's arm out of the way before driving the blade in again and slashing his way out. It couldn't have lasted more than ten or fifteen seconds, but as the guy doubled over at the wall and Matt finally relented, the white and blue paint was stained with splattered thick red blood.

Matt sheathed his knife. With his left hand still blocking the dying man's right hand, he grabbed a fistful of shirt with his right hand and rolled the guy over the wall, where he fell with a thud next to a few scattered bushes and two trees. Cole looked at Matt, unsure of what he should do or say. Matt was breathing hard as he turned to scan his surroundings. Cole then poked his head over the wall and saw that the guy wasn't moving.

"You good?" asked Matt.

Cole nodded, "Yeah, thanks."

"We should go," Matt said, his mouth now open and panting.

Cole asked, "What about him?"

"He's dead. Let's move, I'm parked a few blocks down."

Harley was waiting for them at the Thing. "Dude, you're covered in blood."

"Not mine," Matt replied.

"Fuck."

Cole laughed when he realized that Harley wasn't concerned about Matt—he was upset that he'd missed a fight. As they all climbed in, Harley slammed his door shut, visibly angry.

"Fuck," he yelled again as the Thing accelerated down the road into the dark.

⠀⠀⠀❧

BACK AT THE VILLA, Claire was at the dining room table when they walked in. Standing up from her chair, she looked at Matt with wide eyes and asked, "Matt, are you all right?"

"I'm fine," he replied.

Harley threw a small bag against the wall and went to the refrigerator for a beer. His head was buried as he dug into the back for the coldest of the cans before calling out with a muffled voice, "He had a knife fight."

Matt filled in the details as they all sat down around the table. "Some kid tried to jump Cole as he walked back after dropping off the boat. You didn't miss much, Harley. He had no fight in him."

Harley calmed down a bit and asked, "How'd you get him?"

Matt took a long gulp from his beer and pushed the chair back on its rear legs.

"I tried to keep it to fists, but the guy was stubborn, so I cut his lungs until he quit. From there, it was just a bloodletting to get it over with. Lame, really. You didn't miss anything, bud."

Harley's jaw was clenched as a small smile crept across his face. "Lucky son of a bitch. Over a month and nothing. Out of nowhere, you go and get yourself a knife fight."

Cole was amused at the two of them. Harley was worked up while Matt was trying to downplay the whole affair to keep Harley from getting any more aggravated. Harley seemed on the verge of taking a midnight stroll to find some thug looking for trouble just to even the body count. As he sat there, Cole finished his first beer and went over to the fridge for another round. Returning with six held together in both hands, he looked across the room at the couch where he slept and saw Isabella sitting there, her legs crossed as she rested comfortably, looking out the window.

He dropped the beers on the floor and blinked several times, looking back at the table, then over to the couch again, where Isabella was no longer sitting. Chills ran from the back of his head, down his neck, to his back before they spread out across his entire body. His entire frame shuddered, and his fists tightened to a point where his nails dug hard into the numb and sweating palms of his hands.

"What the fuck, Cole?"

He didn't respond, instead looking intently at the couch for a moment more.

"Cole?"

When he looked back at the dining room table, Harley was staring into the living room as well, trying in vain to see whatever Cole had seen.

"What the fuck, Cole?"

This time, he replied, "Nothing, sorry."

Bending over and picking up the cans, Cole walked slowly back over to the table and set them down.

"Well, fuck it." Harley shook his up even more and popped it open and froth spewed out and all over him. He chugged the rest of it. Matt laughed at Harley's absurdity, while Claire stared intently at Cole.

"What was that all about, Cole?" she asked.

"Nothing. Just tired." It was all he could think to say. He took a few long breaths to steady himself and looked once more at the empty couch.

Claire softly tapped on her beer a few times with her pointer finger before cracking it open and taking a sip. She set it on the table, her eyes still focused on Cole.

He looked at her and smiled. "It's nothing."

She looked upset, or concerned, or frustrated. Cole couldn't be sure which one it was, but he sensed that she genuinely felt some level of sympathy for whatever emotion or ghost always seemed to sneak up on him at the most inopportune times.

Matt spoke up to change the subject. "Did you recognize him, Cole?"

"No, never seen that guy before."

Harley asked, "You think they're trying to get rid of him?"

"Who, Cole?"

"Yeah, gringo sticking his nose into Mexican drug smuggling. Maybe we moved too soon?"

Claire chimed in. "You mean maybe Cole moved in too soon?"

Cole laughed. "Had to do something."

Matt closed out the conversation. "We'll find out soon enough."

Only a few hours separated them from the sunrise, and Matt shut down the evening, recommending they all get some sleep.

Cole looked with some hesitation at his couch, but as the rest of them headed upstairs, he reluctantly rolled a sheet around him and lay down, thinking for a fleeting moment that he smelled Isabella's perfume on the cushion.

THE FOLLOWING AFTERNOON, Matt and Harley hovered outside as Cole walked casually once more into the boot shop. He knocked twice at the back door and pushed the door open, stepping in to find Juan seated at a table, playing cards with three other guys. Cole didn't recognize any of them.

"Hola, Ben. Como Estas?"

"I'm good." In a jovial tone, he asked, "Did you send someone to kill me?"

Juan pushed back from the table and looked at Cole with surprise.

"No, amigo. I didn't send no one to kill you." Juan's tone implied that it was not outside the realm of possibilities.

Cole took a seat at a stool in the corner. "Well, some dude tried to stab me."

Juan nodded at one of his buddies, who then promptly stepped outside with a cell phone.

"I like you, Ben. No drama. You want a beer?"

Cole actually believed him, so he agreed to a beer.

One of the other guys reached down into a dirty cooler, popped the top off from a Dos Equis, and handed it to Cole. He took a sip and looked around the room. There wasn't much to it other than the bits of leather strewn over wooden beams and piles of boxes and boots in each corner.

A minute later, the man walked back and leaned over to Juan. The two spoke for a few moments, and then Juan leaned back and looked up at the ceiling. He stared for a bit, then nodded to himself.

"That was one of my guys that came after you, but I didn't send him."

Cole nodded, his eyes not leaving Juan's.

"So, you are good with a knife?" asked Juan.

Cole nodded again. He had to lie, and lie quick. "Yeah, I can handle myself. Why did he come after me?"

Juan laughed. "You underbid him, mi amigo. He was mad."

It made sense. Cole had made a run for pennies compared to what he knew he could make.

Juan took another sip and said simply, "Sorry."

Cole shrugged it off. It wasn't the first time someone had tried to kill him, and the likelihood of it happening again was all but certain.

"So what's next?"

Juan had picked up his cards, but set them back down on the table and rocked back in his chair. He seemed to be thinking about something before he looked back towards Cole, taking a slow sip from his beer. He nodded to the others then at the door. Slowly, they each got up and left, leaving Cole and Juan by themselves.

"Your timing is interesting, my friend."

Cole asked, "Why is that?"

"I have something else to move, maybe a bit more money for you."

Cole could see that Juan was a bit more serious than he was before. The fact that he'd sent the other guys out was indication enough that something was up.

"So, what is it?"

Juan waited. He took a long breath, staring at Cole. Running his hand across one side of his face, Juan looked down, licked at his lips, and reached for another beer. He pulled two from the cooler and handed one to Cole.

Finishing his first, Cole held his second beer and leaned back against the wall. He felt his nerves getting away from him. *Perhaps this is the moment?* Juan was nervous, which meant the risks were elevated. *Keep it cool,* Cole reminded himself.

Calmly, he asked, "What do you need?"

"Could you take a boat to Corpus Christi?" asked Juan.

Cole smiled. "With enough gas, I can get a boat anywhere."

Juan nodded, still not entirely at ease.

"I need to move some boxes. Wooden crates, six of them—to Corpus Christi. I'll pay you five thousand dollars, for you to move them and also, more importantly, to keep quiet about it."

"What's in the boxes?"

"I don't know, amigo. I don't really want to know."

"Is it your stuff?"

"No, it's for a customer."

"Who?"

Juan shook his head, a stern look across his face, telling Cole it was a dead end.

Cole sat back and replied, "Yeah, I can do that. But I need a good boat."

Juan thought for a second and scratched at the back of his head. "I can get you a boat. What kind do you want?"

Cole smiled. "A fast one."

Juan couldn't help but laugh. Cole did too, and it broke the tension that had formed since the subject had come up. They finished their beers quickly, Cole shaking his head with the last mouthful.

"When do you want me to come back?"

"In two days. Let me round up a good boat for you. And Ben, I am paying you to keep quiet, not just for driving the boat."

Cole looked at him and nodded that he understood.

"I don't want this ever spoken of."

Cole replied, "Understood."

BACK AT THE HOUSE AND once again seated at the dining room table, Matt pressed Cole for details. What specifically had Juan said? Who were the others in the room? Did Juan have any comms gear, phones, computers, or anything at all that Cole could remember? Frustrated, Cole replied that he had not. Their conversation had been brief, and it occurred to Cole that maybe he should have pressed for more info.

Matt asked, "Who picks it up in Corpus?"

Cole shrugged his shoulders. He simply didn't know. Matt's mannerisms and tone were calm, but Cole could tell that inside was a different story. Recognizing that Cole had little to offer, Matt turned to Claire and asked, "What's he moving?"

Claire also shook her head. "I don't know, but it matches up with what I've heard."

"Can you find out?"

She shook her head again.

Matt turned and looked at Harley, who was expressionless, but asked, "You wanna call him?"

Matt pressed the palms of both his hands firmly against his forehead and gritted his teeth. "No, I don't want to call him, but I don't think we have a choice."

Harley retrieved some kind of speaker from one of the Pelican cases and plugged a cell phone into it. He set the contraption down in front of Matt before going to the fridge for a round of beers. Matt took a deep breath and dialed. "Hello?"

Cole recognized the voice immediately. It was Johnson with his nasally obnoxious voice.

"Hey, Sir. It's Matt. We might have something."

Johnson said nothing for a few seconds, then asked loudly, "Well, I don't have all day. What is it?"

Matt and Harley looked at each other, with Harley smiling and Matt just shaking his head. Cole was happy to not be a part of the conversation.

"Cole's making a run in two days. Something about a package. It's not people, and it seems the locals want to keep the whole thing quiet. They want it dropped off near Corpus Christi."

Johnson pressed, "Well, what is the package?"

Matt, still calm, replied, "We don't know."

"Find out."

Matt exhaled slowly before replying, "We can't, Sir. We don't know and probably won't know until it's already moving."

Johnson snorted. "That's unacceptable."

Claire, Cole, Matt, and Harley all looked at each other, each unsure how to respond.

Johnson repeated himself, "That's not acceptable. I need to know what's in the shipment."

After a few more seconds, Matt asked, "Should we turn it off?"

Johnson was quiet for a moment. "No. Can you put a tracker on the boat, or on Cole?"

Harley and Matt both mulled it over in silence. Claire nodded at Matt and mouthed the word, *cellphone.*

Matt scratched at his neck and looked to Harley one more time. They each nodded. "Yes, Sir. I think we can work something."

"Good, but I still need to know what it is. You've got until tomorrow to find out what it is."

Matt smiled to himself and laughed quietly. "We don't even know where it is on the island. If we start probing, I think we're risking the whole thing."

Johnson was quick to reply, "I expect more from you, from each of you. You are not putting me in a good position."

Matt pressed him. "Sir, we can take the boat ourselves if you want. We can deliver it wherever you want, but we'll compromise the whole thing if we don't make the delivery on time."

"No, that's not an option either. You just track it, you tell me where it is and where it's going. I'll handle it once it gets stateside. Don't do anything to risk the op."

Johnson's back and forth had Cole's blood boiling. After a few more stern reminders from Johnson not to fuck up and how displeased he was, he hung up on them with directions to contact him again once the shipment was on the water.

Cole asked, "Should we call Gene Thomas?"

Matt shook his head. "No. That's Johnson's job, not ours."

"So what do we do now?"

Matt looked out towards the windows and the dark evening air. "We take it easy tomorrow, then you drive a boat to Corpus."

CHAPTER 11 – PORT ARANSAS

THEY SPENT THE NEXT morning idling away at the pool. Harley brought out the first round of beers shortly after ten in the morning. By one, all but Claire had opted for a siesta somewhere in the shade. Cole woke almost two hours later and walked inside to find her still at the table, combing through something on her computer. She was always focused, but this time she seemed even more so. "I've got a position."

Cole sat down, still groggy, and looked at her for something more. "What kind of position?"

She looked back at him and almost smiled, as if this development marked something to celebrate. "I think I know the house where they're holed up. We should take a drive."

Cole found Matt and Harley and nudged both of them awake from their hammocks. Harley had his M4 across his lap with his finger resting just off the trigger, so Cole cautiously tapped his shoulder and stepped away. Thankfully, Harley came to quick enough. Once they were all inside, Claire explained further. She'd had a momentary hit from a GPS satellite on a position on the outskirts of Cozumel. It was only for about 30 seconds, but it was something with which to work.

Harley loaded up some extra magazines, and Matt, for the first time since they'd been on the island, field-stripped, wiped down, and reassembled his M4. Feeling a bit underpowered, Cole pulled his revolver from his hip, swung out the cylinder and spun it to verify what he already knew—five rounds of .357. He took a handful of speed strips from a Pelican case and tucked them in his pocket. Claire stared intently at her computer for a few more minutes, then closed it and motioned that she was ready to go.

Armed up with the Thing running, Matt swung the gate open, and Harley inched out into the broken street. Both Harley and Matt sat up front, their rifles tucked against the floorboard and out of sight. Claire quietly called out directions, and they were on their way, the back tires spinning and kicking up dust.

The far side of Cozumel was dirty and rundown. Streets were empty, for the most part, save for the few random cars that rolled slowly along the streets. Houses and buildings all had the same high walls, and many had barbed wire on top to further dissuade anyone from trying to get inside. There were no tourists to be seen. At one intersection, as Harley idled the Thing and scanned the crossing road, Cole watched as a moped crossed in front of them. A man was seated and driving, his young son standing in front of him and held steady by his father's legs. Behind the man was presumably his wife, her right arm tightly around his waist and her left arm cradling a second child, no more than a year old. Cole watched and thought first of the absurdity of four humans sharing a moped, but he also saw the mother's look of contentment as the entire family sped and bounced down the crumbling street. It was an entirely different world from the one Cole knew. One misplaced rock or a swerving car could in a second's time wipe out that entire family, but at the same time Cole felt jealous as he watched the wife lay her head against her husband's back and pull herself in tighter as they neared a turn and disappeared.

After the moped passed, Harley sped across the street and Cole stared down the road at the light plume of white dust left in the moped's wake. He thought of both Isabella and Marie as Harley cursed his way up to fourth gear, a cloud of dirty brown dust billowing up behind them. Minutes later, Claire called out for him to stop halfway down a narrow two-lane road. She scanned the length of it. On one side were graffiti-laced concrete walls, and on the other were lower fences and gates that led into a row of villas.

"On the right, it's the fourth lot down. We're on the backside of it. Can we make one run down this street?"

Matt nodded. "Yeah. Let's get a look at the wall."

Harley drove on and kept the speed at about 20 miles per hour as they passed. It was a six-foot tall wall of unpainted concrete. There was no barbed wire on top, but as they passed it and accelerated further down the street, Matt spoke to Harley. "Looked like there was glass cemented into the top." Harley nodded, not the least bit surprised.

Several blocks further down, they stopped.

"One pass in front?" asked Matt.

Harley replied, "You wanna whack 'em?"

Claire spoke firmly. "No, Harley..."

Before she could finish, Harley turned and looked at her with a smile. "Just kidding, Claire. We know your boy's in there."

She grit her teeth for a second and looked down, almost showing some embarrassment.

Harley chimed in again, "Let's take one pass and get going."

Matt nodded, and Harley spun the Thing around, side-stepping one street over, and as they neared the villa, he slowed again to about 25 miles per hour. Matt held a camera with his left hand and obscured it with his right as they passed. Cole looked briefly, then looked at Claire, who was craning her neck until she caught Cole looking at her. She turned, again trying in vain not to give away her heightened interest in the home.

Back at their own villa, they sat again at the dining room table. The run hadn't provided much more information than they had before. Cole's mouth was dry, so he went to fridge and pulled out a handful of beers, spreading them out across the table. Armed with one in his hand, he sat back in his chair and thought more about Isabella and Marie, closing his eyes and trying to think back to France. Claire talked with Matt and Harley, but Cole paid little to no attention to their conversation.

As the sun set, they were all sitting idly by the pool, Claire dangling her feet in the water. Cole was, like so many nights, on the rough edge of being good and drunk. He grit his teeth and they felt numb in the back of his head. He had long ago forgotten what it felt like to be drunk and happy. Harley and Matt were in the shallow end, a sea of cans floating nearby, and they were in far better spirits than Cole. Cole watched the beer cans, a mix of Tecate and Dos Equis that drifted among themselves like a battle at sea. A gust of wind interrupted the otherwise light evening breeze and pushed a line of Tecate cans closer to Matt and his armada of Dos Equis.

"Tecate has the wind advantage..."

"What the fuck are you talking about, Cole?" Harley was standing in the water expressionless as he stared at Cole.

"Nothing." Cole shook his head to clear his thoughts.

Matt and Harley looked at each other and laughed. Claire, from the edge of the pool, looked at Cole with compassion. Cole worried about himself, too.

Matt asked, "Cole, you good with this tomorrow?"

He nodded. "Yeah, I'm fine." He edged into the water and ducked his head under, then emerged and shook water from his face. Harley chucked a beer at him, and Cole ducked, the beer exploding against the side of the pool and spinning on the surface several times before petering out. Cole laughed, and Harley did, too. By now, Cole understood that it was the only way Harley knew to offer some encouragement. As pointless as it would seem to anyone else, the gesture gave Cole some reassurance that he wasn't going through all of this on his own. He knew that the group had accepted him, flaws and all. They'd grown tight over the past weeks, and while no one ever spoke of the hardships, they each knew when one was nearing their limit.

Cole lay back into the water, his head against the side of the pool, and he looked up at the stars. *Tomorrow,* he told himself, *maybe we'll be one step closer to going home.*

THE FOLLOWING MORNING was painfully slow. Harley disassembled his SP101 down to every last pin and spring and picked at it until the stainless steel looked perfectly new. Claire surprised everyone and took a long nap in a hammock by the stand of palm trees tucked into a corner of the courtyard. Matt was typing something on the computer, but seemed to be taking his time. Cole sat on the couch and chewed on the side of his lip for what seemed like hours. By the time noon rolled around, he opted to cook something for the group rather than sit and idle his mind away.

They ate a late lunch, and as the afternoon sun started its slow retreat to the west, Matt called them all to the table.

"Cole, you keep this phone turned on at all times. It's our only way of tracking you."

He nodded. "Will do."

Matt continued, "We'll be trailing you to the boat, but once you're on the water, it's up to you."

Cole again nodded.

"We'll meet back up once you're back on the island."

Matt paused, then continued, "If anything comes up, you just flip the phone open, dial seven, and hit send. We'll do what we can to get you some backup, but it may not happen quick."

From his tone, Cole could tell that Matt was not entirely happy with the plan. They all worked as a team, but when Cole was miles offshore by himself, there was nothing anyone could do to help him. It was a solemn lesson he'd learned in the previous year of running boats. The ocean was a proving ground, one that Cole had survived, albeit with a heavy toll on his conscience. Corpus was more than 700 miles away, and he could only hope that Juan had a solid plan in place.

He packed up some things into a bag, grabbed his fake passport, smiling briefly at Harley's humor, and threw the backpack over his shoulder just after five in the afternoon. The three looked at Cole as he stood in the living room staring back at them.

"I think I'll walk."

They said nothing. Matt and Harley looked back at him without expression. It was time to go, and there was little anyone could say or do to lessen the unspoken tension. If there was fear, no one would admit it. The mood was certainly beyond the point of any small talk or jokes.

"We'll be watching, Cole. Harley and I will be right behind you."

Cole replied, "I know, right up until I hit the water."

He nodded goodbye, taking a second longer to flash a smile at Claire and do his best impersonation of a Cheshire cat. She didn't seem impressed. *Worth a try at least*, he thought. From there, he turned and started towards downtown.

ॐ

AS SUNSET APPROACHED, Cole was in Juan's personal car. It was a Lexus, white with tinted windows. From the outside, it looked pretty good, but the cracked leather seats inside and disarray of papers revealed the limited extent of wealth for a low-level drug smuggler well outside the more lucrative corridors on the mainland.

Just outside of town, Juan turned down a gravel road and slid the wheels to a halt after driving 100 yards, where the road opened up to a beach. They walked about halfway down the beach, and Juan stopped. Cole could see a handful of men down at the water's edge, and the outline of a boat ten yards offshore bobbing softly in the calm of early evening.

Juan spoke. "She's topped off and should get you about three hundred miles or so before you need gas. I've got two fishing boats along the way. You call them on channel six eight, ok? Ask for Carlos on the radio. They'll know it's you."

Cole nodded, but said nothing, as he stared out at the water and fading sky in front of him.

Juan asked, "You get some sleep last night? This is a long run."

Cole smiled. "Yeah. Don't worry about me. Is the boat loaded?"

Juan nodded. "Don't touch the boxes, OK? Even I don't want to know what's in them. The GPS has positions in it for you. When you get to the beach, look for two white trucks." He paused, then continued. "They'll be waiting for you tomorrow morning."

"Who?" asked Cole.

Juan didn't answer.

Cole nodded, unsure if he'd actually take a look at the packages or not. *Maybe Juan knows who is on the other end; maybe he doesn't.* Either way, Cole tried not to think too far ahead of himself. He kicked off his shoes and waded out into the water, thinking back to the time he'd run up on the beach after dodging the Coast Guard on his first migrant run. *You've got this.*

Juan called out from the shore, "Cole..."

Turning, he looked back and Juan asked, "It's a nice boat, right?"

Cole looked it over for a few seconds, then looked back at Juan. "Yeah, Juan. It's a nice boat. Adios."

One of Juan's guys hopped over the side as Cole walked farther out, and nodded slightly as he passed. The boat was Cole's. As he got closer, now up to his thighs in the warm and dark water, he noted that the boat had Florida registration numbers on its bow. Cole laughed to himself. It was not the first time he'd driven some rich guy's toy in the middle of the night. At the transom, he climbed up and over to the deck and set his bag down beside the console. It was a 32-foot Sea Fox, wearing twin Yamaha 350 horsepower outboards. *Overpowered*, he thought, his mind recalled the graceful lines of a panga. When he fired them both up, Cole felt chills run up his back. It would be fun for the first few hours, but Cole knew by the time the sun was up, he'd still be running hard to the west. There was a part of him that looked forward to the trip, to break up the monotony of the past few weeks. A veteran of the open water, he knew at the same time that his back would ache, his eyes would burn from the salt, and his mind would be stretched to its limit by the time he found the coast of Texas.

He looked over the boat, taking note of the six or eight wooden boxes that were stacked up forward. Each was no more than five feet long and shy of a foot wide. Drugs weren't packaged in wood, of that much he was certain. Nevertheless, he wasted no time in pulling the anchor up and spinning the Sea Fox around until her bow pointed north. The wind was calm, and as he accelerated and felt the boat rise up to a plane, pockets of cool air descended down from the sky, spilling over and into the blanket of warm air that hugged the water's surface. He felt the on-and-off change in temperature, and wondered what waited for him on the other end.

At nearly full throttle, the boat made 44 knots over the ground. It was an insane amount of speed, and Cole smiled as the Sea Fox tore a path across the open water. Not even the slightest ripple stirred as the boat skimmed over the top of an almost indistinguishable ground swell that rolled in from the east. He was on the ocean again, and, at least for the time being, felt a weight lifted from his shoulders. It took over an hour to round the northern tip of Mexico before Cole made an arcing turn just north of west. He pushed buttons on the GPS until it displayed his next waypoint, over 200 miles to his west. He had the gas to make it, and the sky was a wasteland of random stars. He settled against the seat behind him, staring intently to the west and waiting.

Five hours passed before he tried calling out on the radio. "Carlos, Carlos, Carlos." *Nothing*. Ten minutes later, he repeated the call, again with no results. With his fuel at less than a quarter tank, he tried again a few miles further and the radio crackled after his call. Not long after, he had comms with whoever Carlos was. The voice on the other end spoke in Spanish, too fast for Cole to understand. As he settled the boat down to a troll in the exact coordinates on the GPS, Cole scanned but saw nothing. Minutes passed, and Carlos called out again, but spoke no English. Finally, Cole saw what looked like a blinking white light. He turned the boat and edged it further towards the light. Sure enough, well-concealed by the nighttime sky, a small and run-down coastal fishing boat with a cramped cabin up forward was waiting for him.

Carlos called out a greeting, and soon enough, Cole was tied up next to him. Carlos handed over a hose and then disappeared into the cabin, and fuel began to run slowly through the hose. Cole looked up and scanned the horizon in all directions, knowing that refueling posed the greatest risk of being intercepted. It took almost 20 minutes, but soon Cole was topped off and on his way again, waving farewell to Carlos and hoping he'd see the old man again soon on his return trip.

The next five hours passed much the same as the first. He rendezvoused again with another Carlos at the pre-coordinated spot, and topped off the tanks yet again after having made another five-hour sprint. It was nearing four in the morning when he cast off for his third leg to the coast of Texas. A slow hour passed before he saw the sky beginning to change in front of him. He saw lightning in the distance, and as the eastern horizon turned a blood-colored red, he could see that dark skies were between him and Texas. Soon, as the sky edged towards pink, Cole could see the towering cumulus clouds in front. They spread out all around him, their bottoms hung low in the sky, reaching down to the surface of the Gulf. As daylight broke, the sky was a dark menacing shade of grey that looked more like billowing smoke from a fire than it did any sky he'd seen before. Lightning ran low across the clouds like crooked fingers from a skeleton, but not a single drop of rain touched the surface. Thunder followed seconds later, roaring a low groan from somewhere deep in the depths of the clouds.

The storm was still building. A half an hour later, he saw the clouds break to his north and spill their contents into the sea. From a distance, it was a wall of dark grey, as if the cloud itself was driving hard, punching its way into the sea. He was thankful to be clear of the worst of it. Yet even from several miles away, he felt the wind shift from the downpour, and cold air slapped hard against his face, the kind of wind that can only come from tens of thousands of feet above. It was clean and cold, blowing hard enough to give him the chills.

Another hour passed before he was through the worst of it, and the air warmed again. Corpus was two hours away. The sky was still overcast, and the horizon was blanketed by the early morning haze, stubbornly refusing to give way to the sun that now climbed unseen from somewhere far on the eastern horizon. The Gulf was still and flat, as though Cole was tearing across a puddle at nearly 50 knots rather than an open body of saltwater. Strange shades of purple and orange slipped through the haze and softly painted the bottoms of the low ceilings. With the morning's light, he felt his circadian rhythm break free from the fatigue that had clung to him for the last few hours of the night.

An hour passed as the colors shifted from orange to yellow and finally blue, while the Gulf of Mexico lay flat like a pane of glass in front and behind. His wake trailed off for miles behind the boat, and other than his two refueling stops, he'd seen not a single sign of life. The engines screamed, but Cole heard nothing, his ears now tuning out the whine of the motors. Possibly delirious, Cole's mind wandered along with improbable thoughts of where he was. *Lost? Impossible,* he told himself. The GPS showed him nearing the coast, but still he saw nothing on the horizon.

As midday approached and his fuel gauge slipped below a quarter tank for the third time, he sighted the shoreline ahead. The GPS took him north of Corpus Christi, to what appeared first as a barren stretch of beach with a small town at the northern edge where a channel led into Corpus. On the chart, he saw the name Port Aransas.

Soon he could make out the larger structures of the town, and the GPS position led him a few miles outside, to a beach where there was nothing in either direction but dunes. He slowed to ten knots and turned the boat south, scanning ahead for anything on the beach. Creeping closer, he spotted what he thought to be two trucks. Barely discernable, he squinted for a few moments more, then crept in closer to the shore.

The sky was still overcast above him, and the clouds seemed to hang no more than 100 feet above. They looked heavy, as if they too were ready to fall from the sky. The water was grey all around with large circular bands of red seaweed. A breeze, the first of the day, was slowly filling in from the west, disturbing the water and revealing a reddish tint. Cole found it hard to believe that this same dirty sea could be connected to the crystal-clear waters of Mexico. Somewhere over the 700 miles between here and there, the ocean had purged itself of whatever made the water so dirty off Texas.

Cole scanned the depth finder to see that he was only in six feet of water and still 50 yards offshore. He slowed to an idle and crept in another 30 yards until he felt the boat's deep V-hull touch bottom. He trimmed the motors up as best he could to keep the propellers from striking the sand. Several men were standing motionless on the shore, looking out towards him. He waived them to come out, but they didn't move. They were thin, wearing pants and long shirts. Two of them wore sweatshirts with the hoods up over their heads. Cole waived again and could see that they began talking among themselves. Cole counted five of them.

He felt for the phone in his pocket and retrieved it, leaving it on a seat in the back of the boat, giving it a clear signal to any satellite or cell phone tower, hoping that Claire, Matt, and Harley were indeed feeding his position to someone on the shore. He looked back to the beach and saw that two of the men were wading out to him.

As they approached, one kept his eyes on Cole while the other walked up to the bow. The first one, staring at Cole, looked at him with something close to hate. The man's features were one of a fighter, his eyes intense and his face stiff like leather. Cole cautiously walked forward, not losing sight of the one looking at him. The second man motioned up for Cole to hand down the boxes.

The first one was heavy, but not so much that it was full of any one thing in particular. *Weapons*, Cole thought as he handed the first box over. *What the fuck is going on here?* He handed over the second and third boxes. As the two men marched ashore and set the packages down in the back of their truck, Cole scanned the dunes, expecting at any minute to see a platoon of camouflaged men come running with guns at the ready. As the two men returned for the rest, Cole felt butterflies in his stomach. He hesitated to hand over the rest until the first man grew impatient and yelled something at the other. Cole didn't catch it, but it wasn't English.

After handing over the last of the boxes, they walked away without even acknowledging Cole's presence. Wasting no time, Cole reversed back from the shallow water, turned the boat, and got into the relative safety of some deeper water. From there, he waited and watched as the two loaded pickup trucks headed south down the windswept beach. Their tracks blended in with the dozens of others from the past days, and soon enough they were out of sight. Cole waited for some time more, trying to process in his head what was happening.

He asked himself, *Where is Johnson?* Realizing that it was the first time he'd wanted to see the guy since he'd met the fat son-of-a-bitch, he shook the idea from his head and looked down at his fuel gauge. He was at less than an eighth of a tank. Juan had apparently not thought any further than getting the boat to Texas, nor had Cole. *Or was he not supposed to have made it this far in the first place?* Scanning back north before looking south, Cole knew that he was all alone, once again. He looked up the beach one more time, hoping foolishly to hear gunshots or something to that effect, but there was nothing over the whine of the engines and the increasingly gusty west wind.

He turned the boat north and made for the channel leading into Port Aransas. Once inside the jetties, he could see it was a quiet town, late morning not producing much more than a sporadic bit of traffic. To the north and west was nothing but endless low dunes and grass with a solitary ferry landing and some old piers. A few boats motored in and out of the channel, most offering a wave in Cole's direction as he drove in. Ahead and to the south, he turned inside another set of jetties into the main harbor of the town. He needed fuel, and needed it in such a way as not to require any sort of payment, since Cole had nothing but some pesos and a fake passport.

He tied up at an empty slip near the end of a dock and set foot on solid ground for the first time in the better part of a day. The restaurant at the foot of the docks seemed abandoned, and none of the scattered patrons paid much attention to the smuggler from Mexico who'd just illegally set foot in another country. The audacity of it made Cole smile.

He smiled even more when he saw the small white and red Coast Guard flag stiffly flying in the breeze. Rounding a corner, he could see that it belonged to an 87-foot patrol boat, neatly moored to a wooden dock. At the brow, there was a sign that proudly proclaimed the ship to be the Coast Guard Cutter *Steelhead*. Cole did a double take when he read the next line below that, where it listed the commanding officer at Lieutenant David Wheeler.

As Cole stepped closer, a petty officer emerged from the bridge and called down to Cole, "Can I help you, Sir?"

Cole could do nothing but smile. He hadn't been called *sir* by anyone in a long time, and the ridiculous circumstances of his present condition certainly didn't warrant it anymore.

Cole replied, "Is Wheeler the CO?"

"Yes, Sir," replied the petty officer.

"Can I talk to him?"

"I believe he's on a phone call right now, Sir."

Cole hesitated, then smiled. "Would you tell him that if he doesn't come out here now, I'm going to tell you about what he did in Cartagena?"

The petty officer looked confused for a second, and Cole waited until the young guy disappeared down below. Less than ten seconds later, he reemerged from below with a lieutenant right behind him.

From the dock, Cole asked, "Wheeler?"

Wheeler looked down at Cole with shock. "Cole? Good God. What the hell are you doing here?"

Cole gave him a big grin. It was good to see a familiar face. "Think I can get some gas?"

CHAPTER 12: TURNING SOUTH

THEY SETTLED ONTO barstools at a waterfront bar tucked just back from the docks. It was the middle of the week and the middle of the day, leaving the seating area empty, save for a group of teenage girls that were seated near a window in the corner. They incessantly giggled, and Cole couldn't help but turn and watch for a few seconds. On their table, they shared two plates of some kind of fried appetizer and seemed more concerned with whatever gossip kept them smiling and their focus wholly consumed with each others' presence.

"So what brings you to Texas, Cole?" asked Wheeler. His tone implied that Wheeler had correctly assumed that Cole was up to no good.

Cole turned back to the bar and replied, "Just doing some sightseeing."

The bartender came over and stood in front of the two of them.

"Rum and Coke, please. With a lime."

The bartender smirked and turned to Wheeler, who looked at Cole before turning and ordering an iced tea.

"Cole, seriously, what are you doing here?"

Mashing his elbows into the bar top, he casually answered, "I'm just passing through."

"Well, you look like shit."

"I am aware of that, Wheeler. Thanks."

Cole turned back to look at the girls again. They were no more than 18 years old, five of them huddled close, still giggling and whispering. Wheeler turned and looked as well. They carried the kind of youthful exuberance that made it easy to smile and remember better times. One of the girls turned for a moment and looked at the bar, then reached down to her purse. The bartender was still busy mixing Cole's drink. The girl, blond and in a floral-patterned summer dress, looked the part of an innocent debutante. From her purse, she pulled out a flask and topped off each of the girl's sodas, then tucked it back in her bag.

Cole turned to Wheeler with a grin. "You gonna go break that up, Mr. Lawman?"

Wheeler spun back around, turning a blind eye to the girls. "I've got a feeling you're the one I should be arresting right now."

Cole nodded. "You're not that far off." He paused before taking a deep breath and asking, "So, how about some gas?"

Wheeler shook his head. "No, I'm not giving you government gas for whatever smuggling you're into these days."

Under his breath, Cole replied, "So judgmental sometimes…"

The bartender returned and set Cole's drink in front of him on a napkin. Wheeler took a sip of his iced tea. Cole squeezed the lime over the top and stirred it in with his finger before downing the entire glass and smacking it back down on the barstool.

"Cole, you look delirious."

Picking up the glass, he raised it towards the barman and rattled the ice. "Una mas," Cole called out.

"Cole, he speaks English."

"Force of habit. Sorry." Cole watched as his second drink materialized, and he took another long sip, emptying half of it and holding the fizzling sweet taste in his mouth for a few seconds before swallowing. He wiped his eyes with the cold water that had dripped onto his hand from the glass.

"You want some food?"

Cole shook his head. He was feeling the rum at this point and preferred its calming ability to blur his thoughts. He finished the second glass and shook the ice one more time. When the bartender made his way over, he stopped in front of Wheeler and stared at him with a look of concern nearing frustration.

Wheeler, dressed in his working uniform, was the consummate professional, whereas Cole looked like a cross between a lost Springbreaker and a homeless bum.

"Una mas, por favor."

The bartender looked at Wheeler, refusing to even acknowledge Cole's presence.

Wheeler said, "Give him one more. I got him."

Cole spun back around to the girls, watching them in silence. They were smiling, laughing, and whispering at a frenzied pace. Each of them was pretty, young, and vibrant. "You should go tell them."

"Tell them what?" Wheeler asked.

"To enjoy it while it lasts."

The bartender returned with a third rum and coke. Cole drained it before the man could even walk to the other side of the bar. Looking at Wheeler again with wide eyes, the bartender said, "He needs to leave."

Cole stood up, unsteady on his feet, and proclaimed defiantly, "I'm *choosing* to leave."

Wheeler helped him back up and to the door. The sun was still bright when they walked outside. Cole squinted and turned to look away. He asked matter-of-factly, "Where to, boss?"

"The boat."

Cole smiled. "You mean, your boat?"

"Yeah, Cole. My boat."

"I knew you'd get command one day. I'm happy for you."

He meant what he said. Cole thought back to years ago when Wheeler had licked the system and excelled as a newly minted junior officer onboard *Delaney*. For a moment, he almost felt bad for himself, but as they rounded a corner and walked out on the dock, Cole couldn't help but be happy for the guy. Wheeler had worked hard for what he'd become. A young commanding officer of his own cutter. The little interaction Cole had seen with the crew confirmed what he already knew—Wheeler was a good skipper. As they neared the boat, Cole wondered why he hadn't followed Wheeler's example. It had seemed easy enough, but Cole had never found the will to bow down to Potts and all his bullshit. And Walters was certainly one of the worst human beings he'd ever met, hell-bent on catapulting herself to the top and burying anyone that stood in her way. The thought of Delaney gave Cole the chills.

They crossed the brow and Cole stopped midway, firing off a salute towards the bow.

With a laugh, he asked, "I forget. Which way do I salute first?"

"Cole, just get on the boat."

Wheeler pushed at Cole's back. It felt just like it had years ago when they were roommates on *Delaney*. Cole was screwing around, and Wheeler was doing everything in his power not to laugh. He pointed Cole back to the stern and told him to wait. Doing as he was told, Cole sat on the back deck and looked out across the small harbor. He thought back to Carentan, and then to Isabella and Marie. Reaching for the phone in his pocket, he noted that he had half his battery charge left, and dialed her number.

She picked up, and at the first sound of her voice, Cole smiled and looked down at the deck, focusing entirely on the syllables of her hello.

"Isabella?"

"Cole?"

"Oui," was all he could say without laughing.

"Cole, where are you?"

"I'm in Texas."

"Are you coming home?"

The smile sunk from his face and he grimaced. If only he could tell her that he was in fact coming home.

"No, not yet, but maybe soon."

"Cole, are you drunk?"

"A little, yeah. I think I just need some sleep."

"What are you doing?"

He thought for a second, unsure of what to say. "Is Marie there?"

"Yes. She is playing on the rug. She moves all the time now, all over the house. We had to put up a gate."

Cole heard Isabella's voice change as if she fought back a similar sadness. Cole felt it spread, and found himself once again unable to think of anything to say. There were no words that fit the situation.

"Cole."

"Yeah?"

Isabella paused, and Cole could sense the conversation was changing, like it always seemed to do. He ran the fingers of one hand through his salt-crusted hair and took a breath, mad at himself now for getting drunk.

"Isabella? What?"

"Cole, we can't keep doing this."

"Doing what?" he asked, but already feared the answer. Still, in his mind, he refused to admit what was going on. He expected her to ask the same questions she always did. *Who are you with? When will you come home? Is there someone else? What are you doing?* Those conversations always went downhill, and Cole took a longer breath, determined this time to not let it lead to a fight.

"Cole, I don't think we should be together anymore."

No words followed, from either end of the phone. Cole felt a vice clamp down on his throat. He could feel his breathing constrict and his mouth went dry. Isabella said nothing else, which only served to make things worse.

She asked softly, "Cole?" Her tone implied that she still cared about him in some twisted sort of way.

He moved his lips, but no words came out. He tried to say her name, but couldn't.

"Cole?"

He said nothing.

"Cole?"

His mind was detached from his body and spinning in weightless orbits above him. He felt as if he might fall.

"Cole?"

This time, he looked up to see Wheeler standing in front of him.

"You're all right, bud. Come with me."

Wheeler helped Cole up, wrapping one arm around his waist. Cole's entire body was numb, and he felt as if Wheeler had lifted him up entirely off the ground. Wheeler assured him again, "You're all right, bud."

Cole knew better.

✂

IT WAS SOME HOURS when he woke, in what must have been Wheeler's stateroom. He was on the bottom rack, his shoes on the floor, otherwise still wearing the rest of his dirty attire still. The door was closed, but he could hear movement outside. A clock near the wall showed that it was just after six in the evening. Footsteps passed outside the doorway several times. Cole closed his eyes and ran his hands across his face to shake the sleep. He'd gotten a few hours, but knew he was still well behind the curve. As he started to formulate the beginnings of a plan in his head, he remembered Isabella, and his mind fell back into the same emotional pit.

Staring up at the ceiling, he grit his teeth and tried to remember if it had all been a dream. Perhaps it had been, as it would not be the first time he'd woken up from those kinds of things floating around his mind. He pulled the phone from his pocket and flipped it open. The call log was evidence enough that it had been real. Sitting up, he stared at the phone for a few moments then flipped it shut. He felt the same choking feeling take hold of his gut and closed his eyes to shake it all from his head. Burying his head in his hand, an emptiness wrapped itself firmly around him and the room was blurred. *Enough,* he thought. *Enough of this.*

Wheeler pushed the door open gently, then closed it behind him and took a seat at the small cramped desk next to the rack where Cole sat. He took a long breath, but said nothing. Cole could tell Wheeler was looking at him.

"Cole, there's a whole shitload of federal dudes in town. Any chance they're looking for you? We got a call to be on the lookout."

Cole lifted his head, asking, "Lookout for what?"

"An adult male with a stolen boat. Sound familiar?"

The boat, Cole thought. "Where's my boat?"

Wheeler took another long breath. "Tied up next to us, tucked up against the pier where no one will see it." He paused and the two of them made eye contact. "We gassed it up for you."

Cole stared at Wheeler, completely caught off guard that Wheeler would put himself in that kind of position. From a drawer at the desk, Wheeler pulled out the revolver and held it with his pointer finger looped through the trigger guard. It rolled a bit back and forth as Cole looked at for a second or two, then took it and tucked the gun back into its holster.

"Can I go?" He asked the question as if he was already detained.

Wheeler smiled. "I won't stop you, bud. But where are you gonna go?"

Cole looked at the floor, and said contemplatively under his breath, "South. I'm heading back south." Standing up, he asked, "Can I get out without anyone noticing?"

Wheeler stood up with him. "My crew won't say a word."

The two shook hands, and it was understood how much of a risk Wheeler was taking. Holding the handshake and gripping even harder, Cole thanked him again. Back on the main deck, Cole heard sirens in the distance. As the early evening light began to slowly fade, he saw a flashing blue light from around a corner as it made its way towards the marina. *The phone,* Cole thought. He pulled it quickly from his pocket and dumped it overboard into the water. Wheeler watched with curiosity, smiling and shaking his head.

True to his word, Cole's Sea Fox was tucked against the dock and bulkhead, out of sight from anyone unless they were directly over the top of it and looking down.

"Who's looking for me?"

Wheeler dug his hands deep into his pockets. "It seems like all of Texas is looking for something right now."

With reluctance, Cole said, "I should go then."

"Seriously, where are you going?"

"If you really want to know—Cozumel."

"What's down there?"

"Nothing good, but there's nothing good for me anywhere these days."

He fired up the engines and they rattled briefly before settling down. Cole smelled the exhaust, and for a moment he felt some relief from the digging pain in his chest. Next to the console was a six pack of water bottles. Cole pulled one, opened it, and chugged the entire thing in one pull. It gave him some relief from the post-rum cotton tongue. He untied the bow line and Wheeler grabbed the stern line, holding it until Cole nodded for him to let it go. Casting it down to the deck, Wheeler stood motionless on the dock as Cole backed out. He looked back over his left shoulder, cleared some piling, then scanned back to his right before twisting the boat in place and idling forward. He looked back to his left at Wheeler one last time and nodded as the boat motored solemnly on. Wheeler let out a fraction of a smile and nodded back.

The harbor was most certainly a no-wake zone, but as soon as Cole had settled himself, he throttled up and ahead. The bow rose, and he mashed the throttles down as far as they would go. The boat practically leapt out of the water onto a plane. He smiled, knowing that Wheeler was definitely shaking his head and laughing. Nearing a jetty, Cole kept his focus on the closest rocks and steered so close in a sweeping turn that he could almost reach out and touch them as the boat screamed past. He made a hard 180-degree turn to point east towards the channel. To his north sat a windswept and barren island, and to his south sat the northernmost reaches of Port Aransas. He couldn't hear the sirens, but somewhere in the town another set of blue lights were heading towards the harbor.

Another thick overcast layer of dark clouds now hung low over the Gulf. Behind Cole, to the west, the sun was on its evening surrender. Lighter clouds to the west blocked it, but a soft hue dominated by yellow lay across the coast behind him. As he passed the channel mouth, a heavy chop jarred the boat hard from side to side. Whitecaps littered the dark sea ahead of him, and the engines surged and strained to carry the hull onward through the wind and waves. He chugged two more bottles of water over the next hour and let the darkness take hold as the light to the west faded more and more.

He looked back as the sun disappeared, and the yellow turned to a thin fiery orange line before disappearing entirely from the sky. The low clouds were too dark to hold any of the color, and the horizon to his west was little more than a sliver of lost light before Port Aransas faded to black, never to be seen again. There were no stars to guide him, and no horizon to speak of. Whitecaps snuck up from nowhere and slammed against the hull without warning. Sea spray ripped over the top and hit him in the face with the force of small pebbles. He was soaking wet and felt the familiar chill set in, first at his fingers, then his toes, and then soon thereafter deep in his core. Not long after, fatigue set in and had it not been for the violent punches and counterpunches from the rolling sea, Cole would have fallen asleep. As the third hour passed, he looked at the GPS and saw that he was over 100 miles east of Port Aransas. He finished off the water and felt, for the first time in more than a day, adequately hydrated.

He looked down at the fuel gauge, now at just over a half of a tank. It was inevitable that he'd run out of gas. He had not taken the time, nor had he cared to think of any plan other than running. They'd seemingly tracked him to Port Aransas, and Cole was in no mood to deal with Johnson's goons. If they'd caught the trucks, then perhaps Cole's work was done, but he knew there was likely more waiting for him. His intuition had nagged at him for some time, building and solidifying in his mind the likely fact that there was no escape.

He thought back to Gene Thomas' promise of life insurance. Isabella had reached her breaking point, and as hard as it was for Cole to accept it, he couldn't blame her. On one hand he was mad and wanted to lash out, but on the other he knew that it was a mess he'd created. A wave rocked the boat hard to one side and the jolt changed his thoughts over to Marie. He could only hope that Isabella would tell his little girl good things about the dad she'd never get to know. It was hard to accept, but at her age, she wouldn't remember the hundreds of little details that now raced through Cole's mind. Any normal human being would have cried, but Cole's life was far beyond the point of tears. Spray shot across the bow and into his face, blinding him for a second. The wind was now blowing hard from the south, directly in his face. He powered on through the night.

Early into the morning, the Sea Fox ran out of gas. The left engine quit first, and Cole fought to control the boat for a few moments more until the right one quit as well. He tried, foolishly, to start them back up, but the fuel lines were dry. It was a completely black night, without even the faintest bit of light sneaking through whatever clouds hung above him. He sat on the seat and thought about his life, although he admitted that there wasn't much beyond his mistakes, a chemical reaction left unchecked that had gotten him to where he was tonight. He took long breaths of the salt air, and despite the isolation of it, he was content to be on the sea. He laid down up forward, his head propped on a seat cushion, as the boat circled around and bounced from side to side. A lesser sailor would have grown violently sick from the disorganized pitching and rolling.

The rest of the night passed with Cole in and out of sleep. He was jerked awake by a particularly large wave against the hull and noted the first shades of grey above him. Sitting up, he could see that the clouds were beginning to break, and it gave him some hope, although he didn't know what for. Standing moments later, he felt weak on his feet, but looked around at his surroundings. He turned the battery on and the GPS showed that he was over 200 miles from Texas and hundreds more from Mexico. He'd slept for perhaps no more than three hours, and it was rough sleep at that. The day before, he'd caught a few hours more in Wheeler's stateroom. His mind was unable to process anything clearly. He rummaged around the boat, remembering that he'd already drank the water. His mouth dry, he mulled over his options, not liking any of them.

As noon approached, he was sweating under the sun. There was no place where he could hide from the heat, and he was unable to focus on anything no matter how hard he tried. He held his eyelids closed and then opened them to no avail. He blinked more times than he could count, but his eyes were not working as they were supposed to. By the afternoon, his head was swelling and the ensuing headache was nearly debilitating. Opening his eyes only made it worse, so he sat against the rail with them closed and sunk his head into his hands. Some time passed before he reached for the revolver and pulled it from its holster. He slumped lower to the deck in front of him and stared down at it, still unable to discern any of its features other than a silvery blur of stainless steel.

He cursed at the sun and felt his skin tender and red from the exposure. Salt gnawed at his eyes, and he knew that each drop of sweat robbed him of the water that his body needed to keep living. He pulled himself up to his knees, now weaker than he had been in the morning, and gripped his hand tightly around the revolver. He stared around the horizon and then crawled over to the other side and did the same. There was nothing but an endless sea of rolling dark blue water. He made his way back to the console and got up to his feet, his vision entirely gone until the blood caught up with his head. He turned the keys to fire up the engines, but the battery was insufficient to even turn them over. The GPS was dead as well.

A magnetic compass was all he had now to keep his bearings. To the east, one lonely billowing cumulus cloud shot skyward and a mass of grey erupted from underneath it. *Rain*, Cole thought. He watched it as it marched northward, and the top blew off in the familiar anvil shape of a mature storm. He fired the revolver at the cloud in three quick shots. The boat rolled and knocked him off balance. As another wave approached, Cole lowered the gun and fired into the trough in front of it. The bullet's impact shot a spout of water up, but did nothing to stop the wave from rolling the boat sideways and Cole fell back down. There was one round left. He scanned the horizon once more then climbed to his knees, holding the rail with his forearms and the revolver loosely in his right hand. He was mad now. *Just finish this*, he told himself. He looked up at the sky, still unable to focus on anything in particular besides a haze of bright light. His head hurt. His mouth may well have been full of sand. He could move his tongue, but it felt foreign against the dry lining of his mouth.

As the sun dropped further to the west, Cole thought it to be his last sunset. He remembered so many of them from the past. He thought of Key West, and of the Cuban coast at night. He remembered running right over the reef and the desperation that night as he hid under a boat hull from the police. He thought of the drugs, Maria, and *Havana's*. At that, he smiled. The feeling of a boat riding high on a plane soothed his mind for a few seconds more, until his conscience cruelly put Isabella back squarely in his thoughts. At first, it was her in Martinique and the cotton shorts she wore on those warm nights. Then he remembered their afternoon under the palm trees at Le Diamant. He thought next of Marie. *Perhaps it's best that she'll never know her father.* Despite it all, Isabella would give her a wonderful life. Cole was certain of it. He believed that Gene Thomas would keep his word, too.

Cole gripped the revolver tight in his hand, let his head fall in front of him, then dropped the gun over the side. He heard it splash into the water and felt both his hands shaking violently. Dropping to the deck, he begged no one in particular to finish this chapter of his life. As he struggled to stand back up, his right hamstring cramped, and Cole yelled out in pain as he fell once more to the deck. Gritting his teeth, he tried once more on his other leg, but this time his bicep cramped violently and he dropped again. Trying in vain to pull his arm straight and work out the cramp, he tried to scream but couldn't, only a hissing gasp of air followed by a long dull groan emerged from his mouth. He crawled on his stomach to the side of boat and pressed his back against the rail. He remained there for hours more, paying attention to little else than his labored breathing.

Thinking of Marie, he tried to distract himself from the intense and unending pain in his muscles and his head. He felt her touch at his nose, his ears, and his mouth. It worked and soon thereafter he felt nothing at all except the rhythmic up and down of his chest. He then felt himself falling asleep, and made no attempt to stop his body from letting go.

CHAPTER 13: SECOND CHANCES

HE AWOKE IN A SEA OF LIGHT, bright to the point where his eyes instinctively closed to shield themselves. Reaching up to touch his face, Cole felt something tug at his left hand. It stung for a second until he lowered it back down and wiped at his forehead with his right hand. His head no longer hurt like before, but he could tell his body was weak. The sound of rushing water and weightlessness startled him, and he squinted with one eye to take in his surroundings. He was still unable to focus, but the room he was in brought back a foggy memory. His mind still clouded, he closed his eyes once more and took a long breath, hearing nothing but the strain of his lungs.

The sound of rushing water again confused him. *A boat,* he thought. He was unable to formulate coherent thoughts beyond that. He felt himself lifted up and down again and while his mind slowly began to process, he was unable to translate those thoughts into words. Moving his lips, no sound emerged. Struggling to open his eyes, he lifted his head and felt a sharp pain shoot through his neck. His muscles were stiff and in no shape to help him get up. His head fell back down on to a flat and flimsy pillow. It was then that his eyes finally caught up to the light, and he was able to partially look around at his surroundings. Details were still a blur, but he recognized the clock. He was back in Wheeler's stateroom. *I'm dreaming,* he thought. Perhaps it was all an elaborate dream that his mind concocted in a desperate attempt to comfort him in the moments that preceded his death.

Wheeler opened the door. *Not a dream,* Cole told himself.

Sitting in the same chair as the day before, Wheeler took a long and exaggerated breath, saying nothing.

"Where are we?" asked Cole.

"Hundred miles off Cozumel."

"You came looking for me?"

Wheeler took another breath before replying. "They got us underway right after the attack."

Confused, Cole asked, "What attack?"

"Those lights, right before you left—there was some kind of raid going down. A handful of dudes launched a full-on attack in Port Aransas. Apparently they were heading for Corpus, got turned around, and ran back for Port A."

"What happened?"

"They got cornered by the ferry docks and started shooting rockets." He paused for a second, thinking it over in his head, and continued, "It turned into the wild west about fifteen minutes after you left."

"Did they get all the guys?"

Wheeler chewed on his lower lip for a second before replying, "Yeah, they got them. It's Texas, ya know? But not before a good number of people got killed." He paused for a few moments again, his facial expression one of remorse, before continuing. "Some locals, some kids and families—those pricks put a rocket right into a restaurant."

Cole asked, "How many?"

"I dunno. We were told to get underway within half an hour. Supposedly those fucks came in on a boat."

They both looked at each other. Wheeler asked plainly, "You part of that?"

Cole was silent and looked back at Wheeler, his eyes now able to discern the genuine frustration on his face.

"Those guys were already on land. It's not what you think, Wheeler."

"Then tell me what I should think, Cole."

Cole sat up and the blood drained from his head. He lost his vision for a few seconds, but felt otherwise steady enough to sit. As it slowly started to return, he saw an IV drip running into his left hand.

"I got forced into this."

Wheeler asked, "By who?"

"You wouldn't believe me if I told you."

Wheeler pressed the issue. "Try me, Cole."

There was silence in the room. Cole heard the rushing sound of water again, a wave rolling off the bow of Wheeler's cutter. He felt it ride up, over, then back down into the trough behind it.

Cole scratched at his jaw and felt the tender skin, burned from days of exposure to the elements. "I know DHS is involved, and I'm pretty sure the CIA is as well."

"Bullshit, Cole."

"I told you."

Wheeler asked defensively, "Told me what?"

Cole laughed. "That you wouldn't believe me."

Wheeler sat back in his chair and looked at Cole. He had no reason to hide anything from Wheeler, so Cole explained as best he could. He told him about France, about Isabella, about three clowns in suits that gave him no choice other than to get back in the mix. He told him about Cozumel, about Johnson, and his meetings in London and Mississippi. He dropped every name he could to convince Wheeler that he hadn't just fucked his own country on his own free will.

When he was done, Wheeler logged into the computer at his desk and pulled up Gene Thomas' congressional website. Cole nodded. Wheeler then searched for Johnson and pages of articles popped up. Finding a photo, Wheeler clicked on it and Cole nodded again. He felt his body temperature rise when he saw Johnson's stupid arrogant smile.

"All right, Cole. So how does this all end?"

"I don't know, but I think the folks I'm with are good people. I need to get back to Cozumel. Johnson was supposed to stop them at the beach, but no one was there when I rolled up. They unloaded and drove south."

Wheeler sat for some time as Cole felt the cutter ride up and over swells. The swishing sound of water rushing against the hull reminded Cole of *Delaney*. He shook his head back and forth, wishing more than anything that it had all been a dream. He felt for a moment like he might puke.

Wheeler spoke, "Sun's up in about two hours. I should make a turn back to the east."

"What do you want to do?"

Wheeler smiled. "Get back to the coast before they realize I headed out this far. They'd have my ass right now."

It was the second time in as many days that Wheeler had put his career on the line to help Cole. "Your boat is fueled again, by the way."

Cole nodded. "Thanks."

Wheeler grinned. "After today, you're not getting another drop of gas from me."

୫ꞇ

AN HOUR OR SO later, Cole was up on the fantail in the predawn darkness, his Sea Fox tied alongside the cutter. He was fed and feeling as good as he could, given the past few days. His body still ached as he climbed over the Jacob's ladder and down to his boat. Hopping down, he looked at the deck where no more than 24 hours ago he'd resigned himself to die. He again felt almost sick to his stomach, but took a long breath of the salt air and it calmed his nerves. Wheeler tossed down two bottles of water. Two guys from Wheeler's crew looked down at him with a look that was part curiosity and part disbelief. Wheeler had drafted up statements of non-disclosure and had craftily lifted the DHS logo from its website and inserted it on the fake memos he'd had each of his guys sign. They had no clue the memos were fake, but in it Wheeler had specified a 20-year prison sentence if they ever spoke about it. While he didn't admit it, Cole suspected Wheeler got a kick out of the whole affair. Now, to Wheeler's crew, Cole was some kind of international badass. Looking back up at them, he knew better.

୫ꞇ

THE STRONG WESTERLY breeze blew hard on Cole's starboard quarter as he raced for Cozumel. The two-hour trip gave him time to recharge his mind. He stood at the console, his legs spread to steady himself, and he stared east for the first sign of land. Even at speed, beads of sweat formed on his forehead as the morning sun climbed up in front of him and warmed the air. The soft early shades of yellow gave way to blue skies, and the same light clouds that would no doubt bring scattered showers by mid-afternoon. When he rounded the northernmost corner of the mainland, the seas subsided and Cole screamed further south on a calming sea.

The water was dark and blue, disturbed by the wind but otherwise protected from the groundswell. Clusters of orange seaweed marked the meandering tide lines as the lower Caribbean currents pushed through the chokepoint between Mexico and Cuba. With the wind now on his starboard side, he felt a breeze against his face, and for the first time in days, felt something just shy of happy that he was alive. The thought faded as soon as it had surfaced, when Cole brought himself back to the reality of his circumstances. People were dead. *Innocent people were dead.* And as much as Johnson was to blame, Cole had been the one to deliver the rockets. The entire thing was a mess. and Cole grew increasingly angry, thinking back to his last day in Carentan.

He sighted Cozumel just before ten in the morning. Its palm trees and bleached concrete walls were a welcome sight. With the pastel-colored and already-bustling downtown to his south, Cole ran the Sea Fox right up to the rocks on the outskirts and climbed over, stepping onto the seawall. Pushing the boat back out a few feet, he stood there on a dark coral-covered rock for a few moments and looked at it as it drifted south and spun lazily in the wind. He took a long breath and chewed on his lip, thinking for a few moments more of Isabella. A pit formed in his stomach and he pushed the thoughts to the back of his mind.

Ambling back to the villa, Cole blended in seamlessly with the midday street traffic. He pushed open the iron gate and saw the Thing tucked against the corner. It had a new coat of red spray paint on it, most likely from Harley's handy work. Perhaps it was an effort to avoid the police, who were most certainly on the prowl for a blue Thing that sped through the streets on an all-too-frequent basis.

Stepping in through the unlocked front door, he thought it odd that no one was downstairs. He stood a few feet inside the doorway and looked around. Claire's laptop was open on the table and the screen was unlocked, which struck Cole as odd. Just then, he heard movement behind and turned to see Matt with his M4 at a partial draw on him.

"Fuck, Cole. What the hell, man?" He lowered the gun to his side and held it by its pistol grip alone. A look of disbelief and also relief was spreading across Matt's face. Harley emerged from the stairs, his M4 also by his side. Claire followed right behind him. Harley set his gun down and went to the fridge for a beer. Claire moved quickly towards Cole and gave him a firm hug, which caught him entirely off-guard.

She whispered softly, "We were worried about you."

Cole struggled to find words to express what he felt. He gently wrapped his arms around her and patted at her back twice, realizing that she meant what she said. As she was about to let go, Cole pulled her in tight for a few seconds more as he shuddered with the chills running down his back. Cole held her for a moment more and looked directly into her eyes.

"Thanks," was all he said.

Matt set his gun down on the table and took a seat. Claire also sat down, and Harley brought over a round of sweating Tecates. With his folding knife, he hacked up a lime and tossed wedges to each of them.

Matt asked, "What happened?"

Cole filled in the details as best he could. He left out the more personal aspects of the boat and being adrift, but Matt was laser-focused on it anyhow.

Knowing that something didn't make sense, Matt asked, "What the hell were you gonna do when you ran out of gas?"

Cole looked down and shook his head, "I didn't think that far ahead."

They were all quiet and Cole suspected that each of them had a better sense of his mental state than they let on. Thankfully, they dropped it out of kindness. He could tell that none of them wanted to put any more of a burden on him than he already had.

"Do you have the phone? We lost the signal once you hit Texas."

Cole felt genuinely sorry when he told Matt he'd tossed it over the side.

Matt smiled, trying to lighten the mood, "No more phones for you, Cole."

THEY SPENT THAT afternoon glued to Claire's computer, watching updates on both national and international news about the attack on Port Aransas. By the evening, now two days after the fighting, there were increasingly loud calls for more border security and wild claims about the origins of the attack. Some news broadcasts took wild guesses with eyewitness accounts of encounters with the men in locations all over the country. Most, if not all, were speculation at best, and flat-out lies in all likelihood. Cole, Matt, Harley, and Claire were the only ones in the world who knew exactly what had happened.

That evening, as they sat around the table, Matt and Harley tinkered with their guns. Harley had pulled out a vast array of additional weapons and looked like a child who had dumped out the contents of his entire toy chest. Cole watched for some time and thought back to the revolver and how his hands had trembled at the thoughts that briefly crossed his mind.

"I need another gun," he said.

Looking around and settling his gaze on Claire, Harley asked, "Last chance, Claire. You sure you don't want it?"

He dangled the fourth SP101 from his pointer and middle finger.

"I'll be fine," was all she said before turning her attention back to the computer.

"Be a bit more careful with this one, Cole. I gotta fill out paperwork every time I lose a gun."

He slid it across the table and pushed a box of .357 Magnum ammo towards Cole. "Cole," he said.

"Yeah?"

"I mean it. I fucking hate paperwork."

Cole grabbed the revolver and swung the cylinder open, loaded it with five more rounds, and latched it shut. He still had the holster and tucked the gun behind his right hip. A phone vibrated, and Matt stepped out through the door onto the front steps and talked for a few minutes while Cole leaned back in his chair and kicked his feet up on the table. He stared up at the high ceiling and wondered when any of this would ever end.

Matt walked back in and took his seat. Claire stopped typing at her computer and stared at the screen for a few seconds before flatly calling out, "Come look at this."

They all gathered around and she played a recorded bit of some kind of hearing. Cole squinted and leaned in close to make out the details. He caught a faint whiff of Claire's shampoo. The floral scent grabbed him off-guard, and he stood back before he saw that Harley had done the same thing. The two of them, now standing a foot or two behind Claire, looked at each other. Cole was unsure of himself, but Harley had his typical shit-eating grin on his face. He motioned with his nose as if he was taking a deep breath and then smirked at Cole, closing his eyes and enjoying the moment.

Matt asked, "Is that him?"

Claire replied, "Sure looks like him."

It snapped Cole back to his senses, and he leaned closer to see that Johnson himself was testifying either to the House or the Senate about the attack. He used every buzzword in the English language and capitalized on his fondness for kissing ass when questioned by the panel seated around him. He laid out a story of a weak and unenforceable border, hampered by funding spent in non-critical areas, and how his agents were heroes for stopping the attack before it got any further. He called the people of Port Aransas victims of terrorism and emphasized over and over again that funding was the root of the problem. He closed by heaping additional praise on the committee and vowed to do more with the limited resources he had to protect the southern border.

Harley sat back down and let the bolt go forward on his M4 and pulled the trigger with an audible click and ping. "Well, if I didn't like him before, I don't like him any more now."

"That was a blatant fucking lie," Cole said to no one in particular. He was certain now beyond a shadow of a doubt that his role was nothing more than that of a pawn.

Claire was visibly uncomfortable, but true to her character, she opted to not comment on the dishonesty going on in Washington. Matt tapped his pointer finger on the table and stared off across the room. He was not happy about it either, but was organizing his thoughts. "That was Gene Thomas on the phone."

Harley looked at Matt and asked, "What did he want?"

Matt paused again and tapped his fingers some more on the table. "He's coming down tomorrow to talk. Should be here first thing in the morning."

∽

COLE DIDN'T SLEEP much that night. For most of it, his thoughts wandered between Isabella and Port Aransas. He wasn't sure which one made him feel worse, but he made sure to give each of them equal time to beat up his emotions. By the morning, he may have gotten two or three hours of actual sleep. He was groggy, and his body was still on the mend from the Gulf. As the first bits of sunlight snuck through the windows and climbed down the walls of the living room, he was already wide awake.

Matt was down shortly thereafter and did a bit of housekeeping in anticipation of Gene Thomas' visit. Claire tidied up her nest of equipment as well. Harley, on the other hand, inventoried his hand grenades.

Cole watched as he set them out on the small table in the living and inspected each one. There were roughly a dozen from what Cole could see.

"How do they work?"

Harley looked up with a smile. He was more than happy to teach a willing student the ins and outs of blowing shit up. With one resting in the palm of his hand, Harley called out the nomenclature.

Safety Clip.

Pull Ring.

Spoon.

He motioned with his other hand to remove the safety clip, pull the ring, then instructed Cole, "You fucking throw it so it ain't coming back. About four seconds later..."

Harley set the grenade down on the table and made an explosion gesture with both hands. He smiled when he did it. "You should see this thing in a small room. Turns terrorists into a Sloppy Jo-head."

Matt was in the corner, shaking his head and laughing to himself. Harley picked two up at a time and put them back into their foam cut-outs in one of his many Pelican cases.

Around eight in the morning, Matt took another call and nodded a few times, gave the address, and hung up the phone. "He'll be here in twenty minutes."

They all waited quietly around the table. As he looked around the room, the group looked riddled with guilt and betrayal.

The gate creaked open and shut. A quick knock at the door revealed Gene Thomas, looking the part of a tourist. He wore baggy khaki shorts, a Hawaiian shirt, flip flops, and a ballcap from the Bay Waveland Yacht Club.

As he walked inside, Matt stood up and shook his hand, offering Gene Thomas a seat at the table. He took a breath, steadied himself, then stopped just before he was about to speak. He seemed to be struggling to find the right words. Looking down and to the right at the floor, he paused for a moment more, then pressed his forearms against the table and looked up at the rest of them.

"I assume you've seen the news."

They all nodded solemnly.

"And have you seen the hearings?"

Again, they nodded, looking intently at Gene Thomas for some kind of reassurance that things were going to be all right. Gene Thomas took a deep breath and rubbed his thumb against the corner of his mouth. His eyes now wandered around the room, unsure on what to focus.

"The problems our country faces are not made any easier by the bitter partisan reality of our political system." He paused before continuing, "I won't lie to any of you. This whole mission is beyond compromised."

Cole cut in, "But he's fucking lying."

Tension built in the room, and Cole immediately regretted his words. Gene Thomas wasn't the least bit upset by it. "I know, Cole. I know what he's doing. I worried from the beginning that politics would get dragged into this."

Matt, showing his level head, asked "What's his angle?"

Gene Thomas nodded, appreciating the fact that Matt was already up to speed. "He'll use the funding issue to win favors."

Harley tilted his head and asked, "With who? Republicans? Democrats?"

Gene Thomas laughed. "It doesn't matter which side. Men like him want power more than they care to ascribe to either side of the political spectrum. I don't doubt that he's already built some kind of backroom alliance."

Claire looked shocked. "So you're saying this was deliberate?"

Gene Thomas rocked his head from side to side. "It's hard to say how far he wanted to let it go, but it served its purpose. There is a witch hunt on now for anyone in Congress that has blocked funding. Mid-terms are around the corner. Believe me when I tell you, he is a cunning man, Johnson."

Cole said under his breath, "He's a piece of shit. Can we prove he's lying?"

Gene Thomas smiled, but said nothing. It was below him to speak of anyone in such a way. He shook his head. "The working theory is already out there, thanks to Johnson and his briefing."

"But it's a lie."

Gene Thomas nodded. "I agree with you Cole, but the story is out there. History is written by the first man to pick up a pen. The rest is all speculation at best."

"I can prove he lied to Congress."

Gene Thomas thought carefully about his words. "Cole, are you familiar with the grassy knoll?"

"Kennedy?"

"Exactly."

Harley, Matt, and Claire all leaned in, as if Gene Thomas was about to say something incredible. He looked at each of them, smiled just a bit, and said, "I'm not saying it's a conspiracy, but I've shot a lot of deer in my day and I've never seen a bullet turn around. Have you?"

None of them moved.

"It's rhetorical. I don't really know what happened to the poor man, but my point is that once the official story is out, anything after that is immediately discredited as a conspiracy."

Cole leaned back, and looked around the room. All of a sudden, it felt too warm and constricting. Harley was up and grabbing beers from the fridge.

Matt asked, "So what now?"

Gene Thomas thought for a moment with a heavy look on his face. "Are there still men here, in Cozumel, trying to get in through Texas?"

Claire chimed in. "Yes ,Sir. We have a rough location, but not a number."

Gene Thomas nodded. "Good. They will feel emboldened by this. They will try even harder now. Once animals like this taste blood, especially from us infidels as they call us, they'll be after more."

Matt asked, "What about Johnson?"

"All bets are off with him," Gene Thomas said harshly. "Watch yourselves, and if you trusted him at all before, don't trust him anymore. If you need anything, I can help you for a few more months."

"Why months?" asked Cole.

Gene smiled. "Mid-terms, like I said, are just around the corner. I'm a dinosaur, a Blue Dog, and the last of my tribe. There is no room for any middle-ground these days. And I bear some of the responsibility for the funding that Johnson is going after."

Claire asked in disbelief, "So he's after you too?"

He looked at her with fondness, as if he'd known her all of his life, "He's after everyone that stands in his way, Claire." After looking at her for a few moments more, he asked, "How are you holding up?"

"I'm fine, Sir," was all she could say.

"That's good. And the rest of you?" They all nodded. "Cole," he said, "You look like absolute shit. Walk with me to the gate."

Outside, he put his arm loosely around Cole's shoulder. For the first time, Cole didn't mind. Gene Thomas had a calming effect, giving off the sense that he sought only the best for the world. As they walked, Gene Thomas took a long breath and looked around at the sky. They stopped at the gate.

"I need you, Cole, more than any of the rest in there, to make very careful and deliberate choices from here on out."

"What do you want me to do?" asked Cole.

"Keep this country safe, Cole. You may be in the best and only position to do that. I don't want anyone else to get hurt on account of the ambition of a corrupt man. I think you feel the same."

Cole nodded.

Gene Thomas popped the gate open, turned one last time, and said softly, "When you get the chance, I want you to end it, Cole."

CHAPTER 14: NOTHING TO LOSE

THEY WERE DRINKING THAT afternoon around the pool. The mood had shifted among the group, and despite their best efforts, little could be said to bring about a lasting smile on any of their worn faces. Matt had insisted that they stop watching the news, as personal accounts were being played continuously and the sight of mothers, fathers, brothers, and sisters crying into the camera for their lost loved ones did no good. Each was keenly aware of what had transpired, and nothing would change it. The body count sat at nine, with a few more in hospitals. All of the casualties were civilians, some of them kids.

As the late afternoon breeze blew hard against the palm trees and rustled the fronds with unending waves of wind, Cole climbed out from the armada of empty beer cans floating around the pool and dried himself off. Inside, he changed into some clean clothes and sat at the couch, reflecting on the past few days. There was still unfinished business with Juan. *How exactly was I supposed to get back?* Cole asked himself the question over and over. He played it out in his head and came to the conclusion that Juan had not intended for Cole to ever return. *Perhaps he figured they'd kill me?* It would not be the first time Cole had been sent to his death by a drug dealer. The more he thought about it, the more plausible the idea seemed. Juan and David were cut from the same cloth, the only difference being that David was dead. Cole toyed with the idea of a suicide run to the boot shop. It would be messy, but the rage inside Cole pushed him further towards the idea.

He fought back against his own thoughts, trying to find alternatives to his theory, but found none. Standing up and walking over to Harley's toy boxes, Cole took one of the grenades and tucked the spoon inside his belt at his crotch. With a loose button-down shirt, it was almost concealed. At his back right hip, he felt for the revolver and wrapped his hand around the grip momentarily for some more assurance. Stepping outside, Harley and Matt were still in the pool, both leaned back against opposite ends and staring off at nothing in particular. Claire was in a reclined chair with one arm up and over her face. Matt and Harley both had their M4s laid across chairs close by.

"I'm taking a walk," was all Cole said as he started for the gate.

"Cole," Matt called out.

He turned and smiled, nodding at Matt, "I'm good. I'll be back in a bit."

Matt said nothing, simply looking back with a quizzical expression.

Turning down the street, Cole walked slowly and used the time alone to try and organize his thoughts. As the sun dropped low on the far western horizon, shadows spread across the streets and the sky changed from yellow and orange to an ominous deep shade of red. Hues of purple followed as the stars began to appear one by one. Still, Cole wandered farther until he turned to make his way downtown. The streets were bustling with the evening crowd. Cole blended in seamlessly and wandered an even more circuitous route, until after almost two hours, he stood one block away from the boot shop. He was at a bench, staring across the median, the opposite street, and the sidewalk. Amid the foot traffic, he quickly picked up on the half-dozen men that were spread in a crescent around the shop. *Extra security*, he thought. They weren't all that tough looking, most either overly skinny or carrying some extra weight. *Good work is hard to find*, Cole laughed to himself. Nevertheless, they most certainly were armed.

Cole walked a block farther and ordered a Tecate, taking it down to the water's edge to seek some comfort from the sea. He felt the breeze blow hard against his chest and ruffle through his hair. He took long deliberate breaths, and for the first time that day, he thought of Isabella asleep with Marie in Carentan. His stomach was a familiar bottomless pit, but he was concerned by his lack of emotion. He felt empty, a deep aching sadness weighing his body down. Finishing the beer, he held it inverted for a few seconds more and felt the lime touch against his lower lip. Tossing the can in the trash, he stood and walked back to his vantage point looking at the shop.

He glanced at the water one last time, then up at the half moon in the sky, and nodded. Stepping across the median, when he hit the sidewalk, Juan's men were on to him. Two approached and blocked his path. The rest hovered back and watched. Cole, not missing a beat, reached down to his waist for the grenade. As he did, both men reached to their hips and under their loose-fitting shirts. Cole was quicker than them both on the draw and produced the grenade, cupping it in his right hand and showing just enough for both to stop in their tracks, looking at each other for some guidance as to how to proceed.

Cole walked steadily towards them, moving the safety off and looping his left pointer finger to pull the pin. He did it in such a way so that both of Juan's men knew exactly what he was doing. They slid to the side and called out under their breath to him to stop. Cole didn't, and replied back to them simply, "Juan."

At the step leading up to the shop, two more men had been alerted to Cole and stood to block his path. This time, Cole pulled the pin and flicked it towards one of them. As it clinked on the floor by his feet, the guard looked up in surprise as Cole held the grenade up at eye level and stared hard into the man's eyes. The second guy quickly stepped out of the store and disappeared while the first man took a step back to allow Cole inside. The audacity of it all was working far better than Cole had imagined.

At the back door, Cole pushed it open and stepped inside, the grenade still held up and next to his head. The room went silent as he took another step in.

"Puta," one of the older men said softly, not daring to move more than his lower lip as he said it.

"Yeah, fuck you too, hombre."

Juan asked in surprise, "Ben?"

"Yeah, Juan. I'm back. You got some time to talk?"

Juan paused and looked at the grenade. He asked, "Is that thing going to go off?"

"Only if I let go of it. And I ain't letting go unless one of your boys shoots me."

"No one will shoot you, Cole, can you please put the..."

Cole cut him off, "The pin?"

"Si, yes, the pin. Can you put the pin in?"

"I lost the pin. So now we're stuck with a live grenade. You mind if I sit?"

He didn't wait for Juan to acknowledge before taking a seat at the small table. There were some folders and a binder spread out on it and a few more men in the room than Juan's normal group of cronies.

"How was I supposed to get back to Cozumel, Juan?"

He didn't answer, but looked at Cole with a blank expression.

"Better question: Did you think I'd make it back, Juan?"

Juan paused, then answered, "I didn't know if you'd make it back. That's a risk in this business, Ben."

Cole nodded. "I know it is. Believe me, I know."

"But you made it back," Juan said, trying to lighten the mood.

"Yeah, here I am."

Silence fell as the men stared motionless at Cole. He knew that at least one or two of them had closed in behind and out of sight, ready for Juan's signal to try and take him down.

"If I let go of this here little lever, even for a second, we all go boom."

"Please don't let go of the lever, then, Ben."

Cole nodded, and for the first time, smiled at Juan. He wasn't a bad guy, as far as drug dealers went. Sure, it was all part of the business, but Cole had run out of patience with the whole game.

"So what's next?" asked Cole.

"What do you mean?"

"For me, what else you got? What else is going on down here for work?"

Juan looked up to a man his age standing against the wall, and the two of them looked at each other for a moment. The man standing then shrugged, and Juan returned his stare to Cole.

"Some things have changed a bit."

"Go on," Cole said.

Juan cleared his throat, "Some partners of mine have asked that we not make any more runs like yours…"

Cole cut him off. "You mean shipments of rockets to the U.S. to kill Americans?"

Juan nodded. "Yes, and people as well."

Cole thought for a second. "What about people? You didn't say anything to me about people."

"There are some men on the island that were also looking to be transported to Texas. But we have decided not to take them."

Cole asked, "Or have you been told not to take them?" Juan looked confused. Cole continued, "What's with the extra security? You seem a little nervous, Juan."

Juan shook his head to dismiss it, but Cole could smell it in the room. His mind raced to connect some dots before he spoke again. "The big boys on the mainland don't want to get into the terrorism game?"

Juan squinted at Cole, frustration and some embarrassment growing on his face. Cole backed off, so as not to spoil his gains.

"What's going on, Juan?" he asked in a friendly tone.

"My partners asked that we end those trips…" He paused, as if to assert his place at the table before continuing, "and I agree with them."

Cole was now certain that Juan had been told to stand the fuck down. In Cozumel, he may have been a king, but in the hierarchy of Mexican drug bosses, Juan was far from sitting on the board of directors. It explained the extra security. From what Cole had gathered over the years, there were only a handful of families, or cartels, that pulled the big strings. Guys like Juan worked under their umbrella, and so long as they kept moving product, the lower echelons could keep their piece of real estate. If someone in Juan's shoes were to reach out and try to broker a sweeter deal with another cartel, it would either be a shrewd business move or a death sentence. In all likelihood, Juan had made a side deal with whomever these men were, and now that it was plastered across the front pages—his bosses were none too pleased.

It made sense. Pressure on the border meant a loss in profits. Drug cartels weren't good people, but for the most part, they employed quasi-rational thought in their business dealings. Terrorists, on the other hand, were not rational people. And now apparently the ones in Cozumel were trapped on the island.

Juan explained, "My partners will get rid of these 'visitors' and we'll go back to how it was before."

Cole asked, "And me?"

"Maybe you might lay low for a while, too?"

"We need to talk alone, Juan."

Reluctantly, Juan motioned with his chin for the rest of them to leave the room, which they cautiously did. None of them seemed keen to blow up. Alone now, it was Juan on one side of the table and Cole on the other. The heavy smell of raw leather wafted through the dark confined space.

"How are they gonna get rid of these guys?"

"Who are you working for, Ben?"

The question caught Cole by surprise. Juan was smarter than he thought. *Fuck it*, Cole told himself. He asked, "Who do you think I work for?"

"CIA?"

Cole laughed, "Nah, I'm an independent contractor." Juan didn't understand. Cole added, "I work for myself."

Juan smiled, not believing it for even a second.

Cole asked, "How are they going to get rid of these guys?"

Juan, now a little bit more at ease, explained. "A team arrived today from the mainland. They'll hit their house tomorrow night." He wiped both his hands as if the problem would be solved.

"And you?"

Juan shook his head. "What do you mean, and me?"

"You've got a lot of security outside. You worried?"

"No, just taking some precautions."

"You should take better precautions," Cole said.

Juan smirked, looked down at the grenade, then back at Cole.

"Good help is hard to find here. It's a small island."

"Can you call these guys off?" asked Cole.

"Why?"

Cole was now unsure of exactly how to proceed. Juan was smart enough to know that Cole was likely up to more than he admitted to. But he couldn't and wouldn't trust Juan with any information.

"What if I can take care of them?"

Juan asked, "Who?"

Cole, frustrated, raised his voice. "The fucking terrorists you're hiding, Juan. Who the fuck else would I be talking about?"

"So the U.S. wants to come to Mexico and kill people on our soil?"

Cole fired back, "Oh, because all of a sudden, you give a shit about border integrity?"

"Let's calm down a bit." As he spoke, Juan reached down to the cooler and pulled two beers from the ice. Cole, at the same time, switched the grenade to his left hand, reached behind his back and drew the revolver. As he leveled it and pointed the barrel at Juan's chest, Cole cocked the hammer with his thumb. The sound of it locking back was timed perfectly with Juan's eyes connecting. His jaw open, Juan didn't move. He held a beer in each hand, the water dripping off and down to the floor.

"Write down the address where your guys are."

Juan replied, "They're not my guys."

"I don't care who they are. Write it down."

"Ben, you don't want to do that. You can't mess with them."

"I do whatever the fuck I want, Juan. Now write it down or I put a hollow point through your chest."

Juan stared at Cole for a few seconds more, swallowed, and set the beers down on the table. Reluctantly, he tore a piece of paper from the binder and jotted something down, pushing it slowly across the table.

"You don't want to do this, Ben."

"There's a lot of things I don't want to do anymore, Juan."

He thumbed the hammer down, picked up the paper and slid it into his pocket, and smoothly stood up. Backing away to the door, he took a breath and looked at Juan, still seated patiently at his table.

"I'll be in touch, Juan. If I were you, I wouldn't say a word to any of your boys about what just happened. And tell those terrorist dipshits I'll run them to Texas in two days."

Nervous, Juan asked, "What did just happen, Ben?"

Cole smiled, "Well, if anyone asks me, you just sold out your cartel."

HE WAS OUT OF BREATH as he rounded the last corner to the house. He'd chucked the grenade over the seawall a ways down from the center of the city and run the entire way back. His mind raced just as fast as he ran. In less than 24 hours, hitmen were making a move on the house. It seemed easy enough to let nature take its course, but Cole had remembered that Claire's people had someone inside. *Casualty of war*, Cole thought initially, but as he ran, that thought sickened him. Having been left for dead himself, Cole's focus turned to ways of turning off the hit.

As he made his way through the iron gate, it was just after midnight. The lights were on in the house. More than likely, one of them was waiting to see if Cole even made it home. He caught his breath and stepped inside. They were all sitting quietly at the table where, on the far side, Johnson sat, beads of sweat on his forehead, with both his hands crossed in front of him. He looked pissed. Harley, Matt, and Claire all looked at Cole with expressions of uncertainty.

Johnson asked plainly, "Where have you been, Cole?"

"Out," was all he replied as he took a seat and slowed his breathing.

Johnson said nothing, but stared intently at Cole. The tension would have peaked, had Cole given a shit about anything Johnson had to say. He felt himself grow angry as he thought back to Johnson's blatant lies to Congress. Moreover, the four of them were now left with an uncertain future.

Johnson asked the group, "What did Thomas have to say?"

Matt replied, "What do you mean?"

"Don't lie to me. I will end this thing right now."

Good, Cole thought. He suspected the others felt the same way.

Johnson continued, "You've all created quite a mess, and I need to know you're capable of handling it."

Harley stirred in his seat. Cole watched with curiosity as the veins in his neck bulged. Harley was looking ready to snap. It occurred to Cole that he could make quick work of Johnson. Any one of them probably could take on his pudgy frame with no issue. *Fuck him*, Cole thought as he strained not to show the rage growing inside.

Getting control of himself again, Johnson asked calmly, "What is the plan?"

Neither Matt nor Claire stirred even a bit. Harley looked off across the room. Cole took it upon himself to address the matter.

"There's another run, of people this time, and I'm on it."

He concocted the story fast in his head, hoping to see if Johnson had the decency in him to call it off. Blood still drying in the streets of Port Aransas, Cole couldn't imagine that anyone with a shred of decency would let enemies like that anywhere near its border.

"Where to? Are they here in Cozumel?"

Cole answered, "Yeah, they're…"

Johnson cut him off. "How many?"

"I don't know."

"When?"

Cole lied again. "In two days."

Johnson's jaw clenched. He tapped his flattened fingers down on the table over and over as he thought. A ring on his left index finger clanked against the wood each time. Cole looked down at it.

"I'm an Aggie," he said proudly as he looked directly at Cole with an expression that seemed to expect high praise or admiration. Cole had no clue what that meant or what Johnson was talking about. He tapped his ring a few more times to drive home whatever absurd point he was trying to make.

Cole took a deep breath and nodded, feigning an appreciation for Johnson's apparent accomplishments.

"Where will this run go?"

Cole lied, "Probably Texas again, seeing as how the last one seemed to work out."

He was probing for Johnson's reaction. He most certainly got one. With a raised voice, Johnson thundered, "No, it did not work out. We stopped them dead in their tracks."

His piercing eyes stared down Cole for insulting his op. Cole stared back, as blank of an expression on his face as he could muster.

"What I meant, Sir, is that they made it to American soil."

Johnson exhaled forcefully, his nostrils flaring and he looked around the room.

"Let's get something straight. If I need to keep you all on a shorter leash, I will. Now what did Thomas have to say?"

Claire answered with her soft sophisticated English accent, "He was just checking up on us, that was all."

Her voice soothed Cole's temper, and he sensed that it eased the tension for both Matt and Harley as well. Even Johnson seemed to back down. He rubbed at his chin and took a breath.

"I want to know where and when, same as last time."

Matt nodded, acknowledging the plan solemnly.

"And none of you say a word to Thomas. You answer to me." Johnson stood up and walked to the living room, looking out the big windows at the pool outside under the moonlight. He stood there as the rest of them sat quietly at the table. Claire looked at Cole, concern growing in her eyes. Harley and Matt sat with their arms crossed, waiting for Johnson to leave.

"I need a ride to airport. I want to be airborne before the sun's up."

They all looked at each other as if to ask who wanted to spend the next half hour sitting next to the obnoxious fat bastard.

Taking out a phone, Johnson dialed a number, raised it to his ear and said, "I'll be there soon. Have it running for me." He paused and listened, then raised his voice, "Of course I want to go home, where else would I want to go?" Another pause followed by Johnson's now incensed voice, "I don't care how long you've been up. I'm not staying here tonight. Get the plane ready. I'm on my way."

Cole smiled and laughed to himself as he looked at everyone else's similar expressions. *At least he's a dick to everyone.*

"I'll take him," Cole said as he stood up and reached for the keys by the kitchen.

Matt asked, "You sure?"

Cole smiled and spoke quietly. "Yeah. I don't think he'd take too well to Harley pissing off the local cops."

Harley grinned for a second before Johnson cut back in. "I'll be outside. Let's get moving."

As Johnson stepped out the front door to the courtyard, they all breathed a subtle sigh of relief. Matt and Harley looked at each other, with Harley saying softly under his breath, "It's fucking treason, Matt."

Matt nodded. "I know. Easy, bud. We gotta be careful on this one."

Looking at Cole, he asked again, "You sure you're good to drive?" Cole nodded.

Johnson called out loudly from outside, "Let's GO."

"What the fuck is an Aggie?" asked Harley.

Claire replied, "Who gives a shit?"

TWENTY MINUTES LATER, Cole was rumbling down a gravel side road that led towards the main stretch of highway towards the airport. It was dark except for the dim yellowed headlights of the Thing barely illuminating more than ten yards in front of them. Cole sped along with the crunch of gravel under the tires. There were piles of trash stacked along the side of the road, some in bags, but most of it strewn along the edges of the road. Jungle reached up and over from each side and masked all but a sliver of the dark sky above.

Johnson said to no one in particular, "This place smells like shit."

So do you, Cole thought.

Not getting any reaction from Cole, Johnson pressed him for no reason other than his own boredom. Staring out to his right side, he said, "I mean it, Cole. You better keep your shit together."

Cole said nothing. Johnson looked to his left at Cole, and he nodded to acknowledge the veiled threat. Johnson spoke again, this time not mincing any words. "If this thing goes bad, you're gonna have a lot of explaining to do."

Cole could feel his body start to shake. Frustrated, he asked, "Why's that?"

Johnson laughed. "This whole thing has your name all over it. You have a way of creating quite the mess."

"I'm not following, Sir."

Cole ripped the Thing around a corner, half hoping the turn would eject Johnson. The Thing steadied and Cole continued on at a steady pace. Ahead of them, the road went on straight for a ways, the white gravel disappearing into the darkness ahead before it would hit the highway in less than a mile.

"You got lucky back in Panama. I don't really know what it is that Tony saw in you in the first place, but you left that whole city in shambles, against my better judgment. You do that again down here, and I'll make damn sure you don't have that opportunity ever again."

Choking back the burning in his chest, he asked, "Is that a threat?"

Johnson raised his voice, "You know, that's your problem Cole."

Cole cut him off and yelled back at him, "What's my problem?"

"You better watch your tone. You keep your shit in check, or you'll never see France again." Johnson's pudgy face shook with anger then stared back out the side of the Thing. He yelled, "This whole island stinks like shit. Is this the right way?"

"Almost there, Sir."

Cole took a hard left down another gravel road, having no idea where it led. The highway was a quarter mile further in the opposite direction. He sped into the darkness, a fierce anger growing over him, even more so than when they'd taken him away from Isabella and Marie. He forced any thought of the two of them from his mind and focused squarely on his present circumstances.

Panama. Left for dead. And now maybe Johnson was the missing link that had called off Tony's guys.

France. Taken away from him, by none other than Johnson.

Port Aransas. Johnson's fucked up power trip—and now Cole possibly hung out over it.

Johnson was still staring out the side of the Thing. Cole thought back to Gene Thomas' words. *End it.*

Cole accelerated until the fourth gear was screaming.

Johnson looked back over his right shoulder, asking, "Cole, do you even know where you're going?"

Not really, Cole thought as he reached behind his hip with his right hand. He drew the revolver and gripped it tight with his three bottom fingers. His pointer finger was extended over the trigger guard as he smoothly lifted it. Nearing a full draw, he touched the pad of his finger to the trigger and cocked the hammer back with his thumb before wrapping it securely around the other side of the grip. The crunch of gravel was too much for Johnson to hear the subtle click when the hammer latched in place.

Cole took a breath, now speeding ahead with a gun to the side of Johnson's head. He looked at Johnson, ignoring whatever lay ahead in the darkness and said, "Fuck you, asshole."

The blinding flash of orange and concussive blast drowned out the engine and flying gravel as Johnson slumped forward and rolled to his right side. Cole let off the gas, unlatched Johnson's seatbelt, and pushed hard with the revolver still in his hand until Johnson's lifeless body rolled out and thumped on the ground. Blood covered the seat and the dash. His finger now extended again over the trigger guard, Cole wiped at his cheek with the back of his right hand and slowed down until the Thing rolled to a stop. He looked behind him, seeing nothing but black. In front and to the sides was more of the same, save for the dim lights from two worn headlights and low dust that had been stirred up around him.

He spun the Thing around in a three point turn and drove ahead, doubling back on his tracks. Johnson's body appeared first as a dark blob on the side of the road. Pulling up closer, Cole stopped a few yards short of Johnson, pointing the headlights directly at him. He stepped out and walked over.

Johnson was balled up and covered in fine white dust from where he'd unceremoniously rolled to a stop. He was resting on his left side, that arm protruding out from under his torso at an odd angle. His legs were wrapped as if they'd been spun together. Cole stepped closer to see that the right side of his face was gone. White dust and small stones were stained pink, and thick fresh blood pooled in the wound's cavity.

Cole panicked for a second, but then shook his head as his conscience cleared the guilt that had failed to take hold. His ears were ringing, and his vision was still partly blotted out from the flash of burning powder exiting the barrel and exploding in the black of night. He felt an odd sense of calm over his body as he looked up at the stars through the broken canopy of jungle.

Forty-eight hours, he told himself. The clock was winding down. *I've got forty-eight hours to end this.*

CHAPTER 15: BLURRED LINES

HE SPED BACK, reversing his course away from Johnson's lifeless body. Cole left it where he'd fallen from the Thing. Accelerating along in the darkness, small bits of rock ricocheted off the bare wheel-wells and tumbled out with the cloud of dust behind him. It wasn't until he was back on a main road that the sporadic street lights cast a pale light on the mess in the right seat. There was blood all over the seat and floor. The sight of it brought Cole regret. He sped on, farther along the empty early morning stretch of road, glancing every few seconds to his right. The tightly packed houses and buildings were all dark, with the sunrise still an hour or two away.

Nearing the villa, Cole slowed and scanned to his right and left. Halfway up a single lane drive, he spotted what he was looking for. A hose lay neatly coiled against a windowless concrete wall. He motored up and left the Thing running, stepping out quickly and grabbing the hose. Its full discharge was only a weak flow, so Cole mashed his thumb over the end to increase the velocity of the water. Still, it was hardly enough to wash away what was left of Johnson. He sprayed it over a second time, but the water did little more than spread the crimson water around the floorboard. Hearing something farther down the alley, Cole looked up as an older man emerged from behind a gate and looked his way. The two of them stared at each other under the faint yellow light of a dull exposed bulb protruding from the wall. Cole stood motionless, the hose in his right hand while the man looked at him for a few moments more before going back in at the gate.

Cole turned off the hose. He looked once more at the floorboard of the Thing and realized he stood no chance of masking what he'd done. Reluctantly, he climbed back in and continued down the lane until he hit a main street and turned for the Villa. As he neared the drive, he killed the engine and coasted to a stop. He sat there in the darkness, one hand on the wheel and his chin sunk into his chest. Clarity was what he sought, but there was far too much in his mind for it to come easily. He focused on his breathing and remembered as best he could the loose framework of a plan that he'd made.

Inside the house, Harley was still up, seated at the table and drinking a beer. A solitary light was on in the kitchen, but otherwise the rooms were dark. Cole stepped in, walked to the fridge, took two beers in one hand and sat across from Harley. It seemed strange to Cole that he wasn't tinkering with a gun or doing something. It was, in fact, the first time Cole had seen Harley sit still since they'd met.

"Johnson make it OK?"

Cole took a long gulping sip of his beer and passed the second to Harley, looking directly at him. "Nope."

Harley popped the top off the sweating Dos Equis and took a quick sip, setting the beer down and spinning it to examine the label for a second. "What happened?"

Cole swallowed, cleared his throat, and replied, "I killed him."

Harley bit down and chewed on his upper lip for a moment, lost in his thoughts. He took a breath and nodded, accepting the gravity of what Cole had just said. "You shoot him?"

Cole nodded. "Yeah, in the head."

"Where's he at?"

Cole looked down then over to the door, feeling those familiar twinges of regret. "Some gravel road. I doubt I could find it again."

Harley asked, "You bury him?"

With no emotion, Cole replied, "No. I left him for the dogs."

They were silent for the better part of a minute. The first hint of dawn was less than two hours away. Cole's regret faded as he watched Harley mull it all over in his head. The only sound in the room was a fan turning in the living room, clicking with each rotation.

"So what now?" Harley asked.

Cole took another sip as he committed to seeing it all through. He looked at Harley with the faintest hint of a smile and asked, "You think you could kill some dudes for me?"

Harley nodded matter-of-factly. "Yeah," he said, pausing for a second before continuing. "Let's try to keep Johnson between you and me for now."

Cole nodded, knowing that was unlikely, but appreciating Harley's consideration.

Harley looked at him with a sheepish smile. "I'll go get Matt."

HALF AN HOUR LATER, the kitchen table was awash in magazines, gun parts, rifles, pistols, and ammunition. Cole was helping load up the 30-round M4 mags as Matt snugged a load-bearing vest around his torso. He wore a pair of khaki pants, a blue t-shirt, and a pair of hiking boots. Thin leather gloves fit tight over his hands as he affixed a helmet on his head. He was fiddling with the battery pack for his NVGs when Harley came bounding down the stairs.

Matt turned, looked, and stopped what he was doing. "Harley, we gotta go, man."

Harley replied casually, "Gimme two minutes."

Matt looked at him, still not comprehending. "Dude, you getting changed?" Matt asked as Harley slipped his own vest over his chest and cinched it tight.

"I'm good." Harley was also wearing a pair of tan boots with a t-shirt, but instead of pants, he still had on his purple and green board-shorts. Claire looked on from the kitchen, where she was hastily putting together a pot of coffee.

"You're wearing boardshorts." No one was quite sure if it was a question or a statement.

Harley stopped in his tracks and looked squarely at Matt. "Yeah." He then went back to stuffing the pockets of his vest with M4 mags. Across his chest was an angled pistol holster, into which he slid a full-sized Sig pistol. Cole thought it ominous that both Harley and Matt were leaving their revolvers behind.

"Harley, you..."

"What?"

Matt stuttered, "You're wearing...that?"

Harley, now a bit defensive with loaded mags in both hands, replied, "My contract didn't say shit about uniform inspections, Matt."

Matt composed himself, shook his head, and took a breath, going back to his NVGs. Under his breath, he said, "You look like an idiot."

Harley just smiled. "I like these shorts. They're stretchy." He spread his legs out and squatted to the floor and back up, a goofy grin on his face. Cole laughed, but Matt pretended to ignore it. Harley then grabbed his helmet, walked over to the table, and pulled out a set of NVGs for himself.

Now standing side by side, Matt repeated, "Seriously, you look like an idiot."

"No time for that now, boss. Let's get moving," Harley replied as he did another half squat to the floor and repeated, "Stretchy."

They both mounted their goggles on their helmets and Claire handed them each a cup of coffee. They took quick sips, careful not to burn their mouths, as they grabbed the last of their necessities for an impromptu pre-dawn raid on a Mexican drug cartel safe house. Harley and Matt both loaded their M4s, slid the bolts forward, and shouldered their rifles, sighting in against the far wall. Each of them had their own routine they followed that brought them to the same level of preparedness. Matt tugged at his vest one last time and turned to look at Harley.

He asked, "Good?"

Harley smiled. "Yeah. Let's do this."

All four of them huddled around the table. Matt rubbed at his eyes, having been woken up after two hours of sleep at best. Harley hadn't slept at all, and Claire was showing signs of the fatigue that each of them worked hard to conceal.

"One more time, Cole. Just the highlights."

Cole cleared his throat and said, "No idea how many, but they're supposed to move on the house tonight and take out whoever is in there. Juan said it's a team, but I don't have much more than that."

"Have you seen the house?" asked Harley.

Cole shook his head.

Both Matt and Harley looked at each other. Harley grinned. "Well, we've got surprise on our side—and the dark."

Matt countered, "Unless Juan told them."

"No chance of that," Cole replied.

"What's your reasoning?"

Cole looked at Matt and answered, "That'd be a death sentence for Juan. These aren't his boys. They're coming from the mainland. Juan's just a little bitch that pushes some coke in Cozumel. He's got his tail tucked between his legs right now. He'll keep quiet."

Matt nodded. "And after?"

Cole continued, "I think we've got a day, maybe two to finish this and get the fuck off the island. It'll get a bit bloody, I reckon."

Matt took a long breath. "All right, let's get one good pass of the house and take a look."

Outside, Cole climbed in the driver's seat. Matt, Harley, and Claire all paused at the passenger seat. It was still a damp bloody mess.

Harley quipped, "Backseat, I suppose."

Matt looked confused and asked, "What the fuck is this?"

"We'll explain later."

Matt turned to Cole. "What happened?" They all looked at Cole, waiting for an explanation.

"I killed him."

Matt asked, "Johnson?"

"Yup."

Matt turned and stepped away from the Thing, holding his M4's pistol grip by one hand. He took a few steps away and spoke out with frustration in his voice, "Fuck."

His back to the rest of them, Matt huffed and looked down the street. Cole was worried and looked to Harley for some reassurance. Harley shook his head and under his breath, he said to Cole, "He'll be fine. It just needs to sink in a bit."

He then turned to Matt and called out, "We're losing time, buddy."

Matt stood for a moment more, looking down the dark abandoned and dusty street, before turning and walking silently back to the Thing. He looked at Cole, and his facial expression rested somewhere between relieved and frustrated. Cole knew, without a word between them, that there were no hard feelings.

With Claire flanked by Matt and Harley, Cole looked through the rearview mirror and could see that she was squeezed shoulder to shoulder against both of them. Their goggles down, Cole could see their helmets bouncing as Cole roared down the road. He took a few turns and found the road that led to the house Juan had marked on the piece of paper. Cole doubled back and found an alley that passed the back of the small one-story house. It was in the standard lower-income section of far too many houses squeezed into one city block. A six-foot tall cinderblock wall blocked access to the back of the house. With the headlights off, Cole crept down the alley, and Matt stood up in his seat, and then motioned with one hand to continue. Back out on the main street, they stopped several houses short of the target.

"Back entry?" asked Matt.

Harley nodded. "Yeah. Seems easy enough."

Matt continued, "There's a glass door into the house."

"Sweet." Harley smiled.

They sat for a moment more, idling in the street. Harley looked down the empty road, then said, "Just so I'm clear, we're gonna go kill some druggies to save some terrorists? Do I have that right?" He was smiling a toothy grin and looking at Claire.

Claire swallowed, not at all in the mood for jokes. She looked back at Harley, but said nothing.

Harley put his left arm around and squeezed her shoulder. "Don't worry. We got this."

Matt leaned forward and spoke to Cole. "Bring us back around to the alley. Once we're out, head around to the front and wait. If we're not out in five minutes, head back to the villa."

"What then?"

"We'll be out in less than five."

Claire asked, "What if it's the wrong house? What if it's just some family?"

Harley replied, "Then we'll apologize and be out in about ten seconds…"

Cole drove back around, and a minute or two later, he was creeping along the alley again. Matt tapped him on the shoulder and Cole slowed. Silently, Matt and Harley both hopped out of the Thing and moved quickly up to the wall. There was nothing but a solitary sliver of moonlight illuminating the alley. Cole could see the faint green reflection from their NVGs, but otherwise both Matt and Harley were just two silent dark masses against the wall. Harley hopped up on a trash can and swept the back with his rifle. As he did, Matt climbed up and over the wall. Harley followed, making no sound. Both of them were gone. Cole's entire body trembled.

Seconds passed with nothing. Cole waited and stared at the concrete wall. From the backseat, Claire whispered, "Cole, drive around."

He felt like an idiot, and quickly shifted into first gear and crept along the alley. As he passed the wall, he heard broken glass and a series of concussive blasts. As he continued on farther, he thought he heard the quiet *thwack* of both Harley and Matt's suppressed rifles. Out of the alley, he shifted and sped the 50 yards to the intersection where he turned hard to the left and accelerated again to the front of the house. His foot now on the brake, he pulled his SP101 from his pocket and stared at the decrepit iron gate that led into the house. Other than the rough congested hum of the Thing's engine, there was no sound. With the commotion, some lights came on farther down the street in the front of one of the houses.

Cole heard a yell from inside followed by another blast. A volley of unsuppressed fire then erupted from inside. *Must be the right house,* Cole mused. He saw the orange glow through one of the windows inside. He heard yelling followed by more thunderous gunfire. He cocked the hammer on his gun and looked up and down the street. More lights were coming on, and he realized he'd forgotten to hack his watch. There was now a full-on gunfight in the house. Cole heard indistinguishable muffled yells from inside.

Claire spoke quietly and to herself, "Come on, boys...come on."

The house went silent for a few moments before a series of solitary shots rang out. After that, the house went entirely dark. As they waited, not even the slightest movement came from inside. Cole feared the worst as dogs barking in the distance reminded him of Matt's instructions. He gripped the wheel with one hand and the shifter with the other.

Fuck, Cole thought He'd done this, and the blame was entirely his. From the rearview mirror, he caught some movement. Startled, he turned with the gun to see both Harley and Matt at full sprint coming towards him. They both hopped in, out of breath, and Matt gasped, "Let's go, let's go."

Cole didn't hesitate, throwing the Thing into gear and speeding away. As the Thing accelerated, Matt leaned forward to Cole again and yelled out over the wind, "Thanks for waiting." Cole nodded, focused on the road ahead as the first shades of dark red wandered their way into the eastern sky.

"Harley, you're bleeding," Claire called out with concern.

"It ain't mine, darling."

BACK AT THE VILLA, Harley dropped most of his gear by the front door and hurled himself into the pool. The sky was a lighter shade of blue with vivid strokes of orange dotting the tops of cumulus clouds in the distance. The air was still as a few birds began their morning chatter.

Matt and Cole stepped inside, where Matt laid out his gear and inventoried what he had left. His M4 was dusty with carbon stains around the action. He locked the bolt open and set it down with a thud. From there, he dumped empty mags out onto the table and took a seat. He was still breathing heavily with his mouth firmly shut. Claire went to the coffee pot. It was still warm. They'd been gone for less than half an hour.

Harley, soaking wet, dragged his gear in and did the same. The table was a clustered mess of tactical insanity. Cole reckoned there were tens of thousands of dollars worth of weapons and gear. Matt's first task was to strip both his rifle and pistol down, clean them, and reassemble. Harley went for beers from the kitchen, then set out to do the same.

Neither Claire nor Cole knew exactly how to start a conversation in the aftermath of the gun fight. Matt broke the silence. "They had the front door barricaded. We had to head out the back again." He looked up at Cole and smiled. "I'm glad you waited."

Cole just shook his head in disbelief. He asked, "How many were there?"

Harley answered, "Eight." He paused as he withdrew the bolt and charging handle, then continued, "They were serious mofos, too."

Matt nodded, "It was a fight."

The two of them smiled at each other with satisfaction. It didn't last long before Matt asked, "So, what's the angle we take with Juan?"

Cole thought and then replied, "We need to go see him today and make a run tonight to take care of these dudes."

Harley chimed in. "I love this shit. We just killed those dudes to make sure we get the chance to kill some other dudes." He sat there, with his arms over his head, and staring at the ceiling. "Love it."

Matt looked squarely into Cole's eyes. "You going by yourself?"

Cole took a moment to reflect. His mind raced through a thousand fleeting thoughts about his last trip and his own demons. He felt it in his gut—the apprehension and the uncertainty of what might transpire on the open water. He shuddered, then looked down at his lap, unable to hide the pain. Feeling broken all over again, he could not find words to break the silence.

Harley, still smiling confidently, said, "I got your back, brother. I'll go with you."

Cole looked at him and Harley nodded in a soft and genuine act of friendship. Cole's breath slowly returned and he was relieved, although he tried his hardest to mask it. "Yeah. That would help."

"We need some sleep," Matt said as he worked slowly and deliberately with his rifle. Claire brought out some tortillas and a steaming plate of scrambled eggs. They all devoured them, the smell interwoven with that of the gun cleaning solution that Harley and Matt were applying generously to their weapons.

Once Matt had his rifle reassembled, he loaded a mag, chambered a round, and set it aside. He set about cleaning his pistol in the same methodical process. Harley was close behind. They were both moving as if they expected the next gunfight to erupt at any moment.

Fortunately, nothing materialized, and all of them dozed off for a few hours until midday. Cole awoke on his couch with his right arm draped over his chest, the SP101 resting in his hand. He didn't move, but glanced down to make sure the hammer wasn't cocked. His eyes were horribly dried out, and he questioned his ability to even put together rational thoughts. The sleep had made his fatigue even worse. Finding a few uneaten tortillas at the table, he ate two quickly and drank two large cups of water before running his hands under the sink and wiping away all that he could from the past 24 hours.

AN HOUR LATER, Harley was driving the Thing downtown. Cole sat shotgun, a towel over the seat to conceal the crusted remnants of Johnson's blood. They stopped in front of the boot shop. Harley made no attempt to hide from Juan's mediocre perimeter of security. He shut the engine off and leaned over to Cole. "I know you took one of my grenades."

It caught Cole by surprise. He looked at Harley and shrugged in a half-apologetic way.

"What'd ya do with it?"

Cole looked back over to the boot shop. "I used it to get inside."

Harley pressed, "I know that, but what'd ya do with it afterwards?"

Cole looked down the road, towards the strand of craggy trees where he'd tossed it and watched the bloom of water explode. "I tossed it over there."

"You could have brought it back, you know." Harley was almost sounding like a disappointed father.

"I, uh, lost the pin."

"How did you manage that?"

Cole looked at him and continued. "I pulled it to scare those dudes."

Harley shook his head and smiled. He laughed and sat back in his seat. "You're fucking nuts, Cole."

"Did you bring one?" asked Cole.

Harley shook his head. "No. Should I have?"

Cole looked back at the shop. "Might have helped."

"Well, fuck. Let's give it a try."

Cole asked, "You ready, Pancho?"

"Let's roll, Ben."

They made their way at a steady walk to the shop. Two of Juan's men cautiously approached. Cole outspread both his hands in front of him and smiled. Harley did the same. At first it seemed as though they'd try to stop both of them, but as Cole and Harley approached, the men stopped and the two passed without even a word.

Inside the shop, a man opened the door for the two of them. Cole stepped in and Harley followed two steps behind. As Cole's eyes adjusted, he felt a hand slam into his neck and press him against the wall. *Not this shit again*, Cole thought as his head slammed against the bare wall. Not a second later, the hand was gone and Harley had reversed the play and choke-slammed whoever it was down to the ground. Two more men lunged forward, but Harley was quick on the draw and pressed the revolver forward with his right arm tensed. The muscles in his forearm surged and swelled and in the dim light, the men froze in place. Cole coughed, cleared his throat, and had his revolver by his side soon afterwards. Through it all, Juan did little but watch. The one on the floor was moaning as Harley had caught him hard in his windpipe. The other two were late on their draw and stood with their hands empty by their sides.

"You brought company, I see."

Cole nodded to Juan. "Yeah. This is Pancho. He's a friend of mine."

Harley, still with his gun at the head of one of the two, grinned and cocked the hammer, its click the only sound in the room to accompany the low moan from the floor.

"Hola. Me llamo Pancho."

The man on the floor moaned some more and rolled to his side, unable to get up.

Harley looked down, then back at Juan. "He may need some ice for that."

Cole took a breath and steadied himself. "Call your buddies and tell them we're making a run tonight."

Juan stared at him.

Cole continued, "And we need a good boat."

Harley smiled. "A fast one." His smiled faded as he asked Juan, "We good, or do I have to kill one of them?"

Juan swallowed. "We are good." Harley relaxed.

Juan looked suspiciously at Harley. "Did you kill my men, Pancho?" He said it in such a way to indicate his suspicion over Harley's name.

Cole cut in, "They weren't your men, Juan."

Harley repeated Cole's statement, "Yeah, Juan. They weren't your men. We did you a favor."

Juan looked at Harley and tilted his head. "I didn't catch your last name, Pancho."

"Nutz."

Confused, Juan asked, "Nuts?"

Harley didn't miss a beat. "It's German."

Juan shook his head in partial disgust. "They'll send more men, even more than they did this time."

"Who are we talking about? The cartel or the terrorists?" Cole asked.

Juan didn't answer. Cole looked at him in silence. He cleared his throat again, and said, "Tonight, Juan. Tell them tonight. Make the call, right fucking now."

Juan stared, but did nothing.

Cole pointed the revolver at Juan's chest and pulled at the trigger just enough to move the hammer, the barrel shaking under Cole's growing rage. Juan's eyes shifted as he noted the hammer tracking backwards.

"Right FUCKING now, Juan."

Reluctantly, Juan picked up the phone and dialed. He talked in Spanish for a while, and after some convincing on Juan's part, he hung up and nodded. "Six will go tonight. I'll get you a boat."

Cole asked, "How many more are there?"

Juan tilted his head. "I don't know. Maybe another six."

"Are they all together?"

"I don't know, Ben. I've never met them. I'm working through a middle man."

Cole and Harley looked at each other. It made sense, so they didn't press the issue. Cole tried to steady his breathing and relax his trigger finger, realizing the recklessness with which he'd damn near killed Juan.

"Ten o'clock tonight. I want a boat fueled and ready to go. And I want your fishing boats ready for us along the way."

Confused, Juan asked, "You're going to take them all the way?"

"It's a one-way trip for them, but not for us," Cole said as he nodded towards Harley. "We good?"

Juan nodded.

Harley chimed in, "And Juan…"

Juan's eyes tried to mask his anger as he stared back at Harley.

"You fuck this up, Juan, I'm gonna rip every tooth out of your mouth and stuff each one so far up your ass you'll be licking shit off them."

Juan sat back, somewhat bewildered.

Harley continued, "Then I'll gut you like a wild pig, tie a knot around your neck with your small intestine, and choke you until you…"

Cole cut him off. "Pancho."

Harley stopped mid-sentence, and turned towards Cole.

"I think he gets the point."

Harley nodded. "Well, all right then. Ten o'clock, Juan." He pointed the revolver at him, shaking it, and repeated softly, "Ten o'clock."

CHAPTER 16: LIGHT AT THE END OF THE TUNNEL

THEY TRIED TO SLEEP later that afternoon, but Cole found it impossible to rest. Claire was on the phone outside and pacing back and forth as she spoke. Matt too was consumed with phone calls. By late afternoon, they all conferred at the table over a pile of weapons, ammunition, and radios. None of it, however, would do Harley or Cole much good on the open water. Cole sat and silently went about cleaning his revolver, pretending to be focused entirely on the gun and not the alternating dark and dangerous thoughts that were speeding through his mind. He'd only taken one shot, but was sure to pick away at every crevice and nook of the SP101's internal parts, as if he could somehow go back in time to before he'd raised the gun in anger. He tried, in his mind, to tell himself that it had been a calculated and thought-out act, but he knew his temper had played a role as well.

When Cole looked up, he saw Matt staring back at him, more concerned than anything else. Claire looked up from her computer and stared at both of them.

Matt asked, "You all right, Cole?"

"He was gonna pin this whole thing on us."

Matt nodded. "I know."

"You mad?"

Matt shook his head. "At you, no." He paused and took an exaggerated breath before continuing. "Not at all, Cole. Not in the least." Matt's tone implied that he was being cautious with him, picking his words carefully so as to not push Cole any further than necessary.

Matt paused, pondered his words some more, then said rather bluntly, "We all thought about it at some point."

He looked around the room to ensure there was no dissent among the group. There was none.

It was Matt's acknowledgment of everything Cole had been through. Without saying anything too direct, it was clear that no one blamed him for cracking under the pressure. Not just Johnson, but all of it—everything about the past few months was enough to break even the most hardened man. If there was to be a breaking point, it should have been weeks ago. Cole felt it in chest, the weight lifted from him by Matt's simple statement. It did nothing to change the situation, but it reaffirmed the bond between them, and Cole took comfort in it.

He went back to cleaning his gun. Claire looked back down at her computer. Harley came downstairs looking as if he'd managed to get some sleep over the past hour. The sky outside was slowly changing from blue to yellow. It was a chemical reaction, starting off slow before the colors all stirred among themselves and culminated in something fleeting and vivid before the darkness wiped it all away. Cole was distracted, reflecting on it in silence, when Matt said, "They want us to look for Johnson."

Cole snapped back from his daydream. No one said anything.

Matt continued, "DHS knows he's missing, and they're asking us to go look for him."

Harley looked to Matt for instructions.

"What did you say?" asked Cole.

Matt smiled softly, on the verge of a laugh, "I told them we're on it."

Cole nodded in solemn appreciation.

Matt continued, "I don't think we have much time, though." He turned to Claire, "Any word?"

She shook her head and looked down. "Not a peep."

"What does your guy look like?"

She was unsure of what to say, her mouth trying for a moment to find the appropriate words. She struggled, paused as if to admit to herself that enough was enough, then spoke. "Average build, average height." She paused again, took a calming breath to compose herself, and continued, "Brown eyes. He has brown eyes."

Harley asked, "Hair color?"

Claire shook her head to dismiss it. "Could be anything, he knows how to blend in."

"Is he Middle Eastern?"

She shook her quickly. "No, Caucasian."

Matt asked, "Build?"

Claire seemed desperate to answer, but struggled even more, "Could be anything, it's been almost two years." She lost her breath at the end of the statement. They knew to stop pushing her for answers.

Harley reassured her, "We'll find him."

AT EIGHT THAT EVENING, they were still at the table. The rough plan was for Harley and Cole to set out with the boat and regardless of however many were onboard, get themselves a mile or so from the coast and finish them off. So long as Juan thought they were heading all the way to Texas, they could slip back to the island outside of town and make it back to the villa, reassess, and be moving again before anyone knew better.

Harley had a phone that Claire could track. Matt would cover them from the Thing until they were on the water. They planned to be back well before the sun was up. As nine neared, Harley and Cole stepped out the front door while Matt was busy tucking a rifle under the seat of the Thing, a pile of magazines stacked loosely next to it. Overall, Cole felt good about their chances. Harley holstered his SP101 and split up the speed strips between him and Cole. Cole felt down to his crotch, where he'd quietly tucked yet another one of Harley's grenades inside his shorts. With Harley by his side, he felt damn near invincible, but the grenade had quickly become Cole's backup plan. Matt shook both their hands outside the gate as Cole and Harley set off in the early evening air. A breeze blew steady, wandering its way down the street and tumbling off the walls of the surrounding buildings.

As it neared ten o'clock, they stood once again across the street from the boot shop. Its lights were still on, and one young man sat idly behind the counter.

Cole said, "It looks quiet."

Harley responded, "A little tooooo quiet," his voice mimicking that of a narrator from some amateur horror movie. They both laughed.

Stepping up into the shop, the man at the counter kept his hands down low and out of sight. Harley side stepped to his left while Cole moved to the right. He'd learned a bit from Harley and Matt and pivoted so that he was ready to reach for his gun.

"Manos," Cole directed. *Hands.*

Harley didn't move a muscle, but his eyes stared intently at the man. Slowly the guy brought both his empty hands to the counter and set them down, staring back at Cole and Harley. The three of them breathed slowly, but still no one moved. Cole looked to Harley, who motioned with his head for Cole to move forward. He did, and Harley followed suit, keeping a direct line between him and the guy at the counter. When they were standing next to the counter and close to the man, Harley spoke in a deep voice, "Yo soy Pancho."

The guy blinked and seemed unable to discern Harley's intended point. Cole too had no idea what Harley was doing. Now standing next to each other, Cole leaned forward and asked, "What the fuck was that for?"

Harley leaned back towards Cole, his gaze still fixed on the man at the counter, and he whispered back, "It's psychological stuff."

Cole replied, "I don't think he knows English."

Sure enough, the man at the counter just stared blankly at Cole.

Harley stood back up straight and leaned subtly towards the counter, and in a slightly more elevated voice, spoke again, "PANCHO."

The man sat entirely still, his mouth open and his hands resting on the counter. Now convinced that the man posed no threat, Harley turned to Cole and mouthed the words, "See what I did there? I'm fucking with his head." He pointed to the side of his own head and smiled.

"OK. Are you done?"

Harley stared hard at the man once more, then turned to Cole. "Yeah, we're good."

Past the counter, Cole pushed the door open and stepped in, half expecting the earlier encounter to repeat itself. Once inside, and with Harley next to him, Cole found Juan sitting by himself, a dirty short-barreled shotgun resting against the wall. No one spoke. Cole smelled the damp wood and tanned leather, thinking about the impending smell of clean air and open water.

"We got a boat, or what?" asked Harley.

Juan nodded. "Si. I have a boat for you."

"And our customers?"

"Six of them, si. They will be waiting."

Cole asked, "Is that all of them?"

Juan shook his head. "No. They want to split up, a second run next week."

"How many more are there?"

"I don't know, maybe four or five. I don't know."

Cole and Harley looked at each other, acknowledging the first hiccup in their plan rearing its head before they'd even started. *Press on*, Cole thought. "Where's the boat at?"

Juan nodded his head towards the front of the shop. "Downtown, at the wharf."

Juan, Cole, and Harley all set out down the street shortly thereafter. Juan had two of his guys follow close behind. The evening breeze was cool as it rolled off the water, but not cool enough to warrant the thick jackets that each of Juan's men wore. They were both packing something heavy underneath.

Cole looked casually from side to side, confident that Matt, from somewhere unseen, was covering both of them. He felt down to his pocket and pinched with his fingers at the handful of speed strips with extra ammo. Harley seemed less concerned than Cole was.

Sure enough, at the short concrete wharf, a Boston Whaler Cuddy cabin was tied off and waiting. Harley circled wide around the platform until he could peak inside and down below. The boat was empty.

Cole asked, "Where are they?"

Juan looked back up towards the street. "They'll be here."

Juan disappeared back up the sidewalk towards his shop, leaving Cole and Harley with the boat. Cole hopped down and fired up both outboards. They started just fine, and the fuel tanks were topped off. They waited five minutes and both sat leisurely on the aft rail. Cole then got up and shut down both of the engines.

"Might as well save the gas."

An hour passed and still nothing. Nerves were getting the best of Cole, and he struggled to not fidget or tinker with something just to occupy his mind. If Harley felt the same, he wasn't showing it. From his seat at the console, Harley had his feet up and crossed resting next to the throttles. He seemed to be enjoying the midnight air. Had it not been for the terrorists, the drug cartel, and the vast unknown, Cole reckoned he too might have enjoyed the evening.

Suddenly, Harley popped up, something off along the seawall catching his eye. He stood and squinted for a second before smiling. Cole stood up as well and looked, but couldn't make out whatever it was that Harley saw.

"There's Matt," he said casually.

Cole squinted, but still couldn't see it. Harley smiled and continued, "Look just past the street sign on the sidewalk." Cole looked, but saw nothing.

"I don't see him."

Harley laughed. "On our side of the seawall, along the rocks."

Cole looked and saw a tiny bit of movement before he caught the pale green glow from Matt's NVGs. He was tucked up against some rocks, using one of the largest as cover. Crouched down, he blended in seamlessly with the rock wall and had a commanding position over the wharf. Cole immediately felt better. They both looked as Matt raised one arm against the bleached white wall and made a slow chopping motion with a flattened palm towards the other direction.

"They're coming," was all Harley said.

Two minutes later, six figures emerged, casually walking down the concrete steps and onto the wharf. Cole and Harley stood on the back deck of the boat, and the six figures stopped short of the edge. The only sound was the soft rustle of the wind and the light chop slapping against the wharf. Each of the six wore laced-up boots and well-worn pants with loose-fitting and dirty long-sleeve shirts. Three of them carried backpacks, but they were otherwise travelling light for such a long trip.

Harley nodded, smiled, and said, "Hola." Still smiling at the men he would soon kill, he asked, "Estados Unidos?"

The one closest to the boat turned and looked back at the others. Another nodded and they each stepped cautiously onto the deck. Two almost fell as the Grady White bobbed with the wind wrapping around from the north. They were uncomfortable on the boat and huddled near the stern. Cole heard them talk in low whispers, most certainly in Arabic. He shuddered silently, his body going rigid to hide his instinctual discomfort. Even Harley was serious now.

Cole fired up the engines, and three of the six lurched forward, unsure of the rattling and snorting of the motors against their mounts. Cole opened the hatch to the cabin and called out for them, motioning with his hand for them to go below. The first three did, but the fourth man, lighter-skinned and with broad shoulders and a ball cap pulled low on his head, stopped and looked at Cole, close enough so that Cole could hear his thick breathing. Cole nodded, knowing that the man was fighting to establish himself as the alpha male. *Not on this boat,* Cole thought calmly.

"Bueno, Bueno," called Harley and he motioned gently for the fourth man to make his way down. The man stared at Cole for a few seconds more, then ducked his head and went down below. The last two followed. They were packed tight, but each had found a spot on the cushioned seats that wrapped around the cabin below.

Harley ducked down, looked in again, and smiled, saying once more, "Bueno," with a smile. From there, he quickly tossed off both the bow and stern lines and the boat drifted off the concrete wharf and slowly spun to her starboard side. Cole twisted the engines, spinning her smartly around into the wind. He trolled forward, looking back over his shoulder to where Matt had been, but seemed to be no longer. Cole took a breath and grit his teeth, coaxing the small boat further into the darkness ahead.

Once clear of the moorings and the scattering of other workboats at anchor, Harley inched a bit closer to Cole. Over the rumbling of the motors and the steady breeze, they were safe to talk quietly.

"You think that's him?" asked Cole.

Harley nodded. "Yeah, might be."

They were quiet and looking ahead, the wind blowing Cole's dirty long hair across his forehead. Clear of land, the temperature dropped, and after five more minutes, he looked at Harley and asked, "You ready?"

Harley looked at Cole, firm resolve across his face, and nodded. "Do it."

Cole punched the throttles and turned the boat due west. She strained a bit under the weight, but within seconds the boat had lifted itself up onto a steady plane. Cole trimmed it to offset the weight below and looked aft as his wake trailed off behind him, a ghostly moonlit shade of two white streaks that gently rolled off in opposing directions into the darkness. He looked forward again and felt the wind firmly pressing against his chest, drying the sweat that had beaded and dripped onto his shirt. He breathed deep and rhythmically to calm his nerves and sped on for almost five minutes before slowing the boat.

Pulling back gently on the throttles, the bow rose up, pushed a wave in front of it, then sank a bit and settled down to a slow troll. He looked at Harley, then tucked his head down below.

"Amigo, come here for a second."

Harley motioned with his hand and continued, "No, no, him, el rojo, Come here." He motioned again. "Yeah, you. I need some help. Ayuda."

The man now had his ball cap off, revealing thick and crusted greasy red hair. Cole was certain it was Claire's guy. Harley motioned further as the man cautiously followed Harley to the stern. The boat rolled with a wave and the redheaded man nearly lost his footing, reaching down and steadying himself against the rail. He stared, in both anger and confusion, at Harley.

Quietly, Harley asked, "You know Claire?"

The man scowled and shook his head as if he didn't understand the question. Harley looked at Cole, then back to the man, "British?"

The man shook his head, not understanding the question. Harley grinned a bit with one of his mischievous smiles, and asked in a slow exaggerated pronunciation, "J-I-H-A-D?"

Cole, despite their present circumstances, couldn't help but laugh at the absurdity of it, until the redheaded man grabbed at Harley's shirt with both hands and gripped him tight. Harley fought back, trying to counter and break his grip, but to no avail. The redheaded man groaned, nearly picked Harley up off his feet, and slammed him to the deck.

Fuck, Cole thought, as he turned to see the first of the others, now alerted, coming up through the narrow hatch from down below. Cole drew his revolver by instinct, its grip fitting snug in his right hand, and pulled the trigger as he pressed the barrel into the first man's torso. The orange flash was suppressed by his clothing, but still pierced the darkness with a bright and thunderous roar. The man tucked at the waist and fell limp, partially blocking the narrow hatch. Cole kicked him in the head as he fell backwards into the cabin. He heard shouts from down below and looked aft to see Harley struggling underneath the redheaded man.

Still holding the revolver with his right hand, Cole reached at his waist with his left hand and pulled the grenade free from his belt. He fumbled for the pin as the next body emerged from the cabin, trying to climb over his now-dead companion. Cole panicked and fired from a half draw, hitting the man in his forearm as he reached out to grab at Cole. The man screamed in pain, his forearm now broken and hanging at a disgusting angle from where the bones had been shattered. He too now blocked the hatch as the screams and yells from below, all now clearly in Arabic, echoed out into the night air. Cole grit his teeth, steadied his aim as best he could, and hit center mass, his bullet abruptly ending the shrieks. The man slumped forward and collapsed, dark oil-like blood pooling under his lifeless contorted body.

Cole set the gun down on his seat, ripped the pin in one quick pull, and lobbed the grenade down below amidst the howls and hate-filled screams. An eternity passed as Cole retrieved his revolver, dropped to the starboard side of the boat, and shielded his face. The blast, when it finally came, felt as if the whole boat lifted from the water for a second. Cole felt bits of fiberglass falling around him and held his left palm over his eyes. When he opened them again, the left seat of the boat was shredded and pieces of foam were spread out all over the deck. He heard muted moans and labored croaking breaths from down below, but dared not look. Turning aft, he saw Harley on his back, his legs locked around the redheaded man's waist as the man rained down punch after punch onto Harley. Just as soon as Harley could trap one arm, the man, who carried far more mass than Harley, freed himself and threw more heavy hits down at Harley's head.

They were both too tangled for Cole to take a shot, so he dropped his gun, popped up to his feet, and charged across the deck towards the redheaded man. Looping his right arm under the man's neck, Cole pulled himself up onto his back and locked both his legs around the man's waist, holding himself securely on his back. The redheaded man screamed and tried to fight off Cole's arm, but Harley pressed on with his own counterattack and grabbed the redheaded man's left arm with both of his. The man, now carrying the weight of both Cole and Harley, fell backwards with Cole still holding on tight. Just as Matt and Harley had taught him, Cole took a second to wrap his left bicep under his right palm and then snugged his left forearm around the back of the man's head. Not quite confident in his choke, Cole tightened his hold with everything he had, his muscles shaking with every ounce of unchecked violence he could muster.

Harley popped up to his knees, blood covering the left side of his face, and he backed away to take a breath. Drawing his pistol, Harley dove back into the fray and pushed the redheaded man's right arm down before pressing the revolver tight against his skull. Cole, with his own head tucked to his right, turned his head quickly to the left and tucked it firm against his left shoulder, closing his eyes as hard as he could. In an instant, he heard the blast, felt it reverberate into and through the redheaded man's own skull, and felt the life slip from his opponent's body. Cole held the choke for some time, his right bicep cramping under the strain. His ears rang with a steady high-pitched whine, and still he held his eyes closed and his jaw clenched. It was Harley's hand against Cole's shoulder that snapped him back to his surroundings. Over the shrill whine in both his ears, he heard Harley's voice. "Let him go, Cole."

He released his grip and the redheaded man's body rolled to his side. There was blood and bits of disgusting jellied brain on his forearm, and Cole almost felt himself get sick from it. Harley grabbed at Cole's shoulder and turned him so they were staring at each other. Harley had taken quite a beating, but even with his blood-stained teeth, his smile was the same as he asked, "You good?"

Cole took a breath, sat back against the rail, and looked up at the stars above him, then back to Harley. "Yeah. I think I'm good."

He sat as the boat bobbed while Harley cautiously sidestepped to the starboard rail and moved forward, his revolver at full draw. Peeking around the corner and down into the cabin, Harley fired two more shots to silence the last of the dying moans. They were, at last, all dead. Cole felt his heart beating hard against his chest and focused on steadying his breathing.

"Did you steal another grenade?"

Cole looked at Harley, thought for a second, and laughed. "Yeah, sorry."

"Fuck, Cole, what is it with you and grenades?"

Cole just laughed and slowly got up to his feet, blinking and taking long breaths. He looked aft at the dead man slumped against the transom. Harley sat at what remained of the left seat and felt cautiously at his face.

Cole walked forward and sat at the right seat, scanning the instrumentation for a second. He then turned to Harley and asked, "How about you?"

Harley pressed himself further against the back of the seat to rest and nodded. "Yeah. Nothing's broken."

Relieved, Cole pressed the throttles and turned for Cozumel. The boat was sluggish to respond. He looked back at the motors, both spitting out frothy whitewater from their propellers. He straightened the boat and pushed them up, but the boat just surged ahead without lifting up to a plane. The engines groaned, and Cole pulled back the throttles to idle.

What the fuck, he said to himself.

Harley looked down below and said, "We might have a problem."

Cole stepped out of his seat and to his left. In the dim cabin, all but one of the lights were blown out. It was barely enough to make out a shallow pool of crimson water that sloshed around amid the pile of disfigured and bloody bodies. The smell of death mixed horribly with that of the saltwater that now flooded the cabin.

Harley was still feeling at his face as he turned a bit to Cole, who was sitting back in his seat. He asked, "That's a problem, I assume?"

Cole nodded. "Yeah. That's not good." He pushed the throttles up a second time, but still the boat struggled to move forward. As he slowed it, the bow sank lower and Cole looked down below again. The grenade must have split the hull, and with each push of the throttles, the busted seam served only to funnel more water into the boat.

They sat for some time, eventually moving aft and leaning against the transom. Harley tried to make a call with the phone, but they were out of range of any signal. As the bow slowly dropped,, both sat up on the transom, their legs hanging freely underneath, much the same as two kids sitting on a fence in a park.

"What do you think?"

Cole looked over his shoulder, towards Cozumel, the faint lights casting barely a smudge of light to his east. He asked, "Swim?"

Harley looked over his shoulder as well, nodding. "Yeah. Might come down to that." A moment later, he asked, "Sharks around here?"

Cole looked down towards the dead man crumpled at his feet, "Might be pretty soon."

They sat, the breeze light but steadily marching in from the north. It was just after midnight, and the first traces of morning were still hours away. Cole looked forward at the bow, now only a foot or so above the water and sinking farther. The hatch was nearly flooded, with the blood-stained water even darker in the nighttime sky. Cole watched as it slowly crept aft to where both of them sat. Currents of blood swirled around the deck and stained the fiberglass.

Harley laughed and shook his head.

Cole asked, "What?"

"That must have been fucking awesome."

Confused, he asked again, "What was awesome?"

Harley looked forward. "Chucking that grenade in there. I would have liked to have seen their faces."

"So that wasn't him, was it?"

Harley turned and looked at Cole in disbelief. "No, that wasn't him. You serious?"

"I dunno," Cole said defensively.

"No fucking way," Harley replied. "Not even a chance. He must have been Chechen or something. Or his mama got down and dirty with a Russian back in the eighties."

Cole uncontrollably laughed and then caught himself. A sense of calm came over him, one that carried with it memories of better times. He smiled, then turned to Harley. "Shall we?"

Harley replied, "Fuck it. Let's go."

They both kicked off their shoes, dropped their shirts, turned to face the water, and sat in silence on the transom for a moment more. Dark drops of blood ran down and stained Harley's back. Cole was covered by blood as well—thankfully none of it his.

Harley stood up on the aft platform and dove effortlessly into the darkness. He emerged seconds later and shook the water from his face. "Let's go, princess."

Cole smiled, stood on the platform, took one last look over his shoulder at the sinking boat, and leapt head-first into the cool sea.

CHAPTER 17: THE BURNING

THEY WERE TREADING WATER for a minute or so, watching as the transom rose briefly to counter the sinking bow. It rolled gently to its starboard side and sat suspended for a few moments more before the port quarter slipped into the darkness. Some bubbles boiled up on the surface, and bits of debris floated about the chop. Cole turned to Harley, who kicked hard and raised his head, looking off towards what they both hoped was the east.

"Steady pace—stay with me," said Harley as he rolled forward and took his first strong strokes. Cole followed as best he could, struggling to build momentum against the rising and falling waves. Taking full strides into the face of waves was nearly impossible, but he followed along with Harley, determined not to give up. Within minutes he was out of breath and felt as if panic might take hold. Raising his head, he looked forward to see Harley rhythmically cutting ahead, rolling to breathe after a handful of strokes.

Cole couldn't find that same rhythm. Harley stopped up ahead, treaded in place, and looked back to Cole. Breathing forcefully, he asked, "Need a break?"

Cole nodded. He rolled into an almost upright position, treading on his back and looking up at the stars. He took long breaths and coughed to clear some water from his throat. The gun was weighing him down, so he pulled it from its holster. "I gotta let this gun go."

Harley smiled. "I dropped mine ten minutes ago."

Cole released his grip and felt it disappear from his hand. It may have been more imagination than reality, but Cole felt as if he'd lost ten times its actual weight. He took a long breath and leaned farther onto his back, the warm water acting like a pillow under his head. He felt the sea lift him up and gently lay him back down into the trough, rocking him gently like a child. Alone with his thoughts, Cole focused on the moment he was in.

Live or die, he thought. *I'm good with it.*

"You doing yoga over there or what?"

Cole turned to face Harley. "Just enjoying the moment."

A wave lifted Harley up, and he surged again out of the water, kicking hard to get his bearings. As the crest passed, it lifted Cole briefly before sliding underneath him, marching further south and disappearing into the black. He saw the faintest light to the east, its pale glow just above the horizon.

"How far were we?" asked Harley.

"Maybe a bit over a mile."

"We should get moving then. You ready?"

Cole nodded and the two set off again. This time, Cole focused entirely on his breathing, trying not to strain or fight against the water. With some forward movement, he eased his strokes until his muscles moved without much resistance. He popped his head up and saw that he was matching Harley's stride. As his breathing slowed, he kept his head underwater longer, spacing his breaths between every fourth stroke. The water surged and ran against his head, across his face, and rolled down his torso where it slid down his legs and trailed off behind. He'd found his rhythm. Before long, even with the waves, Cole felt as one with the ocean, the cool unending rush of water against his face washing away the stains and the pain that had, up until that moment, clouded and poisoned his mind.

His muscles relaxed, and within minutes, he was in a trance. Opening his eyes with each breath, he caught a glimpse of the black sky above and felt the breeze blowing in strong from the north. Bits of spray lifted off the backs of passing waves, and cooled by the air, they touched the back of his head like tiny bits of ice. He laughed as he swam onward, glancing forward every half a minute to keep tabs on Harley. Half an hour passed, and they stopped once again. Harley was taking deep breaths, but seemed full of energy. Cole felt much the same. He'd slept horribly over the past 36 hours. His life had been primed for a bitter ending just hours before, but now, amid the darkness around him and the stars above, Cole felt euphoric.

As they tread water, the moon emerged momentarily from behind the column of a cumulus cloud, and a vivid but broken reflection danced off the water, giving them the first clear horizon they'd seen. An endless plain of disorganized whitecaps danced on the surface before slipping away on the backs of the rolling waves. Each bit of chop carried a flicker of light for a second or two before the ever-changing landscape faded and a new one tried to stand its ground against the unrelenting sea.

They pressed on. Cole felt a cramp in his hamstring and reminded himself of Harley's advice, *steady pace*. He backed off his kicks for a few seconds and felt his legs along for the ride, flowing effortlessly with the passing water. When he kicked again, the cramp was gone. It was the better part of another hour before Cole felt Harley slowing down. The waves were changing, now stacking up against themselves, disturbed by something below. Harley popped his head up, then disappeared below the surface, leaving Cole by himself.

A moment later, he re-surfaced, the moon highlighting a smile across Harley's face. "Ten feet of water—maybe less."

Harley turned and took another stroke towards shore. As Cole did the same, he saw a light on the horizon to their right. Ten minutes later, more lights, all to the north, confirmed that they were close. Cole took longer strokes, advancing until he was next to Harley. He was startled when his hand touched something hard and craggy below him. Harley must have hit it as well, because he abruptly stopped and rolled onto his back. Cole did the same, and set his knees down on the rock before rolling over and sitting chest deep in the water. Waves broke to the south, rolling in with the familiar sound of whitewater. A larger wave rolled in towards Harley and Cole, knocking them off the rock and into deeper water. When they both reemerged, they laughed like two children playing in the waves.

They swam another 50 yards, across a deeper lagoon, and then stood delicately in knee-deep water, their bare feet inching ahead to avoid the unseen coral heads. Cole found a bit of sand and sunk his toes deep into it. It confirmed what he had so far refused to believe. *We made it.*

Once on the shoreline, just above the tideline, they sat nearly shoulder to shoulder and looked out at the featureless and desolate sea. The wind rustled palm fronds behind them and weaved a meandering course along the shoreline. Out over the water, it blew steadily from the north, and Cole wondered how they'd made it through the whitecaps and the waves. He was physically exhausted, but his mind felt strong, almost as if he could go out and do it again. Wiping the salt water from his face, he ran both his hands through his hair and lay back on the cool sand. The sun would be up in a few hours, and Cole's eyes walked a circuitous path across the night sky, stopping briefly to stare at the moon.

"Feels good, right?" asked Harley.

Cole nodded. Nothing else was said.

THEY MAY HAVE BEEN there for an hour, but neither tracked the time. When the sun was up, they might start making their way back to town, but it made no sense to struggle more than necessary in the dark. Cole nodded off briefly before Harley shook him and motioned to be quiet. Cole rolled softly onto his left side and looked up towards the tree line, where Harley was staring. Neither of them dared to make a sound. A stick broke somewhere beyond the perimeter of the jungle.

Harley called out, "Matt?"

Two more quick snaps of twigs followed some intense rustling of leaves and a figure emerged from the brush. Harley smiled.

"I swear you two picked the absolute worst fucking spot in the entire fucking world."

Harley smacked Cole's back squarely between the shoulder blades and popped up to his feet. Matt walked casually down to meet them, wiping away the dirt and grime that he'd accumulated. The two shook his hands. Matt had his goggles on and held his M4 loosely by his side. Two more mags were affixed to his belt. His pants were filthy, covered in mud and sand. His shirt was soaked in sweat and torn in several places.

Harley pulled the phone from his pocket. Holding it in his hand, he flipped it open. "Wasn't sure this thing would even work."

Matt laughed. "Glad you didn't give it to Cole."

Smiling, Cole turned and looked once more out at the sea and chewed on his lower lip. He was thankful to be alive.

Matt caught a glimpse of the side of Harley's face, and he grimaced. "You look like shit."

Harley nodded. "Yeah. Old boy knew how to fight."

"How many?"

"Six," Cole replied.

"One was a ginger," Harley added.

Matt looked at them without a word. Harley assured him, "It wasn't him. Not a chance. He was trying too damn hard to kill both of us."

Matt took a breath and exhaled. "So there's more of them?"

Cole nodded. "Yeah, maybe another five or six."

"That may explain it."

"Explain what?" asked Harley.

"The town's a warzone. Come on—I'll show ya."

They crept back into the jungle. Cole was more concerned about snakes and critters in the mud than he was for the sharks in the water. If Harley was concerned, he didn't show it. It took them another 30 minutes to make it back to the gravel road where Matt had parked. Hunkered down just out of sight, Matt swept up and down the road with his goggles before motioning them to come out. Cole's feet were cut, but not nearly as badly as he'd feared traversing the unkempt jungle. He felt his own sweat burn against some open scratches on his arms, torso, and legs, but otherwise he was all right. Matt fired up the Thing and both Harley and Cole sat in the back. They quickly emptied the half dozen bottles of water that Matt had brought along. Cole drank two and poured the last one over his head, washing away the stinging salt from his eyes and lifting his head against the cold breeze as Matt sped north along the road, back towards town. Harley's M4 was on the floor and he picked it up, pulling the handle back to see the moonlight reflect off the brass case in the chamber. He set it across his lap and finished his last bottle of water.

As they passed the first familiar landmarks, Cole got his bearings. Matt kept the speed up and stayed off the main drag, weaving a course back and forth among the dark side roads. Most were empty with crossing traffic sporadic at best. Fifteen minutes later, he slowed on an alley that led out to the main road running along the beach. Cole heard sirens in the distance. Matt took off his helmet and goggles, then passed them back to Harley who tucked them under the seat. He then pulled his M4 tight against his side. Harley wrapped his right hand around the grip of his pistol and rested his left palm over the handguard to keep his rifle out of sight.

Matt turned and joined the spaced-out traffic running south along the road. Orange flames leapt into the sky from somewhere up ahead and to their left. The lights from downtown were enough to make out the thick black smoke that billowed from wherever the fire burned. Cole's eyes confirmed what he already suspected. The boot shop was ablaze. As they passed the shop, Cole trembled at the sight of three charred bodies hanging from light poles. Police cars and fire trucks had formed a loose perimeter around the crime scene, but the firefighters seemed to be merely waiting for the fire to die.

As he passed the scene and sped on, Matt turned and looked back at Cole briefly. He drove a different route back to the villa and tucked the Thing against the inside wall. Once inside, Harley and Cole ate all but a few of the remaining contents from the refrigerator, washing it all down with a few beers.

As they ate, Matt asked, "Cartel or our friends?"

Cole looked up and chewed, thinking as he did. "Hard to say, I guess."

"Both of them have a thing for burning people," Harley added as he stuffed his face with leftover rice and beans.

Matt pulled a chair around to a far wall with a direct view of the front door. With his M4, he sat and leaned back, saying softly, "Why don't y'all get a few hours of sleep. Today might be a long one."

CLAIR WAS IN THE kitchen making coffee when Cole woke up. The clink of a mug against the tile counter was the first sound he recognized. Sprawled on the couch, he came to and blinked several times without moving. He smelled the coffee and pushed himself up, stretching his muscles as he stood and arched his back. A giant yawn seized his jaw. Despite the past two days, he felt better than he expected. He walked slowly across the room, past Matt who was still seated at the same chair, and leaned against the counter. Claire pushed a mug towards him, turning as she did, and asked, "What did he look like?"

"Who?" Cole asked.

"The redhead."

"Taller than me by a bit, broad shoulders, crazy eyes." Cole paused and thought about it before he continued, "He had crazy fucking eyes."

Claire nodded, relieved.

"Not your boy?" Cole asked.

Claire shook her head. "No. He's your height."

"Oh." Cole added, "He seemed dead set on killing the both of us."

Claire laughed. "Well, then—that's not him."

Cole took a quick sip of coffee, jealous of whatever man Claire was so concerned about, and walked out from the front door. Matt called out, "Cole, don't go too far."

Turning back, Cole replied, "Just sitting right here."

He took a seat at a thick wooden bench that backed up against the villa's wall. In the balcony's shade, the morning was cool. A pastel blue blanket of light hung low over the red horizon, where from somewhere beyond the sun would soon rise. Cole wrapped both his hands around the mug and crossed his bare feet in front of him, his heels resting on the smooth Spanish-tiled walkway. He thought back to waking up on the back of a southbound trawler, somewhere in southern depths of the Caribbean. It had all been so new and exciting to him then. His mind then wandered to man and woman whose charred remains he'd solemnly buried with a borrowed shovel. Staring up at the sky, he wished that he'd simply played along with Potts' stupid games on *Delaney*. *Maybe I'd be the CO of a boat by now, like Wheeler.* He also thought of Matt, and how the two of them shared a wild streak, a freak gene perhaps, that kept men like them from following stable and predictable paths in life. Minutes later, he squinted when the first blinding light pierced the sky, followed by the familiar warmth of the Caribbean sun. The temperature rose almost immediately and Cole listened as the birds stirred to life.

His mind snapped back to Carentan, and his heart trembled, fearing the onset of the sullenness that always came with those memories. But as he sat there alone, Cole felt a clarity that he'd been denied up until that moment. For the first time, he didn't need to force thoughts of France from his mind. He dwelled on them for a few more minutes, taking evenly spaced sips of the coffee and feeling its warmth against his chest. The fiery colors of the morning light faded, and Cole heard dogs in the distance. He smelled the dirt and dust in the air as the early morning bustle of trucks and motorcycles drove by outside the gate. He felt content to live in that moment and that was enough to make him happy.

After about an hour, Matt called for Cole to come back in. Huddled around the table, Harley was the last to come downstairs, a pair of boardshorts around his waist and his M4 gripped by his left hand at its forend. He smacked Cole on the back and smiled as he walked around to the far side and sat down. Claire offered him a cup of coffee, which Harley readily accepted.

"Do you want some ice for that?"

Harley touched his cheek, swollen and red with a dark blue center just below his eye. "Oh, this—it's nothing. You should see the other guy." He winked at Claire with his swollen eye as he spoke. She shook her head and poured second cups for Cole and Matt.

Taking a sip, Matt put down his cup and swallowed. He waited several seconds before speaking. "We need to talk."

He looked around at each of them, took another sip, and carefully set the mug back down before continuing. "They're threatening to hold Gene Thomas in contempt."

"What does that mean?" Cole asked.

"They know Johnson is dead. The cops found him last night. Effective immediately, we are shut down and supposed to get out tonight after dark." No one spoke as the gravity of it all sank in.

Harley asked, "What do they want from Gene Thomas?"

"Whatever he'll give them, but he's staying quiet."

Claire added, "And knowing him, he'll stay quiet."

Matt turned to Cole and looked squarely into his eyes. "Cole, no one here blames you for Johnson."

He scanned to Harley and Claire, who both nodded to affirm the statement. Cole looked up and away from them, the guilt weighing on him again. Matt continued, "This thing was out of control before it started, Cole."

Cole nodded, still not entirely convinced.

"Cole, he sold us all out to get a shot at the top."

Harley added, "Dude had it coming, Cole. He sold out his own fucking country."

Perhaps it was their swim the night before, but for Cole, Harley's words carried the most weight, having triumphed together under such adversity the night before. His thoughts and words often seemed laconic at best, but Harley had a way of saying little while conveying more than anyone else could. Cole trusted that they weren't just trying to make him feel better.

Claire offered up, in her own comforting way, "My mother will not be sad to see him go."

As was so often the case, it tipped the conversation in the right direction as they all laughed, almost embarrassed at the humor over Johnson's fate.

Cole inhaled deeply, held his breath for a moment then exhaled, and felt better. "I fucking hated that guy."

Matt, now assured that Cole was managing his mind, smiled and nodded. "Now, how do we finish this?"

Cole thought about the question for some time. They debated whether it was the cartel that had burned Juan, his shop, and his companions or the remnants of the cell. Or perhaps it was the unknown middleman that brokered the deal between the two of them. If the cartel knew their own men had been slaughtered, it was probably them who'd gone after Juan. And if they killed him, they likely tortured every last bit of information out of him before they strung him from the light pole and doused him in gasoline. On the other hand, if it was the cell that did it, they too were likely pulling information in uncomfortable ways from Juan before they ended his suffering. The safest assumption was that there were, at a minimum, two different groups on their tiny island looking to burn some more bodies.

Harley said, "I think we should run."

Matt turned, a disapproving look on his face, and asked, "What?"

Harley grinned, the joke at Matt's expense, and answered, "Come on, bud. I'm just fucking with you. Let's go kick in their door and make some bad guys bleed."

"Which door?" Claire asked, seemingly all right with Harley's bullish plan of attack.

Harley nodded, acknowledging that he didn't know for certain of any doors that hid any of the guys they were up against.

"Are they still in that house?"

Claire shook her head. "I haven't had a good mark in over a week."

Matt finished his coffee and leaned back, his hands crossed over his head as he stared up at the ceiling. He thought for a while, then leaned back down and pressed his forearms into the table. "Claire, are they online?"

"What do you mean?" she asked.

"Chatter—can you see their conversations?"

She rocked her head and replied, "Not directly, but we see spikes in some targeted sectors. So much of this is a guessing game."

"Let's get this place ready to close out for now. One way or the other, we're heading out tonight."

They set about collecting all of their maps, papers, and bits and pieces they'd collected over the past months. Harley lit a fire in the middle of the grass and went about burning it all to ashes. Claire tossed one of her laptops out as well, keeping her second up and running at the table. When they were done, Cole took a long shower, standing for what seemed like an eternity under the hot running water. Each time he thought he'd rinsed the salt from his hair, he'd feel it burn again in the corners of his eyes and repeat the process. Once he was certain he was clean, he finally stepped out and dried off, changing into a pair of jeans and pulling his boots from the closet. He had one clean pair of socks, and he pulled them over his feet before sliding them back once more into the worn and dusty leather. He found a linen shirt, pulled it across his back, and buttoned up the bottom three buttons. He stopped to look in the mirror. So much had happened in his short life, but if it had aged him, Cole couldn't see it. He thought far back to *Delaney* and how he'd looked at himself the morning he'd been kicked off the ship. *If nothing else,* he told himself, *I ain't easy to kill.*

BY LATE AFTERNOON, there was a smoldering pile of ashes on the lawn. All their clothes, except for those on their backs, were burned as well. Sheets, pillows, towels, and anything else that could be burned was gone. Every magazine they had was topped off as well, spread out on various tables around the room. Cole was now stuck with a short-barreled shotgun, having disposed of the two revolvers in his charge. The shotgun held six rounds of buckshot, and he wore a bandoleer across his chest like some desperado from a western. *Fitting*, Cole thought. Matt and Harley carried their M4s with their vests and pistols attached at their chest. Harley had even opted to put on a pair of pants in anticipation of a good fight before they left.

Claire was sitting patiently at the table, watching her computer. She'd made several phone calls, each time returning to her computer. Harley and Matt were eating and Cole was in the corner, seated at a chair with his feet up and crossed in front of him, the bandoleer loose and over his chest.

"They're talking," she said, so softly that none of them caught on at first.

"Who?" Matt asked.

"It's them," she replied. She read quickly, her eyes scanning back and forth. She read for a few seconds more, then continued, "They're concerned the others didn't make it."

From the corner of the room, Harley grinned at Cole. Cole couldn't avoid smiling as well.

Matt asked, "What are they saying?"

"They're asking someone for instructions. They want to know what happened, but it's just a bunch of back and forth."

Harley spoke. "Tell them we killed their buddies."

Claire shook her head to dismiss the idea as childish.

Matt looked at Harley for a second, then back at Claire, "No, maybe that's an option."

Claire looked up and countered, "What good will that do?"

Matt nodded, solidifying the idea in his head, "They're on the defense right now, and they're confused. We can capitalize on that."

"That's a bit of a stretch for standard protocol."

"Claire…"

"What?" She asked.

"Is any of this the 'protocol' that you're used to?"

"No, I suppose not." She thought for a moment. "What should I type?"

Matt smiled. "We killed your boys."

She hesitated, shaking her head, then slowly typed out the words and mashed the key to send, then reached up to rub her lips with her thumb. A few seconds passed, and Claire perked up in her seat.

Harley walked over and leaned in, saying enthusiastically, "Oh, they don't seem to have liked that."

Claire's phone rang and she answered. She nodded her head several times, then finished the call with a promise. "Yes, we are leaving now." When she hung up, she shook her head, saying, "Well, now I've done it."

"Who was that?" Matt asked.

"Back home. They didn't like our little love note."

"So everyone is watching this shit?"

"Probably more than you think," Claire replied.

Her phone rang again and she rolled her eyes when she looked at the number.

"Hello, Mother."

Claire nodded several more times, then spoke. "Yes, I know." She paused for a few moments and continued, now a bit frustrated. "We are leaving, yes. Well, I didn't see any other way."

She hung up the phone and turned to Matt. "Well, now I have some explaining to do."

Matt grinned and asked, "Back to our boys, anything more?"

"Well, as a matter of fact, yes. They want to know who we are."

They all paused, now seated back around the table. Looking back and forth, Matt's eyes stopped at Harley. He asked, "Thoughts?"

Harley's focus intensified. "Reel 'em in."

Matt turned back to Claire, "Tell them."

"Tell them what?" she asked.

Matt tilted his head, then replied, "Our address."

CHAPTER 18: THE FIGHT

MATT AND HARLEY pre-positioned ammo throughout the house and hid a few more magazines outside around the courtyard's perimeter. They moved quickly and within 20 minutes, they were all standing around the table. Claire was packing up her computer as Matt and Harley tugged at straps on their vests and made their final adjustments to their gear. Cole, with his shotgun in one hand, fidgeted with the bandoleer across his chest. He had never prepared for a fight like this before and tried hard to hide the apprehension creeping up on him. *Buckshot is straightforward enough,* he told himself.

Matt asked, "You sure they're coming?"

Claire looked up at him, closed her laptop and tucked it into a bag, and nodded. "Yes, they are coming."

Harley adjusted the stock on his M4 and shouldered it a few times in rapid succession, content with his setup. Matt let go of his M4 and it hung loosely by his side, attached by a single-point sling across his chest. He thumbed at the hammer of the Sig holstered also across his chest.

"I'll take upstairs," Matt said as he extended his hand to Harley. They gripped firmly and pulled each other in to a momentary embrace. Matt did the same to Cole, then he hugged Claire and said softly, "See ya in a bit."

Matt hustled up the steps and set up by one of the windows. Harley and Cole hung out downstairs, Cole by the table and Harley standing halfway inside the door, casually looking and listening for the first sounds of movement. Claire had on a pair of pants and shoes with a loose-fitting t-shirt over her tall and slender frame. She looked as if she was ready for a photo shoot, but her face told an entirely different story.

She smiled at Cole, then looked away. He felt some comfort in the fact that she was also trying to hide the same apprehension.

Harley perked up when he heard a door slam shut outside on the road. He knelt down and shouldered his rifle, but nothing happened. A minute passed, and he let it back down, standing again by the doorway. Half an hour passed with not much more than the occasional truck speeding by or dogs barking down the road. The waiting and the unknown was killing Cole. He felt a lump in his throat and pulled back gently against the bolt to verify for the fourth or fifth time that a round of buckshot was indeed ready to go.

Harley pressed against his ear with his finger, then turned to Cole and Claire, saying, "Showtime."

Cole moved across the room to the opposite side of the large window in the living room. From across the room, he quietly asked, "Where?"

Harley motioned with his hand towards the far back concrete wall that bordered up against the narrow side street. With Matt covering the wall, Harley was keeping his eyes towards the gate out front. On the ground floor, they all heard a car come to a stop, its tires crunching against the loose rocks of the broken driveway. Cole could hardly breathe and felt his vision narrowing. He forced air into his lungs and told himself, *Steady.*

A single loud crack of a gunshot echoed out from beyond the gate, followed by what sounded like a fight. Harley slowly took a step out, his rifle sighted in at the gate, as he took a look before ducking back inside. He turned to Cole and shrugged his shoulders, then spoke into the microphone attached to his helmet. Harley and Matt were on the same page, and it reassured Cole that they still held the advantage.

Several more thuds came from just beyond the gate, and Harley turned to Cole again, motioning for him to move forward as Harley stepped out. Cole moved and kept his barrel just to Harley's right as the two of them moved cautiously forward. A yell startled them, as there was clearly a fight just out of sight beyond the gate. From behind the two of them, Claire emerged running forward at the gate. Harley tried to call out to her, but Claire was up on top of the hood of the Thing before either of them could react. With a stainless Walther PPK in her hands, she steadied her aim downward and took two rapid shots, then hopped over the gate and disappeared.

"Fuck," Harley called out as he sprinted forward to the gate, kicked it open and rounded the corner. Cole was right behind him. On the ground in front of a dirty old sedan was a body with blood running out from under the head. It was face down on the concrete, with mangled black hair and soiled clothing. Not five feet beyond that, Harley drew down on a lanky figure that was bashing in the head of a second body with the butt of a Kalashnikov rifle. The muffled crack of his skull crunching echoed from each downward thrust of the rifle.

"Harry," Claire called out, trying to catch her breath.

The wild-eyed man put his entire weight behind one final *coup de gras*, and then he lowered the gun before turning to Claire. His finger now on the trigger and muzzle towards the unknown man, Harley called out to no one in particular, "What the fuck?"

Standing up with his rifle in one hand, the man nervously turned to Claire, who was tucking her Walther back in the small of her back. Seconds later, they embraced firmly and the unkempt figure came to life and nearly picked her up, twisting from side to side as they embraced. His hair was disheveled and it nearly stood vertically on its own before falling in varying directions over his back. He had a lengthy beard and was in khaki dress pants that were so dirty, they'd been stained entirely brown. He wore plain leather shoes and a loose green pullover shirt that was also disgustingly soiled.

"Claire," he called out as they continued in their embrace. His accent was British.

"You smell horrific, Harry."

He smiled, held the hug for a moment more, and defended himself, "Hygiene hasn't been a priority—sorry."

When they finally released their grips, they still held each others' hands. Claire hugged him again, releasing her embrace before turning to Cole and Harley, introducing Harry to the others.

"My brother, Harry," was all she said with tears welling in the corners of her gorgeous dark eyes.

"Fuck me," Harley said as he pivoted and checked down each side of the road before lowering his rifle. He extended a hand, and the two cautiously shook. Cole stepped up and did the same. Harry's face was thin but chiseled, hardened no doubt by nearly two years of malnourishment and whatever else he'd endured. Still panting, Harry looked back down at the two men he'd just killed.

"Thanks," he said to Claire as he took a gulp of air and exhaled calmly through his nose before continuing, "The bloody thing jammed on me. Can you believe that? An AK of all things."

"You're welcome," she said, unable to contain the smile as she looked him over.

Harry was still perturbed about the gun, shaking his head disapprovingly and adding, "I've told them for two bloody years to clean these damn things."

"Where are the others?" Harley asked.

Harry quickly replied, "They're coming from around back. Can we get back inside?"

"Yeah. Follow me."

The four of them moved quickly back to the gate, where Harley scanned cautiously around the courtyard then motioned for them to move. As soon as they were inside the courtyard, the low wall now behind them and the front door of the villa ten yards away, the far side of the courtyard opened up with gunfire. Cole, Claire, and Harry dove to their left, behind a row of waist-high cement flower pots. Cole heard and felt the bullets fly just over his head. Bits of cement dust drifted down as bullets chipped away at the pots. Claire had drawn her Walther again and crouched down, keeping her head below the ledge of the pots. Cole struggled to bring his shotgun around to his shoulder.

From above, Matt was dumping an unending and steady rate of fire into the far wall, with his empty brass clinking against the tiled walkways below. While the three of them had ducked back, Harley had somehow made his way halfway across the courtyard and was crouched behind a column, also firing back at the wall with steady and precise fire. Cole sensed the returning fire shifting towards Matt and Harley, so he popped his head up momentarily, but could see nothing but muzzle blasts, perhaps from two different positions on the wall. He rolled to his side towards Harry and Claire, yelling over the gunfire for them to move.

Still doubled over, they sprinted towards the door of the villa. Halfway between, and fully exposed, they fell to the ground as the whole villa shook with a massive explosion. Cole had tripped over his own feet as he ran, but stood quickly again as Harry was busy helping Claire back up before all three of them made it inside the door.

Claire asked, "What was that?"

Harry looked around the door towards the courtyard and yelled out to Harley, "They've got vests."

Harley had by now regained his footing and moved forward once again, his rifle still drawn on the far wall amidst the thick smoke and ash of debris drifting down.

Harry turned to Claire and Cole back inside. "The blast was outside the wall, but it knocked a hole in it." Claire looked confused as he continued, "Most likely that was Khalid."

Cole asked, "Who is Khalid?"

Harry shook his head, disapprovingly, and yelled over the increasing volley of gunfire, "The village idiot." He was silent for a moment before continuing in a thick British accent, "I told them *not* to give him a vest. They've got one more vest, and there might be two more if Khalid didn't blow them up." He looked around the room for a weapon of his own.

Cole went to the door and peaked outside, asking, "Harley, you good?"

"I'm out of ammo. Cover me."

Cole stepped out and sprinted towards the column where Harley was crouching. The entire lawn was awash in dust and dirt swirling around in the air. The far wall had been blown open, a brown haze sitting low against the ground and moving slowly with the midday breeze.

Matt called out from above, "Ammo."

Cole turned back towards Claire and Harry, yelling out, "Can you run ammo up to Matt?"

"On it," Claire replied as Cole turned back to Harley.

"Cover me, I'm going for ammo."

There was a fruit tree 20 yards farther towards the wall where Harley had stashed more magazines. They now had the advantage, with most of their assailants either shot or blown up. Two remained at most, likely tucked somewhere behind the wall. Cole hoped that they'd both been blown up, but he knew better than to count on it. He shouldered his shotgun and held the front bead on the crumbled portion of the wall, moving forward another ten yards to a large concrete pot.

Harley sprinted ahead and three steps into it, a dark figure emerged from the settling dust, running towards the center of the villa. Once clear of the rubble, he opened fire towards Harley, and Cole pulled the trigger without thinking, the recoil snapping the shotgun back and upwards before settling back down. He placed his right foot behind him to steady himself and fired until the bolt locked back in the open position. He'd stopped the guy's advance, at least momentarily, but the buckshot was out of range to kill him. Whoever had run into the courtyard was now tucked behind a palm tree and yelling in Arabic. Harley had ducked against a wall, five yards short of his extra ammo. Cole was busy reloading as Matt fired single well-placed shots at the tree. It wasn't big enough to fully conceal the figure behind it, and with his third shot, Matt connected and hit the gunman in the back, sending him forward and reeling in pain. As he emerged from behind the tree, Matt sent one final shot into his chest, and the man slumped backwards, collapsing to the ground.

Topped off, Cole stood up and moved slightly to his right to cover Harley. Matt called out from above them, "I'm out, I'm out."

Just as he did, a second figure emerged from behind the wall at a full sprint towards the center of the courtyard. He carried no weapon, but ran fully exposed towards them, leaping over the concrete rubble as he moved closer. Harley was moving again by now, but not towards his ammo. Leaning forward and accelerating, he leapt over a chair as Cole drew his sight on the attacker. His finger on the trigger, he caught a glimpse of Harley in his line of sight and moved the barrel away so as not to hit him.

Harley and the charging man collided on the cement walkway around the pool. Wrapping his arms firmly around the attacker's torso, Harley spun 270 degrees, every striation of muscle in his arms nearly busting out from his skin as he lifted and twisted his opponent. With a fluid movement, Harley steadied both of his feet, his arms now trapping both arms of the man and lifted him up and over his head as the two of them fell backwards into the pool.

A wall of whitewater exploded into the air and knocked Cole backwards where he fell onto his side. A shower of water followed and soaked him and all the surrounding area. Cole struggled to stand up, falling down to his knees with a pulsing dizziness in his head. Water rushed past him and he blinked as he tried to focus on the wall that he was leaning up against. There were bits of glass on the patio behind him from the windows being blown out. He pushed himself up to one knee and opened his mouth wide to try and ease the ringing in his ears.

From behind, Harry sprinted towards Cole and pulled him over to his other side, running his hands up and down Cole's torso and legs, checking for wounds but finding none. He said, "You're good, mate. You're good," before he ran farther ahead, holding a pistol at full draw. Ducking against a tree, Harry looked up and called out, "Matt, I'm moving."

Matt, back at his perch, called out, "Go," with no emotion in his voice.

Harry moved forward in an arcing sweep of the courtyard to the far wall where he moved along it towards the bombed-out portion. He stopped for a second, then pivoted and disappeared behind it into the unsettled dusty haze. Still unsteady, Cole got to his feet and held the shotgun in one hand, walking in disbelief towards the pool.

A dark red stain towards the center cast shades of pink out towards the edge of the pool. The water was still disturbed by the millions of rising bubbles that lay a thin film across its surface. Cole looked down, unsure of what to do. He tried to breathe and felt as if he'd just run a marathon. The entire fight could not have lasted more than five minutes, but the destruction left behind seemed to indicate otherwise. He said nothing out loud, but in his mind, he heard it over and over again, *Harley.*

He'd been right in front of Cole thirty seconds earlier, fearless and defiant as always. But now as the water settled, there was nothing left. Still Cole waited, as if somehow Harley would miraculously pop up, shake the water from his face, and head in to the kitchen for a beer.

From around the wall, Harry reappeared and walked slowly back to the center of the courtyard, motioning to Matt that the fight was indeed over. Claire was soon out and running towards Cole, her expression saying more than any words ever could. Standing by his side, she looked over and down into the pool before turning to Cole and burying her head into his shoulder. He slid his left arm firmly under her right shoulder and pulled her tight, with his right hand still cupping the shotgun. Harry joined them and looked on solemnly, saying nothing, as he knew the bond between them all was something fierce.

Matt was the last to come outside, having topped off his magazines. Cole let go of Claire as she turned to her brother, and the two stood side by side. Harry ran his hand against the back of her neck and he looked up at the now-clear midday sky above. Cole turned and walked back towards Matt, the silence becoming increasingly uncomfortable.

"We gotta move," was all Matt said.

From the edge of the pool, Claire asked, "What about Harley?"

"He's gone, Claire. There's nothing left."

She knew it to be true and took a deep breath, looking one last time at the water, perhaps in her mind thinking too that Harley would pop up any second, revealing that it had all been just a prank.

Matt moved towards the Thing, which had been damaged, but started just fine. The windshield was cracked in several places and bullets had torn open the metal panels. With it running, Matt looked underneath before standing back up and climbing in.

"Nothing's leaking," Matt said as he shifted into gear and stared straight ahead. Cole could tell that the loss of Harley was setting in for Matt as well, despite his efforts to focus on the mission. Cole walked up to the gate and pushed it open, taking a moment to stare at the dozens of bullet holes that had ripped up the concrete wall. How they'd survived the initial gunfire, he had no idea. It was even more amazing that Harley had moved forward under all that fire. He had seemed superhuman.

Cole ran back into the villa while Harry and Claire climbed in the Thing, Claire in the backseat and Harry sitting shotgun. Inside, Cole swept his arm across the table and gathered the last of the spare magazines into one Pelican case. From the far side of the room, he gathered the remaining grenades, taking a moment to think about Harley, and slid each of them against his belt. There were small bloodstains on his jeans and he fought back the confused thoughts from his mind. Grabbing the case with magazines, he slung the shotgun over his back and ran for the Thing, jumping in the backseat as Matt pulled out and onto the street.

Idling, Matt asked, "Any ideas?"

Cole was quick to answer, "The water, just head for the water. We'll find a boat."

Matt spun the tires, struggled to get her into third gear and accelerated wildly down the street. In a spray-painted and bullet-ridden Volkswagen Thing, four gringos speeding through downtown Cozu-

mel were quickly drawing unwanted attention. And it was nearly impossible to hide the handful of pistols and rifles they carried. *Maybe
bringing all this ammo wasn't such a good idea,* Cole thought. Just as Matt
slowed at a busy intersection, a truck up ahead veered hard to its right,
directly at Matt. Reacting immediately, Matt turned hard and accelerated up over a concrete median and into opposite traffic. The truck followed, with at least two men in the cab and three standing in the bed,
pointing wildly and yelling.

The chase continued for several more blocks as Matt yelled out
over the wind, "Who they fuck is that?"

"Not the cops," Cole replied as he looked over his shoulder.

"Cartel?" Claire asked, as she drew her PPK calmly once more
from her back.

Cole looked at her and asked, "How long you had that?"

Claire smiled, "The whole time."

Laughing for a moment, Cole instinctively ducked as he heard gunfire from behind. He crouched and turned to see that the men in the
cab were firing at them. Claire turned and fired off evenly spaced shots.
Over the swerving of the Thing and the jolting from the pock-marked
road, neither's shots were connecting. Harry didn't bother returning
fire, opting to sit calmly up front and look on ahead as Matt was wholly
consumed by driving.

Cole steadied himself and turned, propping one knee up on the
seat and his back against Harry's seat. He pulled the first grenade,
gripped it as Harley had shown him, and pulled the pin, waiting for the
right time to hurl it backwards. Exploding mid-air and behind the truck,
Cole pulled a second and lobbed it down at the street. The truck
swerved as the grenade blew up just as it passed.

Matt asked, "How many more of those you got?"

"Five," Cole replied as he pulled the pin on the third and waited. A
shot connected with the back of thing and made a pinging noise as it
tore through the back panel. They were trailing them now from 50 or

so yards back, outside the range of the grenades, but still within shooting range. Out of frustration, Cole chucked it and the truck swerved again. It was at least distracting the truck and keeping them from making better shots.

"Give me your rifle," Harry said to Matt.

Unclipping the sling, he slid it over and Harry shouldered it.

"I have an idea. Take a turn up ahead and drop me off. Go another fifty yards or so beyond that and stop, as if you're stuck."

Cole chucked another grenade to push the truck further back. Matt nodded and accelerated to build some distance. As an alley approached, he slowed, but then sped on as it was straight-walled and had no places to hide. Two more times he slowed, but then continued on. Cole hurled all but the last grenade at each turn, obliterating trash cans and blowing open the windows of the shops with each blast. At the fourth turn, Matt was satisfied that it might work and took a hard left, nearly ejecting Cole out the side. Once out of sight, he slowed even more and Harry leapt out, not missing a beat as he ducked behind a pile of old boxes and wooden pallets.

Matt sped on another 50 yards and nosed the Thing against a wall, jumping out with Claire and Cole, then taking cover behind it. When the truck stopped at the intersection, Cole felt a pit in his stomach. They fired a barrage of shots at the Thing as all three of them ducked behind the tires, shielding their faces from the ricochets. Cole passed the remaining grenade to Matt and they nodded. The air smelled of gasoline that was now leaking from their fuel tank.

The truck backed up, turned, then drove at a slow clip down the narrow street, firing inconsistently, their bullets ricocheting off the high walls and dirty street. Cole tilted his head slightly around the back of the Thing and saw Harry crouching calmly, the rifle across his chest. As his head emerged, two more rounds passed close enough that he felt the displaced air. He ducked back and shuddered, feeling pinned and uncomfortable. As the truck neared his position, Harry smoothly pivoted, stepped out, and fired exactly five rounds to one-by-one wipe each of them out. He moved to the back of the truck to double check his work, then called out towards the Thing, "Clear."

Standing up, they moved a good ways away from the Thing, Matt taking a moment to lob a grenade under the Thing, then hustling away. The blast was hot against their faces as the Thing lifted up as if it was startled, then settled back down in a fiery blaze. Once they all reconnected at the truck, Harry passed his rifle back to Matt, who motioned with his hands for him to keep it.

"We may need you again," he said as he climbed into the cab of the truck, now nosed up against a wall, and pulled the body out, letting it fall like a sack to the ground. Once inside, Claire held the passenger door open as Matt kicked at the second guy, until he too fell out and collapsed on the pavement. Claire sat shotgun this time while Harry and Cole climbed into the back. They each helped the other to roll the dead up and over the side. Matt turned the truck around, not avoiding driving over the bodies, and pointed for the waterfront, the sound of sirens growing in the distance.

"So who were they?" Harry asked.

Cole replied, "Probably the cartel guys."

"What do they want?"

Cole laughed. "To kill the guys back at the villa."

"The ones we just killed?"

Cole nodded. "Yeah. And you, I suppose."

Harry processed it all for a moment, then replied, "Well, this whole thing is a bloody mess."

That more or less sums it up, Cole thought as Matt accelerated and turned for the waterfront.

Past the burned-out boot shop, where yellow police tape still marked off the crime scene, Matt pulled up to a parking spot and stopped, the engine rattling the doors of the beat-up truck. No one seemed to look twice at the four of them in a bullet-riddled truck with bloodstains running down the sides.

"All right, Cole, what now?"

He scanned down the shoreline at the makeshift anchorage, surveying the fleet of fishing boats, pangas, dive boats, and others. A tall mast rose up a quarter mile down the road, rolling gently back and forth against the north breeze. It was large enough to get them to open water.

"That one, over there," he said.

CHAPTER 19: BROAD REACH

AS THE SUN ROSE in the distance off the starboard bow, Cole looked back over his shoulder at the dark and featureless blue horizon. The sky had slowly turned a shade or two lighter than the deep blue water of the Gulf. Whitecaps spilled over the tops of the disorganized sea behind him, as the appropriately named *Rum Runner* held a course just north of east. A strong wind blew in from the northwest and dictated to Cole the course he would sail.

They'd waited until the sun went down the previous night before slipping from the mooring ball with their borrowed prize ship. Under the cover of darkness, Cole had set the main once they cleared Cozumel, and the Beneteau had rolled slowly to her starboard side, her nose coming down softly from the northerly course they had motored for the first part of the evening. With help from Harry, he'd set the jib as well, then tidied up the sheets to where the boat held her course with little interference from the autopilot.

As he sat motionless on the high side, Cole focused his energy on the moment before him. The breeze was fresh and cool, filling the sails and driving the boat onward to the east. To the south, the coast of Cuba was barely discernable as a thin rising sliver of black against the yellow dawn. He felt the boat rise and settle with each swell that passed underneath them. Harry sat silently by himself a bit farther forward, his back against the cabin as he looked out to the north. He also seemed lost in the moment, and Cole dared not disturb him.

The colors morphed from yellow to a soft orange as the sky above lightened to a pastel shade of blue that slowly erased the stars one by one. He took a long breath, smelling the salt and collecting his thoughts. Claire emerged from below, two cups of coffee in her hand

and she passed the first to him. Crawling forward, she handed the second to Harry without a word, then disappeared back down below for a moment before she re-emerged with her own cup and took a seat near Cole.

"Is he all right?"

Claire nodded, still looking at Harry, and replied, "He'll be fine. He just needs to decompress a bit."

"Was it really two years?"

She nodded and took a sip before turning back towards Cole. "Yes. He was supposed to break off if they moved from Africa, but for whatever reason, he went with them."

"Is that why you got us involved?"

Claire looked at him. "Partly, yes—but these things are never that simple."

"Why do you think he stayed?"

"Same reason you did, I suppose." Claire smiled.

Unsure as to what she meant, Cole asked, "Why is that?"

"Following his conscience."

They sat for a while longer until Matt also emerged, looking somewhat rested from a few hours of sleep. Claire slid over, and Matt took a seat next to her. Harry, seeing them assembled, made his way back and sat on the low side of the cockpit, putting his feet up across the bench. No one spoke as the boat gently rolled and pitched as a wave rolled underneath.

"Where we headed, Cole?" asked Matt.

"Key West, if this breeze holds. Maybe three days."

The mainsheet groaned under the strain from a gust of wind that collided against the mainsail, and the boat surged another knot or two ahead. Cole smiled, a chill rolling up his back to his neck.

Harry said, "I am sorry about Harley."

No one knew what to say, and Harry's tone implied some sense of guilt on his part.

Matt shook his head firmly. "No, no, man. It's part of the business."
He paused for a second before continuing. "Harley of all people knew
that."

Claire looked down at the deck, her mind busy. Cole reached over,
nudged her shoulder, and smiled. She smiled back, then stared south,
the wind grabbing hold of her hair and masking her face before she
reached up and tucked it behind her ear.

Harry asked, "What's in Key West?"

Cole smiled and replied slyly, "Who knows for sure—but I've got
a few ideas."

CHAPTER 20: SIXTY FOUR EAST

MONTHS HAD PASSED. They sat quietly at a small coffee shop just outside Arlington, the first hints of fall in the air. Matt was in good spirits, having spent the down time catching up with his family. They listened as he detailed the minutiae of his days as a stay-at-home dad. Cole knew it wouldn't last forever, but he was happy for him. Claire wore a skirt down to her knees and a sweater hung from her shoulders. Unlike Cozumel, she'd spent considerable time that morning to put herself together, and to Cole, was now an entirely different level of pretty. He found it difficult to not stare at her, just as when he'd first seen her in Chiswick, and shook his head to wrestle his eyes free.

Cole had on his typical jeans with a printed shirt tucked in that he had selected for the occasion. The night before, he'd cleaned and polished the old boots that now covered his two feet. He crossed his legs and looked up as a gust of wind blew a handful of earth-toned leaves from a tree above the shop. As somber as it was, none of them let the day take away from their fierce friendship.

Matt had brought them to Langley early that morning, well before the morning rush. In the lobby, they had the brief opportunity to see Harley's star on the wall. The three of them stood there, not a word between any of them. It was a short and unofficial ceremony, just as Matt had intended. A formal ceremony had taken place days before, but Matt had recommended that they stay well clear of the formal event. Even by agency standards, Cozumel had been messy. In the aftermath, DHS had tried to pin the entire thing on the CIA while the agency had, in typical fashion, denied any involvement or knowledge.

Johnson had been made out to be a hero, dying in the line of service as he fought terrorists on foreign soil. Prominent authors and pundits inside the beltway were busy trying to crack into the entire ordeal and score interviews with anyone that claimed to have knowledge of the operation. For his part, Gene Thomas kept quiet, and soon resigned from Congress amid a growing backlash from his party. Whatever power play Johnson had been trying to make soon fell apart with attacks from both sides of the aisle. Cole hated to see Gene Thomas take the fall, but at the same time, he held the man in immense regard. Cole had received a paycheck a week after returning to the States from an investment firm in North Dakota, of all places. He wanted badly to thank Gene Thomas, but knew that was not possible, at least not for some time.

"So who actually knows about all of this?" asked Cole.

Matt smiled. "Not too many folks. Hardly anyone, really."

"Someone's got to know if they cut him a star," Cole said.

Matt nodded, took a sip from his coffee, then looked at Claire. He explained, "I wrote a summary of action, more than half of which was redacted before the ink had even dried."

"Johnson?" Cole asked.

"Strangest thing. I never saw the guy in Cozumel. Didn't even know he was on the island."

Claire tensed up for a second, then sighed and looked away, still not entirely comfortable with the level of deceit that lingered.

To her, Cole asked, "How about your side?"

"We got Harry back. That's as far as anyone in the UK has dug into this one. Frankly, I don't think they want to know much more."

Matt asked, "How's old Harry doing by the way?"

Claire rolled her eyes and replied disapprovingly, "He's shagging his way across the free world as we speak. Said something to us about a lot of catching up to do."

Matt and Cole laughed. Even Claire was finding it difficult not to smile.

"So what's your plan?" asked Matt.

It stung for a second, as Cole sensed the question was subtly hinting at Isabella.

"We've talked a bit," Cole said. "She wants me to see Marie this winter."

Matt and Claire looked away from Cole, not wanting to press the issue. To ease their minds, Cole added, "It's good. We're talking now, so it's better. I don't think it'll ever be the same, but at least we're talking, and I'll probably head that way for a bit before the holidays."

Matt nodded, happy to see that Cole had found some kind of balance in his life. He asked Cole, "So what's your plan until then?"

Cole grinned and looked at Claire who stared back at him, waiting for his answer. "I rented a little shack on the Outer Banks for a few weeks. It's quiet this time of year. We're gonna go take it easy for a bit."

Matt flashed a devilish grin at Cole, and asked, "We?"

Claire, defensively, quipped back at Matt, "Purely platonic."

Cole turned back to Matt and shrugged his shoulders, smiling.

"Good for you both," was all Matt said in response as he too smiled and laughed.

Claire added, "Well, someone has to keep him out of trouble."

Shortly thereafter, they stood and each took their turn with firm hugs and promises to keep in touch. Matt did a doubletake as Cole clicked his keys and a dark blue Ford Mustang chirped in the parking lot.

Shrugging his shoulders again towards Matt with a sly grin, Cole moved to open the passenger door for Claire. Matt laughed, shook his head, and climbed into his truck, calling out one last, "See ya, bud."

With that, they unceremoniously parted ways.

I-64 EAST WAS a familiar route for Cole, one that he'd driven hundreds of time in his prior life. Fall colors dominated the tall stands of trees on each side. With the sporadic midmorning traffic, Cole enjoyed the throaty exhaust of his new toy. Claire, in the passenger seat, seemed relaxed as she played with the stereo.

"What shall we listen to?"

Cole gripped the leather steering wheel with his left hand and draped his right over the shifter. He replied, "Rock and Roll, if you can find it."

"Such an American," she said with a smile.

Up ahead, as the highway made a gentle turn to the right, Cole saw the hood of a police car tucked in against the trees. Instinctively, he let off the gas for a second and Claire looked up as well. For a moment, Cole's mind flashed back to Cozumel and thoughts of Harley flooded his brain. Feeling sadness creep in, he turned quickly to fond memories. Claire looked at the cop a half mile ahead and then towards Cole, who looked at her briefly before he dropped the Mustang into fourth gear.

"Cole, what are you doing?"

He mashed the pedal down and released the clutch as the car surged and accelerated.

"Cole, is that the police?"

Cole looked ahead, squinted, and replied, "Probably a State Trooper." He accelerated more as the distance closed to less than a quarter mile.

She asked again, now with growing uncertainty, "What are you doing?"

Cole smiled, grit his teeth, and shifted into fifth gear. "Pulling a Harley."

Claire shuffled in her seat, tugged at the seatbelt to firm it up a bit, and replied, "Well, you'll have to go faster than this."

He glanced at Claire one more time, returning her smile. As they sped past the trooper at nearly 100 miles per hour, his blue lights flashed, and a look of bewilderment was clear on the officer's face as both he and Cole made momentary eye contact.

Cole laughed loudly, an uncontrolled grin across his face, and sped on, south and east towards the coast.

ABOUT THE AUTHOR

BRIAN BOLAND is a 2003 graduate of the United States Coast Guard Academy and holds a Master of Arts in Military History from Norwich University. After an initial assignment at sea, he completed Naval Flight Training and was designated a Coast Guard

Utah Beach, June 2017

aviator in 2008. With more than a decade of operational experience, he has deployed extensively throughout the Caribbean, Central America, and the eastern Pacific, supporting search and rescue, migrant interdiction, and counter-narcotics missions.

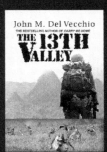